A word from Chris Riddell

I first read *Don Quixote* as a student, and loved its labyrinthine plot twists and digressions, but must admit to finding it rather dense and dusty. Martin's retelling is wonderful, blowing the dust away and uncovering a sparkle and wit that I'd forgotten. When I read it I couldn't wait to saddle up and join him in tilting at windmills.

Very early on I decided to approach the book light-heartedly, to reflect its humour – *Don Quixote* is a great big book that satirizes great big books, an epic romance that pokes fun at epic romances. I looked at the paintings of Velázquez and used costumes and settings from his great royal portraits to give the illustrations a seventeenth-century air, but I wanted them to have a fantasy feel too, and the giants and monsters came from my own imagination. The illustrations came tumbling out in a great avalanche over a period of three months but before that I'd sketched and scribbled with a stubby pencil, roughing the book out. I wanted the drawings to complement the text, not get in the way, which is why the black-and-white artwork is behind the text boxes. It feels playful and allows me to use scale to dramatic effect.

Illustrating a great book is a privilege and endlessly fascinating, and in doing so one discovers just why certain books have become classics. *Don Quixote* is a classic because it is funny, playful, inventive and poignant. This new retelling brings it gloriously to life for a contemporary audience and I hope my illustrations, like Sancho Panza, help a little.

Miguel de Cervantes

Don Quixote

Retold by
MARTIN JENKINS

Illustrated by
CHRIS RIDDELL

WALKER BOOKS
AND SUBSIDIARIES

LONDON • BOSTON • SYDNEY • AUCKLAND

THE NIECE

VOLUME ONE

In which we meet the following characters...

THE
HOUSEKEEPER

SANCHO PANZA
DON QUIXOTE'S SQUIRE

FRESTÓN
THE MAGICIAN

THE PRIEST

THE BARBER

THE
SHEPHERD BOY

MARCELA

MARITORNES

GINÉS DE
PASAMONTE

DOROTHEA

DON
FERNANDO

CARDENIO

LUSCINDA

PANDAFILANDO

LELA ZORAIDA

DON LUIS

DOÑA CLARA

... and many more

PART ONE

≈ Which begins by introducing our hero, the famous but not quite sane Don Quixote de la Mancha, and his long-suffering horse, Rocinante ≈ In a village, the name of which I don't quite remember, in La Mancha in the middle of Spain, there lived a country gentleman whose surname was Quesada or Quixada. He was nearly fifty and was tall and scrawny, though with a strong constitution. He had little money, and lived on simple food. He was looked after by a housekeeper and had a young niece not quite twenty. In his spare time – of which he had plenty – he took to reading books on chivalry set in ancient times, full of brave knights who roamed the land fighting evil sorcerers and rescuing damsels in distress.

Eventually he became obsessed with these books and started selling off bits of his land so that he could buy more and more of them. The more he read the more he began to believe the fantastic tales they contained, until finally he went quite mad and decided that he himself would become a modern-day wandering knight, or knight errant.

He found an old suit of armour mouldering in a corner and cleaned it up as best he could. Instead of a full helmet, there was just a simple metal cap, so he made a visor and face guard out of cardboard, which he attached to the cap. He tested out his handiwork with a thwack from his sword, and succeeded in smashing it to pieces. He carefully rebuilt it, adding some metal bars, but thought that perhaps he wouldn't test its strength a second time.

Then he decided he must christen his horse, which was almost as skinny as he was. After pondering for four days he chose the name Rocinante. Having given his horse a chivalric name, he realized that he too should have one. He thought for eight whole days, and eventually decided to call himself Don Quixote, adding "de la Mancha" as an afterthought.

Lastly he needed a lady love, someone to admire from afar and for whom he could perform his deeds of derring-do. He had once been besotted with a peasant girl called Aldonza Lorenzo, who came from a nearby village, El Toboso. She would do nicely, but she too needed a courtly name. Don Quixote decided that Dulcinea del Toboso would suit her perfectly.

Everything was now ready; and so, early one hot July morning, Don Quixote put on his armour, took up a lance and an old leather shield, mounted Rocinante and set off in search of adventure. Almost at once an awful thought struck him – he hadn't been properly knighted. This meant that according to the laws of chivalry, he was not yet a true knight errant and so couldn't possibly fight with any other knights that he encountered on the way.

All day he and Rocinante travelled on under the burning sun. As night was falling, an inn came into view, which Don Quixote took for a castle with shining silver turrets, a moat and a drawbridge. He assumed his arrival would be greeted by a fanfare of trumpets from the battlements and waited expectantly. At that moment, a swineherd in a nearby field happened to sound his horn to round up his pigs, and Don Quixote, satisfied, marched up to the inn. Two travelling women were sitting outside the door and immediately took fright at the sight of the crazy knight. Don Quixote, thinking they were courtly ladies from the castle, addressed them in flowery language that they could hardly understand. The women started laughing, which rather offended him, though he tried to stay polite. The innkeeper then came out and told him that he was welcome to spend the night there.

Don Quixote dismounted, very stiff after a whole day in the saddle, and the women helped take off his armour, although he refused to remove his visor, which was tied on tightly with green ribbons. He sat down to a meal of revolting salt cod and mouldy black bread, which had to be passed through the gaps in his visor by the women. He ate happily, however, convinced he was dining on the finest trout and freshest white bread.

≈ Don Quixote gets himself knighted and becomes a real knight errant

Don Quixote was still very worried that he hadn't yet been knighted. And so, when he had finished his meal he fell on his knees in front of the innkeeper, whom he took to be the nobleman in charge of the castle, and begged to be knighted the next day, after he had kept watch all night in the castle's chapel. The innkeeper, who was happy to egg Don Quixote on in his fantasy, explained that the chapel was currently being rebuilt. However, Don Quixote would be welcome to keep watch in the courtyard.

He then asked Don Quixote if he had any money on him. Don Quixote replied that he certainly hadn't, as he had never read in any of his books that knights errant carried money. The innkeeper retorted that of course knights errant always carried money, and ointments and spare clothes – or rather had their manservant or squire carry these things for them. This was so obvious that the authors of the old romances hadn't bothered to mention it. Don Quixote agreed and said that he would do this in future.

He then took up his watch in a yard by the side of the inn, piling his armour on a water trough and patiently marching to and fro, clutching his lance and shield. People stole out of the inn to watch the knight's mad antics in the moonlight. After a few hours, a mule keeper staying at the inn decided to water his mules, and began to remove Don Quixote's armour from the trough. Don Quixote was furious and roared at the muleteer, who ignored him and flung the armour onto the ground. Don Quixote raised his eyes to heaven, called on his lady Dulcinea and walloped the muleteer on the head with his lance.

The muleteer fell to the ground, stunned. Don Quixote picked up his armour, put it back on the water trough and calmly began pacing to and fro again, as if nothing had happened. Shortly afterwards another muleteer, who had not seen the first incident, came up and made as if to move the armour. Without saying a word, Don Quixote walloped him on the head too. The muleteers' companions, seeing this, began hurling stones at Don Quixote, who tried to fend them off with his shield while roaring insults at his attackers and at the innkeeper. He sounded so fierce that he made his attackers rather nervous, so they picked up their wounded friends and retreated.

The innkeeper decided it was time to call a halt to all this, and said he would now knight Don Quixote. He hurried off, returning with a big accounts book, a small boy carrying a stump of candle, and the two women who had met Don Quixote earlier. The innkeeper made Don Quixote kneel in front of him and then pretended to read from the accounts book, muttering away as if he were praying. He cuffed Don Quixote on the neck and hit him on the shoulder with the sword.

One of the women then buckled his sword around his waist and said, "May God make you a most lucky knight, and grant you good fortune in your battles."

The other woman fixed Don Quixote's spurs to his ankles.

Don Quixote could now consider himself a true knight. He couldn't wait to be off and, thanking the innkeeper profusely, he mounted Rocinante and rode away. The innkeeper was so glad to see the back of him that he didn't bother asking for any money for his meal and lodgings.

≈ Don Quixote's first attempt at being heroic and its unfortunate consequences

It was daybreak. Remembering the innkeeper's advice, Don Quixote resolved to return home for some money and other necessities and to find himself a squire. He was riding along when he heard moaning coming from a nearby wood. He decided that whoever was making the noise was in immediate need of his protection, and rode over to investigate. In the wood he found a farmer beating with a belt a youth who was tied firmly to a tree. The farmer's horse was tied to another tree, which had a lance leaning against it.

Don Quixote shouted at the farmer, "Scurvy knight, how dare you attack someone who can't defend himself! Get on your horse and take up your arms and let me teach you a lesson."

The farmer began quaking in his boots and replied, "Sir, that boy is one of my own servants, who is supposed to look after my sheep. But he is so careless he loses one every day. I am punishing him for this. The boy says I'm a miser and am just trying to find an excuse not to pay him, but that's a lie."

"How dare you accuse anyone of lying in my presence!" roared Don Quixote. "I'm tempted to impale you on my lance. Now, untie the boy and pay him what you owe him at once, and don't say another word!"

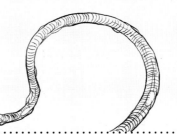

The farmer immediately did as he was told. Don Quixote asked the boy how much he was owed.

"Nine months' wages at seven reals a month, sir."

Don Quixote scratched his head and worked out that this came to seventy-three reals. The farmer responded that he had no money on him but would pay the boy, whose name was Andrés, if he would go home with him.

"Not likely!" retorted Andrés. "He'll skin me alive as soon as we're alone again."

"No, he won't," said Don Quixote. "Under the laws of chivalry he is bound to obey my orders."

"But he's no knight," said Andrés. "He's just Juan Haldudo, a rich farmer from Quintanar."

"That's not important," replied Don Quixote. "He can be a knight in deed." And turning to the farmer he said, "But remember that if you don't pay, I, Don Quixote de la Mancha, will seek you out and punish you terribly." He then spurred Rocinante and rode off.

As soon as he'd gone, Juan Haldudo turned to Andrés and said, "Come here, my boy, and let me pay you."

"You'd better," replied Andrés, "or that good man will come back and sort you."

"Oh, I'll pay all right," said the farmer, "but first, as I'm so fond of you, I think I'll increase my debt a bit." And he grabbed Andrés, tied him to the tree and started flogging him again with all his might.

When he'd finished, he released the boy and said he was welcome to go in search of his kindly protector. Andrés crept off, whimpering and declaring he was about to do just that, leaving his master laughing heartily.

≈ Don Quixote's first beating

Don Quixote, meanwhile, was feeling very pleased with himself about the terrible wrong he had righted. He was riding along thinking of this and his lady Dulcinea del Toboso, when he spotted a party of people. They were in fact six merchants going from Toledo to Murcia to buy silk, accompanied by four servants on horseback and three footmen. Don Quixote decided, of course, that they were knights errant and needed challenging. So, clutching his lance and his shield, he took up position on Rocinante in the middle of the road.

As the men approached he declared loudly, "None of you shall pass until all confess that the most beautiful maiden in the world is the empress of La Mancha, Dulcinea del Toboso."

The merchants were taken aback by this strange figure, whom they immediately took to be mad. They were curious to see what would happen, and one of them said, "Sir Knight, we don't know this worthy lady, but if perhaps we could see her and she is as beautiful as you say, then we would gladly admit it."

"No," replied Don Quixote, "the point is that you have to take my word for it."

"But then we might risk insulting some of the other fine ladies around here. Look, just show us a portrait of her, however small, and we'll say whatever you like – even if she's blind in one eye and oozes sulphur from the other."

"She doesn't ooze anything, you lying knaves!" roared Don Quixote. "Prepare to pay for the terrible insult you have hurled at my lady."

And, lowering his lance, he charged straight at the man who had been speaking. Fortunately for the merchant, Rocinante

promptly tripped and fell, leaving Don Quixote sprawling in the dust, quite unable to get up because he was so tangled in all his armour.

"Just you wait!" he shouted at the merchants.

One of the servants then grabbed Don Quixote's lance and smashed it into pieces. Picking up the bits, he laid into Don Quixote with them, until he grew tired and went back to his masters, who set off again on their journey.

Don Quixote was so bruised and battered that he could not move. He began to recite to himself a poem from one of his books in which a knight called Baldwin lies wounded and dying in a wood. As luck would have it, at that moment, a farmer from his own village passed by. The farmer stopped and asked Don Quixote who he was and what was wrong. Don Quixote just went on reciting the poem.

The puzzled farmer prised off the visor and wiped the dust off the knight's face. He recognized him at once and said, "Señor Quixada, who has done this to you?"

But Don Quixote just continued reciting the poem. Taking off Don Quixote's armour, the farmer carefully lifted him onto his donkey. He then tied the armour to Rocinante and set off for La Mancha. Don Quixote kept sliding about on the donkey and sighing loudly. He forgot all about Baldwin and began to go on about Abindarráez the Moor and Rodrigo de Narváez. The farmer became exasperated and declared that he was not Rodrigo de Narváez, but Pedro Alonso, a humble farmer, and that the Don was not Baldwin or Abindarráez the Moor but Señor Quixada from La Mancha.

"I know just who I am," retorted Don Quixote. "I can be any one of those and a hundred other knights, because my deeds will outdo them all."

And so they went on, until it was evening. The farmer decided to wait for darkness before leading Don Quixote into the village, so that no one would see what state he was in.

≈ Introducing two very important characters, Don Quixote's friends the village priest and Master Nicolás the barber

In the village, Don Quixote's house was in uproar. The priest and the barber, who were good friends of Don Quixote's, were there, as were Don Quixote's niece and the housekeeper, who was shouting, "Oh, what am I to do? My master's been gone for three days, and he's taken his horse and his armour with him. I'm sure his brain has been addled by all those terrible books he reads. The devil take them all!"

The housekeeper's cries were echoed by Don Quixote's niece, who told how her uncle would spend two whole days and nights reading one of his books and then, throwing it down, would slash the walls of his room with his sword, declaring that he'd just killed four giants.

"It's my fault," she groaned. "I should have told everyone about those books, which should all be burnt."

At that moment, Pedro Alonso arrived with his load. The niece and housekeeper fell on Don Quixote, who was carried upstairs to bed declaring that his bruises had been got in a battle against ten of the fiercest giants on earth.

The next day, the priest and the barber came to inspect Don Quixote's library. The housekeeper and the niece maintained that all the books should be burnt immediately, but the priest thought they should at least check the titles first. The first few they looked at were called things like *The Mirror of Chivalry*, *Florismarte of Hircania* and *The Exploits of Esplandián*.

Most of them the priest handed to the housekeeper, who threw them out of the window into the courtyard, to be made into a bonfire. Some of the books, though, the priest thought might not be too wicked. He gave these to the barber and told him to hide them in his house, so that they could decide about them later. One of them was called *Galatea*, by Miguel de Cervantes.

"Ah," said the priest. "He's a good friend of mine. That book is fine but it doesn't really end properly. Perhaps one day he'll write a second part."

The priest and the barber decided that while Don Quixote was still in bed they would seal off his library and tell him that a sorcerer had carried it off, books and all. Perhaps this would cure him of his madness.

Two days later, Don Quixote finally got up and immediately went to look for his books. All he found was a wall where the library door had been. He stared at it for ages and then went to his housekeeper and asked her where his library was. She replied that the devil himself had taken it and all the books in it away.

"No, it wasn't the devil," said the niece, "it was a sorcerer called Muñatón, who says he has a grudge against you."

"Ah, that must have been Frestón," said Don Quixote. "He hates me because he knows that one day I will defeat him."

≈ Introducing an extremely important character, Don Quixote's neighbour, the friendly but not very bright Sancho Panza, and recounting the amazing tale of the windmills that Don Quixote mistook for giants

For the next two weeks, Don Quixote stayed at home, talking about knight-errantry with the priest and the barber, who were still hoping to cure him. During this time, though, Don Quixote had set to work on a neighbour of his, to try to persuade him to become his squire.

This neighbour, whose name was Sancho Panza, was poor but honourable, though he certainly wasn't the cleverest man in the village. Don Quixote promised him all sorts of things if he would become his squire. He was sure, for instance, that one day he, Don Quixote, would win an island in an adventure; when that happened, he would name his squire as the island's governor. Sancho Panza had no idea what an island was – he'd never been near the sea in his life – but was still so convinced by this that he agreed to become Don Quixote's squire.

Don Quixote then set about raising money by selling some of his belongings. He borrowed a little round shield off a friend of his and repaired his broken helmet as well as he could. Then he told Sancho Panza to get ready to go. Sancho Panza said he was going to bring one of his donkeys, as he didn't fancy going very far on foot. Don Quixote couldn't remember any knight's squire having a donkey in any of the books he'd read, but finally decided that this was probably all right.

When everything was ready, they set off in the middle of the night without saying goodbye to anyone, Don Quixote on Rocinante and Sancho Panza astride his donkey, with saddlebags and a big leather bottle dangling beside him.

They rode for hours, talking of this and that. Sancho Panza brought up the island that he would one day get to govern.

"I was thinking," said Sancho, "if one day I become a king, does that mean that my old lady, Juana Gutiérrez, will become a queen?"

"Without doubt," replied Don Quixote.

"I'm not so sure she'd be very suitable as a queen," said Sancho.

"I shouldn't worry about that," said Don Quixote. "Everything is bound to come out fine in the end."

While they were talking they caught sight of thirty or forty windmills on the plain ahead of them. Don Quixote turned to Sancho and said, "We are in luck. Here are at least thirty terrible giants whom I intend to fight and kill. The booty we take off them will help to make us rich."

"What giants?" asked Sancho.

"Those ones over there, waving their enormous arms about," replied Don Quixote.

"They're not giants; they're windmills," said Sancho.

Don Quixote sighed. "It's clear you know little about real adventuring," he said. "They are definitely giants, and if you're frightened you can take yourself out of the way and pray while I fight them."

Don Quixote then lowered his lance and, urging Rocinante on, charged full tilt at the nearest windmill. As the lance ripped into its sail, a gust of wind turned the sail so violently that the lance was yanked up and broken into pieces, while Don Quixote and Rocinante were sent tumbling over the ground.

Sancho came rushing up on his donkey. "For heaven's sake, sir," he said, "didn't I tell you they were just windmills?"

"Nonsense," said Don Quixote. "The sorcerer Frestón, who has a grudge against me, obviously turned the giants into windmills at the last minute, to cheat me of victory."

Sancho Panza helped Don Quixote back onto Rocinante and they continued on their way, Don Quixote riding rather lopsidedly because of the bruises he'd received.

"You must be very sore," said Sancho.

"I am," replied Don Quixote, "but knights errant never complain of their wounds, however bad they are."

"Me, I'm going to moan whenever I feel like it," said Sancho.

Don Quixote laughed and said that that was fine by him.

They spent the night under some trees, and in the morning set off towards the Pass of Lápice, where they were sure they'd find some adventures.

≈ DON QUIXOTE'S FIRST REAL FIGHT
(NOT COUNTING THE WINDMILLS)

Don Quixote and Sancho Panza reached the Pass of Lápice that afternoon. Almost immediately they spotted two friars on the road ahead, riding big mules. They were dressed in black, and their faces were covered in masks to protect them from the dust and sun. Behind them was a coach with four or five horsemen and two footmen. In the coach, it turned out, was a Basque lady who was travelling to Seville to join her husband.

Don Quixote turned to Sancho. "Look, those black figures must be wizards who are kidnapping a princess in that coach. We must rescue her."

"Oh dear," said Sancho, "this is going to be worse than the windmills. Look, the figures are just Benedictine friars, and the coach is probably carrying ordinary travellers."

Don Quixote ignored him and rode up to the friars. "Wicked monsters!" he cried. "Release the princess you are kidnapping at once, or prepare to die."

The friars were very taken aback. "Sir," they said, "we're not monsters but Benedictine friars, and we have no idea who's in that coach."

"Pah!" said Don Quixote, and without waiting any further he charged at the nearest friar, who flung himself off his mule just in time. The other friar took fright and galloped away. Sancho ran up to the fallen friar and began stripping off his clothes. Seeing this, the friars' servants came up and asked him what he was doing.

"These clothes are my rightful booty," said Sancho. "They have been won by my master in a fair fight."

The servants didn't see the funny side of this, and proceeded to beat Sancho black and blue. The friar, having got his breath back, then remounted his mule and dashed off to join his companion, who was waiting some distance off. They both quickly rode away without waiting to see what would happen next.

Don Quixote went up to the lady in the coach and said, "Your serene highness, I have saved you from this dreadful fate in the name of my beloved lady, Dulcinea del Toboso. I implore you to turn back to El Toboso and tell her what I have done."

One of the horsemen with the coach, a Basque, overheard this and, riding up, said to Don Quixote, "Go knight away, or me kill you."

Don Quixote was outraged and, throwing down his lance, took up his sword and advanced on the Basque. The Basque grabbed a cushion from the coach to defend himself, drew his sword and struck Don Quixote an almighty blow. If Don Quixote hadn't been wearing armour he would surely have been split in two. He reeled, then recovered and, raising his own sword high, advanced on the Basque, determined to risk everything on a single blow. The Basque put up his sword ready to defend himself. All the bystanders were watching, terrified, and then...

...and then the story stops.

"Impossible!" you cry. But it's true: at this point the writer of the story declares that he has found nothing more to tell of the adventures of Don Quixote.

PART TWO ≈ In which we discover the true author of the extraordinary story of Don Quixote de la Mancha ≈

We left Don Quixote and the Basque about to try to split each other open. I could not believe that the story could possibly end there, and that there were not more exciting adventures to be told. The trouble was, I had no idea where I might find the missing parts.

Then, one day, I was in the middle of Toledo, when I came across a young boy with some scraps of paper and notebooks to sell. I picked up one of the books and saw that it was written in Arabic, a language I can't read. I soon found a Spanish-speaking Moor who could translate for me. He opened the notebook in the middle and, reading a bit, began chuckling.

"What's so funny?" I asked.

"This sentence, written in the margin," he replied. "It says: *I've heard that this woman Dulcinea del Toboso was ace at salting pork.*"

I was dumbfounded – Dulcinea del Toboso!

"Quick!" I said. "What's written on the title page?"

"History of Don Quixote de la Mancha, written by Cide Hamete Benengeli, an Arab historian," he told me.

I immediately rushed back to the boy and bought all the other notebooks and pieces of paper. I only paid half a real for the lot – the boy could have got ten times that at least, if only he'd known how much I wanted them. I then offered the Moor a good price to translate the whole story, which he did in just over six weeks.

And here it all is. I'm sure none of it has been exaggerated in the least.

≈ THE STORY CONTINUES...

So, Don Quixote was bearing down on the Basque, who had his sword in one hand and the cushion in the other. Don Quixote stood up in his stirrups, grasped his sword in both hands and brought it down with all his might on the cushion and the Basque's head. The Basque swayed to and fro, and blood began to trickle out of his mouth, nose and ears. His terrified mount began galloping about and quickly dumped him on the ground.

Don Quixote jumped off Rocinante and ran over. He put the point of his sword between the Basque's eyes and called on him to surrender. The Basque was too stunned to reply, but fortunately the ladies in the coach, who had been watching from a distance, hurried over and begged Don Quixote to spare his life. Don Quixote replied that he would, provided the Basque went to El Toboso and presented himself to his lady Dulcinea. The ladies quickly agreed.

Meanwhile, Sancho, rather bruised from his encounter with the friars' servants, had got to his feet and was watching, also from a safe distance. He ran over and knelt before Don Quixote, kissing his hand and saying, "Sir, now please make me the governor of the island you've just won in this frightful battle."

To which Don Quixote replied, "I'm afraid this wasn't really an island kind of adventure. Be patient, though, and you'll get your reward in time."

Off they went, Don Quixote on Rocinante going at quite a lick and Sancho struggling to keep up on his donkey.

"Sir," Sancho gasped as they rode along, "I think perhaps we'd better take refuge in a church. If the Holy Brotherhood hear of the way you attacked that man, we'll be in terrible trouble. They're bound to arrest us and throw us into prison."

"Nonsense," replied Don Quixote. "I've never read of a knight errant being arrested and tried, however awful the things he's done. Stop worrying. Now, Sancho, I want you to tell me whether you've ever read of any knight more valiant than me."

"Well, I can't actually read or write," said Sancho, "but I've certainly never served a braver master than you. By the way, you must treat that ear of yours. It's bleeding horribly. I've got ointments and bandages in my saddlebags."

"If only I'd remembered to make up some balsam of Fierabras," said Don Quixote.

"What's that?" asked Sancho.

"Well, if I were in battle and got cut in two – as quite often happens – then all you'd have to do would be to join the two bits carefully up again and give me a couple of mouthfuls of the balsam, and I'd be completely fine."

"If that's true," said Sancho, "you can forget about giving me an island and just give me the recipe – I could make a fortune selling that stuff."

"All in good time," replied Don Quixote. "Now, let's see to this ear of mine, which really is rather sore."

Don Quixote then discovered that his helmet was in a terrible state as the result of his fight. He was outraged, swearing vengeance on the man who had damaged it and declaring that he would not sit down at a table to eat or sleep under a roof until he had taken from some other knight a helmet at least as fine as his had been. Sancho was not at all sure that this was such a good idea.

They then ate some onions, cheese and scraps of bread, which was all the food they had on them. Sancho was concerned that this was not good enough fare for a distinguished knight, but Don Quixote assured him that knights errant normally ate such food, except when sumptuous banquets were prepared in their honour.

Having eaten, they hurried on to find somewhere to spend the night. Eventually they reached a spot where some goatherds had set up camp. The goatherds welcomed them and invited them to share their meal of goat stew. They provided Don Quixote with an upturned bowl to sit on. Sancho stood near by, ready to serve his master. Don Quixote said that they should share the food as equals, and asked Sancho to sit down beside him.

"To be honest, sir," said Sancho, "I'm much more comfortable eating my own food, however plain, by myself rather than eating fancy food in polite company, where I can't relax. So I respectfully decline the honour of sharing your food with you."

"Just sit," returned Don Quixote, pulling him down by the arm.

The goatherds watched in silence as their two guests stuffed themselves with meat, washed down with copious amounts of wine, followed by sweet acorns and hard cheese.

When they had finished, Don Quixote held forth at length about the golden age of chivalry, when everything was shared freely and people roamed at peace through the beautiful countryside, drinking from overflowing fountains and feeding on honey and wild fruits. The goatherds listened to all this in amazement. When Don Quixote had finished, they thanked him and said that they would like to entertain him by calling on a friend of theirs who could sing and play the violin, and even read and write.

Shortly afterwards a young man in his early twenties appeared, called Antonio. He sat down on a stump, tuned his violin and sang a song he had written about his love for a girl called Olalla. Don Quixote asked him to sing another one, but Sancho declared that after all that wine he, for one, was quite ready to go to sleep.

"Fine," said Don Quixote, "but before we do, can you have another look at this ear of mine, which is still hurting."

One of the goatherds took some wild rosemary leaves, chewed them up, mixed them with salt and applied them to the ear, which he bandaged tightly, assuring Don Quixote that this would heal it once and for all. And indeed it did.

≈The sad tale of Grisóstomo and Marcela

A young man then turned up, bringing provisions from the nearby village. He was very excited.

"That rich student who dressed up as a shepherd, Grisóstomo, died this morning – everyone says out of love for Marcela. He's left instructions to be buried by the cork-oak spring, where we think he first saw Marcela. The village priest is furious, but Grisóstomo's friend Ambrosio – you know, the one who used to

dress up as a shepherd with him – insists that the funeral will be carried out exactly as Grisóstomo asked. It's tomorrow. I can't wait."

Don Quixote then asked the young man, whose name was Pedro, to tell him more about Grisóstomo and Marcela. Pedro explained that the dead man had been a student at Salamanca University for many years and had then come back to live in the village.

"His father died," he went on, "and he inherited a lot of property. He was a clever and honourable man, and very popular in the village. Marcela had also had a rich father, who had died when she was young. She was brought up by her uncle, a priest, who kept her quietly indoors. Nevertheless, fame of her beauty soon spread, and she began to be plagued with suitors. Her uncle begged her to choose one, but she said she was still too young, so he stopped pressing her.

"And then, one day, to her uncle's consternation, she suddenly decides to become a shepherdess and sets off with the other village shepherdesses. Of course, all the shepherds immediately fall for her. She's very polite to them until one of them proposes, when she sends him off with a flea in his ear. Grisóstomo saw her a while ago and fell in love with her too. Then he started dressing up as a shepherd, taking Ambrosio along, so that he could follow her about."

Don Quixote was fascinated by this story, but Sancho was very keen to go to sleep. He suggested that Don Quixote spend the night in Pedro's hut, while he settled himself down between Rocinante and his donkey.

The next morning, they all set off for the funeral, leaving one of the goatherds in charge of the goats. Soon they came across six shepherds also heading for the funeral, wearing black sheepskin jackets and with mourning wreaths on their heads.

With them were two gentlemen on horseback, accompanied by three servants. The men had heard the story of Grisóstomo and Marcela and were very keen to witness the funeral.

One of the gentlemen, whose name was Señor Vivaldo, asked Don Quixote why he was riding about so heavily armed in such a peaceful part of the country. Don Quixote said that he was a knight errant.

Señor Vivaldo asked what a knight errant was, and Don Quixote explained at great length, telling him about King Arthur and the Knights of the Round Table, and Amadis of Gaul and other famous figures. Señor Vivaldo and his companion quickly concluded that Don Quixote must be quite mad, but to while away the journey they continued asking him about knight-errantry, debating whether all knights errant had to have a lady love to perform their deeds for, and other important questions. They asked Don Quixote about his own lady love. He told them about Dulcinea del Toboso.

"Is she from an aristocratic family?" asked Señor Vivaldo.

"Well, it's not a very renowned family now," replied Don Quixote, "but it could become so in the future."

"Strange I have never heard the name," mused Señor Vivaldo.

Sancho, who otherwise believed everything Don Quixote said, also thought it odd that he himself had never heard of a princess called Dulcinea del Toboso, even though he lived very near El Toboso.

Just then they caught sight of another group of about twenty shepherds, all dressed in mourning. Six of them were carrying a bier covered in flowers, on which Grisóstomo lay. He had obviously been very handsome in life. Scattered about the body on the bier were lots of books and pieces of paper. The procession stopped and Ambrosio gave an impassioned speech about his dead friend, telling everyone how good and honourable he had been and how he had loved someone but been cruelly rejected. He explained that Grisóstomo had written about his love but had stated in his will that all his writings were to be burnt once he was dead.

Señor Vivaldo declared that it was wrong to burn the dead man's writings. He reached out and picked up some of the papers lying on the bier. Ambrosio said that he could keep those, but that all the others were to be burnt. One of the papers had a long poem on it, which Ambrosio said was the last thing Grisóstomo had written. It told of his despair at loving Marcela, who did not love him back. Señor Vivaldo read it out to all the mourners.

Then, to everyone's amazement, Marcela herself appeared on a rock above where Grisóstomo's grave was being dug. Ambrosio accused her of having come to gloat over her dead admirer. Marcela declared that she had not, but rather had come to defend herself.

"It is not my fault that I am considered beautiful," she said, "nor can I force myself to love someone just because they decide that they are in love with me. I do not need to marry for money, and I have never encouraged any man in his pursuit of me. I love my freedom, and am never happier than when alone in the countryside or with just my fellow shepherdesses and my animals for company. I do not understand how you can think that I have done anything wrong." And saying this, she turned and disappeared at once into the nearby woods.

Some of the mourning shepherds made as if to follow her, but Don Quixote grasped the hilt of his sword and declaimed, "Marcela has shown clearly that she is not to blame for Grisóstomo's death. She does not deserve to be persecuted, but rather to be honoured as a pure and noble woman."

With that and Ambrosio telling them they had to finish the funeral, no one left the spot until Grisóstomo had been buried and his papers burnt. There were many tears, and the mourners strewed flowers all over the grave. Don Quixote, Sancho Panza and the two gentlemen travellers said goodbye to their hosts. The gentlemen urged Don Quixote to accompany them to Seville, where there were sure to be lots of adventures; but Don Quixote refused, saying he would remain to clear the mountains of robbers. The gentlemen then went on their way, and Don Quixote determined to go in search of Marcela and offer her his services.

But things didn't quite turn out that way.

PART THREE ≈ WHICH BEGINS WITH DON QUIXOTE AND SANCHO PANZA'S SECOND BEATING EACH, ALL THE FAULT OF ROCINANTE ≈

DON QUIXOTE and Sancho rode off into the forest where Marcela had disappeared. They looked for her without success for a couple of hours and then came across a lovely grassy meadow with a stream running by. They stopped to rest in the heat and to have a simple meal, turning Rocinante and Sancho's donkey loose.

As ill luck would have it, some men from Yanguas had let loose a herd of mares to graze in the same meadow. Rocinante galloped over and there was immediately much biting and kicking. The men from Yanguas appeared and laid into Rocinante with the heavy sticks they were carrying.

Hearing the commotion, Don Quixote and Sancho came running up.

"These men are not knights but ruffians," said Don Quixote. "Come, Sancho, we must punish them for the beating they have given Rocinante."

"How on earth are we going to do that?" asked Sancho. "There are more than twenty of them and only two of us."

"I am worth a hundred men at least," said Don Quixote, drawing his sword and attacking the nearest man, whom he cut badly on the shoulder.

41

But Don Quixote and Sancho were no match for the men from Yanguas. They were thrown on the ground next to the prostrate Rocinante and severely beaten. Their assailants then loaded up their animals and left.

After a while Sancho groaned feebly, "Don Quixote, sir, you wouldn't happen to have any of that balsam stuff on you, would you?"

"Do you think we'd be lying here all battered if I did?" replied Don Quixote.

"When do you think we'll be able to move?" asked Sancho.

"I have no idea," said Don Quixote, "but I will admit that it's all my fault. Those men were clearly not knights, and I have broken the laws of chivalry by attacking them. In future, Sancho, if you see common men about to assault us, don't wait for me, but draw your sword and plunge in. I for my part will undertake to defend us both from any knights who might attack us."

Sancho was not convinced. "I'm a peace-loving man, sir," he said, "with a wife and children to support. So I'm afraid I won't be attacking anyone, however much they might insult me."

"I'm not sure that attitude will do you much good when you get an island to govern," retorted Don Quixote.

"Yes, well," said Sancho, "enough of all this. Let's try and get up, and give Rocinante a hand, although I'm not sure he deserves it as he's the cause of all our trouble."

Sancho wearily got to his feet, though he was too bruised to straighten up properly. He harnessed his donkey, helped push Rocinante upright and then managed to manoeuvre Don Quixote onto the donkey, where he lay slumped across the saddle like a sack of corn. With Rocinante tied behind the donkey, they set off. After a short while they came across a road, by the side of which was an inn, which Don Quixote immediately insisted was a castle.

"It's an inn," said Sancho.

"No, it's a castle," declared Don Quixote.

"I tell you it's an inn," retorted Sancho, and on they went, bickering away until they reached the gate.

≋ THE INN (NOT THE FIRST ONE, WHERE DON QUIXOTE WAS KNIGHTED, BUT ONE WHICH HE ALSO MISTAKES FOR A CASTLE AND WHERE LOTS OF IMPROBABLE THINGS END UP HAPPENING)

As soon as Don Quixote and Sancho arrived at the inn, the innkeeper appeared at the door. Seeing Don Quixote lying across the back of the donkey, he asked Sancho what was wrong.

"Oh, he's just had a bit of a fall," said Sancho.

The innkeeper's wife, who was (unusually for innkeepers' wives) quite a kindly person, immediately told her daughter and another girl, an Asturian called Maritornes, to help Don Quixote. Now, Maritornes wasn't that bad-looking, if you ignored her coarse, matted hair, squashed-in nose, several chins and hunched back.

The two girls went off and prepared a bed for Don Quixote in the hayloft. It comprised a thin, lumpy mattress and threadbare blanket on four rough planks of wood, but it was better than nothing.

The innkeeper's wife and daughter then tended Don Quixote's wounds while Maritornes held the lamp.

"Are you sure this was just a fall?" asked the innkeeper's wife. "It looks more like a beating to me."

"No, it was just a fall onto a particularly bumpy rock," said Sancho. "But would you mind keeping a few bits of bandage for me – I seem to have come out in bruises in sympathy with my master."

"So who is this man?" asked the innkeeper's wife.

"He's Don Quixote, a knight errant," replied Sancho.

"What's one of them?" she asked.

"Someone who's beaten to a pulp one minute and crowned king the next," explained Sancho.

Don Quixote had been listening to all this, and, raising himself up in bed, began to address the innkeeper's wife in his flowery way, as if she were the lady of an important castle. Neither the innkeeper's wife nor her daughter nor Maritornes could understand Don Quixote, but they did realize he was trying to compliment them. Thanking him profusely, they left.

Don Quixote wasn't the only guest staying in the inn's attic. A muleteer had also made up a bed there, further away from the door. Sancho laid out a mat between Don Quixote's bed and the muleteer's and, wrapping himself in a blanket, lay down to sleep. All was quiet and dark.

≈ Don Quixote and Sancho's third beating

Now, Maritornes had secretly promised to come and keep the muleteer company during the night. She crept into the attic in the pitch black. Meanwhile, Don Quixote, who could not sleep because of his bruises, was lying there, thinking about the day's events. Believing that he was in a castle, not an inn, he had decided that the innkeeper's daughter was in fact the daughter of the lord of the castle and had fallen in love with him. He was sure that she would come to him in the night to declare her love.

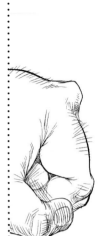

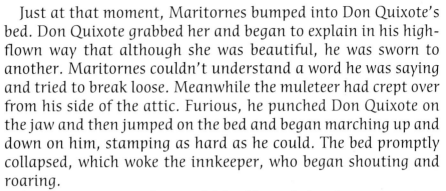

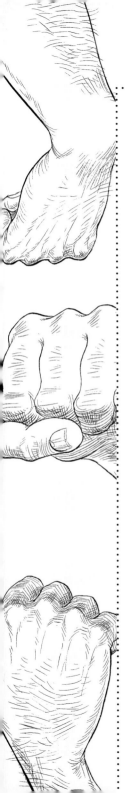

Just at that moment, Maritornes bumped into Don Quixote's bed. Don Quixote grabbed her and began to explain in his high-flown way that although she was beautiful, he was sworn to another. Maritornes couldn't understand a word he was saying and tried to break loose. Meanwhile the muleteer had crept over from his side of the attic. Furious, he punched Don Quixote on the jaw and then jumped on the bed and began marching up and down on him, stamping as hard as he could. The bed promptly collapsed, which woke the innkeeper, who began shouting and roaring.

Maritornes, sure she would be blamed for the commotion, darted under Sancho's blanket and curled herself up into a ball. Sancho, who by this time was fast asleep, woke thinking he was being attacked and laid into Maritornes with his fists. Maritornes immediately retaliated. The innkeeper burst in holding a lamp and ran over to try to punish Maritornes. The muleteer, seeing what was happening, waded in and started to beat up Sancho. Fists were flying in all directions, when the innkeeper's lamp went out. Everyone simply continued lashing out in the dark.

By chance, one of the other guests in the inn was a member of the Holy Brotherhood. Hearing the noise in the attic, he came up to investigate and stumbled against Don Quixote's bed. Feeling on the bed, he grabbed Don Quixote by the beard and shouted, "Assist me – I am an officer of the law!"

Don Quixote, after the further beating he'd got from the muleteer, could no longer move at all and did not answer. The officer assumed he'd been murdered and that the others in the attic were his murderers.

He yelled downstairs, "A man has been killed here. Shut the inn door and let no one out!"

Alarmed by all this, everyone stopped fighting and crept back to their respective beds. The officer then went downstairs to try to find a light.

Don Quixote came to and called out feebly, "Sancho, my friend, are you awake?"

"How could you imagine I'd be asleep, when all these devils have been assaulting me?" retorted Sancho, who was furious.

Don Quixote then told Sancho of the beautiful maiden who had visited him, and declared that he thought the castle they were in must be enchanted by some wizard.

The officer had meanwhile found a lamp, and came back up to see what was happening. He was amazed to see Don Quixote and Sancho chatting away to each other.

"Are you OK, old chap?" he asked Don Quixote.

"The impertinence!" returned Don Quixote. "How dare you address a knight errant in such a familiar way!"

The officer was furious at this response and promptly smashed his lamp down on Don Quixote's head, bringing up two huge bruises and plunging the room into darkness once more. The oil from the lamp was trickling down Don Quixote's face, and in the darkness he thought it was his own blood.

"That must have been the wizard or ghost who enchanted the castle," said Sancho.

"I'm sure you're right," replied Don Quixote. "Now get up and call the lord of this castle, and get me some oil, wine, salt and rosemary so that I can make that balsam I was telling you about – my head is bleeding terribly."

The innkeeper gave Sancho the ingredients for the balsam and Don Quixote pounded them together and boiled them up. He then swallowed down a couple of big glassfuls and put the rest in an old oil can. He was immediately badly sick and broke out in a great sweat. The others wrapped him in a blanket and left him to sleep.

He woke a few hours later feeling very much better – indeed, he was convinced that the balsam had healed him completely after his beatings. Sancho was sure that his master's cure was a miracle, and he too then gulped down a large amount of the liquid. He quickly collapsed in a terrible state, and writhed around retching and groaning. After a while he was sick and started sweating horribly. This went on for two hours, during which he began to think that he would surely die. When the spasms finally stopped, he was so weak he could not stand.

"I think that balsam probably doesn't do much good to those who are not knights," said Don Quixote.

"Why didn't you warn me of that before you let me drink it?" asked Sancho indignantly.

≈ The famous incident of Sancho and the blanket

Feeling fit and well, Don Quixote was determined to be off. He saddled Rocinante and helped Sancho to dress and get onto his donkey. Everyone at the inn was gathered watching them. Don Quixote then summoned the innkeeper and addressed him in lofty tones.

"Sire," he said, "I am eternally grateful for the magnificent hospitality I have received at your castle. If I may repay you in any way – by taking revenge on some ruffian who may have offended you, for example – pray let me know."

The innkeeper replied, "Sir, I am quite capable of taking my own revenge if I need to. I would, however, like you to pay for your board and lodging."

"Is this an inn, then?" asked Don Quixote.

"It is, and a very respectable one," replied the innkeeper.

"I have made a mistake," said Don Quixote, "and I must ask you to forgive me for not paying you – I cannot possibly go against the laws of knight-errantry by paying for my keep."

"I'm not interested in knight-errantry," retorted the innkeeper, "but I am interested in the money that you owe me."

"You're just a foolish, grasping publican," said Don Quixote, grabbing a pikestaff from the wall to replace his broken lance and riding straight out of the inn's gate without looking behind him.

The innkeeper then hurried over to Sancho and demanded that he pay the bill. Sancho maintained that the same rules applied to knights' squires as to their masters. Unfortunately for Sancho the innkeeper didn't agree. Even more unfortunately, some of the other people staying at the inn had a rather rough sense of humour. They rushed indoors and came out with a big blanket. They hauled Sancho off his donkey and, tipping him into the blanket, began tossing him up and down.

Sancho yelled so loudly that his master heard him. Thinking that some new adventure was afoot, he turned Rocinante and trotted back to the inn. As he approached he got a marvellous view over the yard wall of Sancho repeatedly rising and falling. If he hadn't been so cross he would probably have laughed; instead he began hurling abuse at the men holding the blanket. He even tried to climb off Rocinante onto the wall but was too weak to do so.

For all Don Quixote's shouts, the men didn't stop their game until they were completely exhausted. They then sat Sancho on his donkey, and Maritornes, who had quite a kind heart, gave him a jug of wine to drink.

Don Quixote cried out, "Don't drink that; I have some of that balsam for you."

To which Sancho replied, "You know perfectly well what effect that stuff has on non-knights. Just leave me alone."

With that he rode out of the inn, secretly delighted at having got away without paying. In fact, the innkeeper had taken the saddlebags off the donkey by way of payment, but Sancho hadn't noticed.

They rode along, with Sancho slumped on his donkey, battered and exhausted.

"That castle was obviously enchanted," said Don Quixote. "That's why I couldn't come and rescue you."

"I don't know about any enchantments," said Sancho, "but I do know that all that comes out of knight-errantry seems to be regular beatings. We haven't won a single battle yet, unless you count that one against the Basque, and even then you lost half an ear and most of your helmet. I think we'd be better off going home, especially as it's harvest time."

"What we need is Amadis's magic sword," said Don Quixote.

"Knowing my luck, it'll be as useful to non-knights as that balsam," muttered Sancho.

≈ DON QUIXOTE BEATS UP SOME SHEEP, IS FELLED BY SOME STONES AND ENDS UP WITH FEWER TEETH THAN HE STARTED WITH

Don Quixote and Sancho rode slowly along, and after a while spotted a huge cloud of dust coming towards them down the road ahead.

"Fortune has smiled on us," declared Don Quixote. "That is a vast army approaching."

"In that case, there's another one," said Sancho, turning and pointing to a dust cloud on the road behind them. "What are we going to do?"

"Help those that need it," replied Don Quixote. "That army in front of us is led by the great Emperor Alifanfarón, lord of the island of Taprobana. The leader of the one behind us is the king of the Garamantes, his mortal enemy, also known as Pentapolín of the Turned-Up Sleeve." And then he launched into an account of the two armies, naming the knights they contained and describing their armour and the emblems on their shields in immense detail.

"Funny," said Sancho, "I can't see any knights in all this dust, and all I can hear is the bleating of sheep."

"What," said Don Quixote, "can't you hear the banging of drums, the call of trumpets and the neighing of horses? It must be because you're afraid." And so saying, he spurred Rocinante and charged into the dust cloud, his pikestaff at the ready, shouting, "Fear not, Pentapolín of the Turned-Up Sleeve. I will help you vanquish the evil Alifanfarón of Taprobana!"

"Come back, please, Don Quixote, sir!" yelled Sancho. 'There aren't any armies; they're just sheep. Lord have mercy on our souls."

But Don Quixote ignored him and began laying about at the sheep with his pikestaff. The shepherds who were guarding the flocks, seeing this madman in their midst, began firing stones at Don Quixote with their slingshots. One hit him square in the ribs. Don Quixote got out his bottle of balsam and began drinking from it. Almost at once, another stone hit him in the mouth, crushing two fingers, breaking the bottle and knocking out several of his teeth. The force of the two blows caused Don Quixote to slide off Rocinante. The shepherds ran up and, seeing him lying on the ground, thought they had killed him. They quickly rounded up their flocks, picked up the dead sheep, of which there were several, and made off.

Sancho appeared. "I did warn you that they were sheep not armies, sir," he said.

"It's that accursed enchanter Frestón again," replied Don Quixote. "Just as I was about to win, he turned the armies into sheep. If you don't believe me, just follow them for a while. They'll soon turn back into armies when they think no one's looking. Meanwhile, come and tell me how many teeth I've lost."

Sancho peered inside his master's mouth. Just then the balsam had its effect, causing Don Quixote to be sick all over Sancho. This caused Sancho to be sick in turn all over Don Quixote, leaving them both in a very sorry state. Sancho stumbled over to his donkey to look for something in his saddlebags to clean himself up with and bandage his master's wounds, only to discover that the saddlebags were missing. This was the last straw. He stood there mournfully, cursing the day he had ever decided to become a knight's squire, and determined to go back home at once.

Don Quixote, seeing the state Sancho was in, tried to cheer him up by saying that all their misfortunes were a sure sign that their luck was about to change.

Sancho was not very convinced. "In any case," he said, "we've got to find somewhere for the night, and there'd better not be any blankets or blanket tossers or wizards there, or I'm giving up adventuring for good."

"Fine," said Don Quixote, "but before we set off, just feel in my mouth to see how many teeth I have left on this right side at the back."

Sancho stuck his fingers in. "Two and a half, as far as I can work out," he said.

"Oh, woe!" lamented Don Quixote. "That means two and a half have gone. I'd rather have lost my left arm than those precious teeth."

It was now Sancho's turn to try to cheer Don Quixote up. They rode on, chatting away until it got dark, getting hungrier and hungrier – all their food had been in the saddlebags that the innkeeper had kept. Then they saw coming towards them on the road ahead a mass of moving lights that looked just like stars. Sancho began to quake with fear, and even Don Quixote could feel the hairs on the back of his neck standing on end.

≈The dead knight and how Don Quixote became known as the Knight with the Face in a Sorry State

"This will be our greatest adventure yet," declared Don Quixote.

"Oh no," groaned Sancho. "If there are ghosts involved this time too, I don't think my ribs will be able to stand it."

"This time I will protect you," said Don Quixote stoutly.

As the lights approached, Sancho became even more afraid. There were about twenty ghostly figures, all draped in white and holding flaming torches. Behind them was a chariot decked out in black, and behind this six figures on mules, dressed in mourning.

Don Quixote immediately decided that the chariot was carrying a dead or wounded knight, whom he had a duty to avenge. He positioned himself in the middle of the road and as the party approached called out, "Stop, you knights or whatever you are. Tell me who you are, where you have come from, where you are going and who is on that chariot."

"We haven't got time for long explanations," said one of the men in white. "The inn we're heading for is still a long way off." And he spurred his mule to move off.

Don Quixote was offended by this reply and grabbed the mule's bridle. "Mind your manners," he said, "and reply to my questions, or I'll challenge you to mortal combat."

The mule, startled by being grabbed, reared up and fell backwards on top of its rider. One of the attendants on foot started to curse Don Quixote, who, furious, began attacking everyone around him, wounding at least one of the mourners badly. The men in white soon ran off, but the mourners, who had heavy robes on, couldn't move as fast, and Don Quixote gave them all a good beating. Sancho was amazed at his master's performance, and at the speed and agility of Rocinante, who was like an animal transformed.

Don Quixote then came up to the man who was trapped under his mule. He put his pikestaff to the man's face and ordered him to surrender or die.

The man declared, "I've given up already – one of my legs is broken. If you're a good Christian, I beg you not to kill me, for I have just become a priest."

"And what the devil brings you here then?" demanded Don Quixote.

"My name is Alonso López," replied the man, "and I live in the city of Baeza. My companions and I are taking the bones of a gentleman who died in Baeza some time ago to his home town of Segovia to be reburied."

"Who killed him?" asked Don Quixote.

"God, with a fever," replied the man.

"In that case I won't have to avenge his death," said Don Quixote. "You should know that I am a knight from La Mancha, called Don Quixote, whose profession is to wander around righting wrongs."

"I don't know how you can say you're righting wrongs when you've badly wronged me for no reason, and broken my leg, which won't ever be right again."

"Well," replied Don Quixote, "the problem was that you all appeared out of the night, looking like evil beings from the next world. I had no choice but to attack you."

"In that case, can you at least help me out from under this mule?"

"Why didn't you ask me earlier?" said Don Quixote. "We might have gone on talking all night."

Don Quixote then called Sancho, who ignored him as he was busy rummaging through the packs on a mule belonging to the men from Baeza. The packs were full of good things to eat and Sancho wrapped as much as he could in his coat, which he tied to his donkey. He then came over, and he and Don Quixote freed the trapped priest. They helped him onto his mule and, handing him his torch, sent him off to join his companions.

As he was leaving, Sancho said, "If by any chance your companions want to know who it was who committed this offence against them, say it was the famous Don Quixote de la Mancha, also known as the Knight with the Face in a Sorry State."

As soon as the man had left, Don Quixote turned to Sancho Panza and asked him what on earth had possessed him to call him that.

"Well," said Sancho, "I was looking at you in the light of the torch that poor soul was carrying, and I thought that you, sir, had the sorriest-looking face I'd seen for ages – it must be because of all the teeth you've lost, or because you're so tired after all this fighting."

"Actually," said Don Quixote, "lots of knights had names of that sort in the past. I'm sure that whoever it is who will write of my deeds has decided that I too need a title like that. I think that when there is time, I will have a very sorry face painted on my shield, so that people will know how to refer to me."

"You don't need to waste any time and money on that," replied Sancho. "All you have to do is uncover your own face, and everyone will immediately know what to call you."

At that moment, Alonso López returned and said, "By the way, because you laid violent hands on something holy – me – you are to be excommunicated." He then started spouting in Latin.

"I don't understand that Latin," said Don Quixote, "and in any case it wasn't my hands but this pikestaff. What's more, I didn't think I was attacking a priest or anything else holy."

Alonso López rode off without replying. Don Quixote then wanted to check that the chariot really was carrying a skeleton, but Sancho stopped him.

"We should leave while we're ahead," he said. "You've got out of this adventure more safely than any of the others and we don't want to push our luck. My donkey is carrying supplies, there are mountains near by and we're both starving hungry. So, to the grave with the dead, and to the living some bread, is what I say."

≈Don Quixote's scariest adventure yet and Sancho Panza's desperate efforts to stop him setting out on it

Don Quixote and Sancho continued their journey. They soon came to a wide, sheltered valley full of green grass, where they stretched themselves out and ate their fill. Unfortunately, the one thing missing was anything to drink.

Sancho said, "Surely, sir, all this grass means there must be water near by. I think we should go a little further as we're bound to find somewhere where we can quench our thirst."

Don Quixote agreed. They loaded up the remains of their feast and set off, feeling their way carefully through the dark, leading Rocinante and the donkey by the reins. They had only gone a little way when they heard a roaring sound, as if a mass of water was rushing over a high cliff. They were cheered by this, but then over the top of it they heard another, even louder noise, a great rhythmic crashing accompanied by the clanking of chains. They had also happened to walk under some tall trees, whose tops were swaying about in the wind, making an eerie rustling noise which added to the general cacophony.

What with the pitch dark, and the wind, and the awful noises, anyone but Don Quixote would have been terrified. That includes Sancho, who was indeed terrified. But Don Quixote wasn't scared. He leapt onto Rocinante and, grasping his lance and shield, began to hold forth.

"Sancho, my friend," he said, "knowest thou that I was born in this dull time to revive the glorious golden age of knight-errantry, to carry out valiant deeds." And on he went, declaring that this was yet another trial designed to test his mettle and show that he was braver than any of the knights of old. "Tighten up Rocinante's girth," he ordered Sancho, "and wait here for me. If I have not returned in three days, go back home and then to El Toboso, where you must tell the glorious lady Dulcinea that her knight died performing deeds truly worthy of her name."

As soon as Sancho heard this he began to weep. "Oh, sir," he sobbed, "I don't understand why you want to set off on this terrible adventure. It's night, no one can see us and there's no one to accuse us of being cowards if we just turn round and go away. You, sir, have had a load of miraculous escapes already – you haven't been tossed in a blanket like me and you've just got away from ever so many enemies scot-free.

"If that doesn't convince you, then think of me. As soon as you've gone, I'll be so scared that I'll be ready to give up the ghost just like that. To think I left my wife and children just to serve you, believing I might be better off, not worse. And now, just as I thought I was about to get my hands on that pesky island thing you promised me, I find that I'm going to be left alone in the dark in the middle of nowhere. If you must do it, please *please* wait until morning, which I'm sure is less than three hours away."

But Don Quixote was unmoved. "I'm afraid, Sancho, that as a knight I cannot allow tears and pleas to dissuade me from doing what I must. So I beg you to shut up and tighten Rocinante's girths. I'll soon be back, alive or dead."

Sancho, seeing that words could not persuade Don Quixote, decided to take action. While he was tightening up Rocinante's girths, as Don Quixote had ordered, he secretly tied two of the horse's legs together with his donkey's harness. When Don Quixote tried to set off, he found that Rocinante could only hop feebly.

Sancho saw that his trick had worked. "Goodness, sir," he said, "heaven has taken pity on me, and has cast a spell on Rocinante."

Don Quixote began to despair, as, however hard he tried, he could not make Rocinante budge. Eventually he calmed down and decided to wait, either for daybreak or until Rocinante was able to move again.

"Don't worry, sir," said Sancho, "I'll entertain you while you're waiting by telling stories, unless your grace would like to dismount and lie down to rest on this soft green grass."

"What, me sleep in the face of danger?" retorted Don Quixote. "You can sleep if you like, for that's obviously what you were born to do, but I'm staying here, in my rightful place."

"I didn't mean to offend," said Sancho, who, still terrified by all the noise, had grabbed the front and back of Don Quixote's saddle and was standing pressed up against Rocinante's flank, not daring to move an inch.

Don Quixote said that Sancho could tell a story to amuse them.

So Sancho launched into a long rambling tale about a goatherd and a shepherdess. "Well, you see, somewhere in Estremadura, there was this goatherd – you know, a person who looks after goats. And this goatherd I was telling you about was called Lope Ruiz. Now, Lope Ruiz, the goatherd I just mentioned, was in love with a shepherdess called Torralba. This shepherdess called Torralba was the daughter of a rich farmer. The rich farmer—"

"If you go on telling the story in that way, repeating everything twice, we'll be here for days," said Don Quixote, rather exasperated.

"It's the only way I know how to tell stories, sir," replied Sancho, who then carried on as before. He told how the goatherd had fallen out of love with Torralba just as she had fallen in love with him.

"Just like all women," put in Don Quixote. "They can't stand any man who loves them and love any man who loathes them."

Sancho Panza went on to explain that in order to get away from her, the goatherd had decided to flee with his three hundred goats to Portugal. He got to a big river where there was just a fisherman with a small fishing boat, which only had room for one person and one goat. Torralba was following and had nearly caught up. The goatherd arranged for the fisherman to ferry his goats across.

Sancho continued, "The fisherman got into his boat and ferried one of the goats across. Then he came back and ferried another goat across. He came back again and ferried another goat across. Now, sir," he added, "you must keep track of how many goats the fisherman has carried across, because if you miss one the story will end. Oh, and I forgot that the landing stage on the other side was all muddy and slippery, so it all took ages. In any case, he came back for another goat, and another goat and another goat..."

"Oh look, just say that he took all the goats across," said Don Quixote.

"How many have gone across so far?" asked Sancho.

"How on earth should I know?" replied Don Quixote.

"Well, that's ruined it," said Sancho. "I said you should keep count. Now there's nothing left to tell, because I've forgotten everything that happened next, although it was all very interesting."

"Well, that's the oddest story I've ever heard," said Don Quixote. "Now let's see if Rocinante can move."

But he couldn't, so they all stayed put.

Just then, perhaps because of the cold, or because of something he'd eaten, or because that's the normal way of things, Sancho felt an urgent call of nature. But he was much too scared to move away from his position clinging on to Don Quixote's saddle. So, very carefully, he let go of the back of the saddle with his right hand and loosened his trousers. He then stuck his backside out as far as he could and proceeded to unburden himself. Unfortunately, as he was doing this, try as he might he couldn't help making a noise. It wasn't a loud noise, but it was different from the background crashing and roaring, and Don Quixote heard it distinctly.

"What's that?" he asked.

"I don't know, sir," replied Sancho. "It must be some new adventure."

Now, Don Quixote's sense of smell was as good as his hearing. Soon some of the fumes from Sancho's effort drifted up to him. Pinching his nose, he said in a rather muffled way, "I think you must be rather scared, Sancho."

"As a matter of fact I am, sir," replied Sancho, "but why have you said that now?"

"Because you smell more than usual, and not very nicely."

"You probably think I've done something I shouldn't have done," said Sancho.

"Yes, and I'd be grateful if you'd move a few steps back," replied Don Quixote, but Sancho stayed just where he was.

Eventually the sun began to rise. Before Don Quixote had seen anything, Sancho carefully pulled up his trousers and unhobbled Rocinante, who immediately began to paw the ground. Don Quixote, seeing that Rocinante could now move, was determined to carry on with his adventure, despite Sancho pleading once more that they should beat a retreat. Don Quixote would have none of it, and off they went, heading towards the source of the terrible noise with Don Quixote mounted on Rocinante and Sancho leading his donkey by the harness. Soon they came out of the trees and looked across a small meadow to some cliffs, over which a great waterfall was plummeting. At the foot of the cliffs was a collection of tumbledown buildings. It was from these that the clanking noise was coming.

They advanced towards the buildings, Sancho staying close behind Rocinante and peering through the horse's legs to keep an eye on what was ahead. They rounded a corner and there, in front of them, was the source of the racket. It was six great mill hammers, pounding away.

Don Quixote fell quite silent, stiffened in his saddle and then sank his head onto his chest, looking utterly dejected. Sancho began to shake with laughter. To make matters worse, he then started to mock his master by imitating him, repeating most of what he had said when they had first heard the terrible noise. "'Sancho, my friend, knowest thou that I was born in this dull time to revive the glorious golden age of knight-errantry, to carry out valiant deeds...'"

≈ Sancho's fourth beating
(not counting the blanket-tossing)

Sancho's mockery was all too much for Don Quixote, who raised his pikestaff and began to beat Sancho furiously on the back.

"Sir, sir, please calm yourself," said Sancho. "I was only joking."

"Well, I am not," replied Don Quixote coldly. "You, sir, should admit that had they not been mill hammers, but some real danger, I would have been as brave as was needed to defeat them."

"It's true I was a bit too quick to laugh, but you must admit that it was pretty funny, us being so terrified and everything."

"I confess that it was amusing," said Don Quixote, calming down, "but there's no need to tell anyone else about it. Other people don't always understand these things."

"What I understand," said Sancho, "is that when important gentlemen shout at their servants, they sometimes give them a pair of trousers afterwards. I don't know what knights errant are supposed to give their squires when they've beaten them, but perhaps it's an island, or something of that sort."

"It's quite possible," replied Don Quixote. "You must forgive me for what just happened, but you're an intelligent fellow and know that people sometimes react too quickly. Now, though, you've got to stop chattering to me so much. In all the books of chivalry I have read, I have never come across a squire who talks to his master as much as you do to yours. You should show more respect."

Sancho promised that he would never again make fun of his master, but would only speak in order to honour him.

≈The marvellous helmet of Mambrino

It began to rain, and Sancho wanted them to shelter in the mill, but Don Quixote had taken such a dislike to the hammers that he refused. They turned right and found themselves on another road. Soon afterwards, Don Quixote spotted a man riding towards them wearing something on his head that shone as if it were made of gold.

Don Quixote turned to Sancho and said, "Those old proverbs are always true, especially the one that says 'When one door closes another one opens.' Last night Fortune closed a door on one adventure, but now she's opened another. If I'm not mistaken, that man ahead of us is wearing the enchanted helmet of Mambrino."

"I just hope it's not another set of mill hammers," sighed Sancho.

"What on earth have mill hammers got to do with enchanted helmets?" asked Don Quixote.

"If I was allowed to talk as much as before, I'd explain," replied Sancho. "All I'll say is, that's a man on a donkey just like mine, wearing something shiny on his head."

In fact, the man approaching them was a barber making his way from one village to another, carrying a brass shaving basin along with other bits of equipment. He had put the basin on his head to protect his hat from the rain. But Don Quixote saw a knight on a dapple-grey horse, wearing a marvellous golden helmet. He lowered his pikestaff and, urging Rocinante on, charged at the barber crying, "Defend yourself, or surrender to me what is rightfully mine!"

The terrified barber leapt off his donkey and sprinted away, leaving the basin lying on the ground. Sancho picked it up and handed it to his master, saying, "This is a good basin. It must be worth a bit of money."

Don Quixote put the basin on his head and began to turn it round and round, looking for the visor. "The heathen for whom this helmet was made must have had a huge head," he said. "What's more, half of it is missing."

Sancho began to chuckle, but, remembering the last time he had laughed at his master, quickly stopped.

"The helmet obviously fell into the hands of someone who didn't recognize its value," continued Don Quixote. "They must have melted half of it down for the gold. I'll have it repaired as soon as we find a blacksmith, but in the meantime I'll wear it as it is."

"And what are we going to do with this here dapple-grey horse that looks just like a donkey to me?" asked Sancho.

"I have never believed that a knight should take a horse from another knight, unless it's in battle," said Don Quixote. "I think you should leave this horse, or donkey, or whatever you think it is, as its master is bound to come and retrieve it when he sees we've gone."

"If you say so, sir," said Sancho, "though the rules of chivalry do seem terribly strict. But what about its packsaddle and other stuff? It's in a much better state than my donkey's. Couldn't I at least swap them over?"

"Well," mused Don Quixote, "I'm not sure about that. As I'm uncertain of the proper rule, then I think you can exchange them, if you really think you need to."

Without further ado, Sancho swapped his donkey's trappings for those of the barber's. Don Quixote and Sancho Panza ate and then set off, wandering wherever Rocinante happened to take them. While they were riding along, Sancho asked Don Quixote for permission to speak, as he had a lot on his mind.

"Very well," replied Don Quixote, "but for heaven's sake be brief."

"Well, I've been thinking," said Sancho. "It seems to me that we're not getting much profit or fame from our current way of adventuring in out-of-the-way places. Wouldn't we be better off finding some great emperor who's waging a war, and offering our services to him? We're bound to be well rewarded, and there'll be someone there who can commemorate all your brave deeds in writing."

"You have a point there, Sancho," replied Don Quixote, "but before a knight can turn up at an emperor's court he has to wander the world to prove his worth. Then, when he finally arrives, his reputation will have gone before him."

Don Quixote then described in great detail what would happen next – how the knight and the emperor's daughter would fall instantly in love, and secretly swear themselves to each other; and how the knight would cover himself in glory fighting battles on the emperor's behalf and return and ask for the princess's hand; and how the emperor would be reluctant at first but would agree when he discovered that the knight came from an aristocratic family. After some time, the old emperor would die and the knight would become emperor in his place and would reward his trusty squire with a large estate, and the squire would marry one of the princess's ladies-in-waiting.

≈ How Don Quixote released some unfortunate souls from their chains, including the handsome but notorious Ginés de Pasamonte

They were discussing how all this would take place, when Don Quixote looked up and saw coming towards them a party of twelve men, shackled to a great iron chain. Accompanying them were two men on horseback armed with pistols, and two men on foot with swords and spears.

"Look," said Sancho, "a gang of convicts, being forced by the king to go to the galleys."

"What, does the king use force to make people do things?"

"That's not really what I meant," said Sancho. "They've been found guilty of crimes and are now being made to serve their punishment in the king's galleys."

"That still means they're not going by their own free will. It's obvious I have to act here, as my duty is to right wrongs and offer help to the wretched," said Don Quixote.

At this moment, the chain gang came up and Don Quixote politely asked the guards who the men were. One of the guards said that Don Quixote was welcome to ask each of the convicts what crimes he had committed.

The first one said he was there because he had been in love.

"You can't possibly have been sent to the galleys for being in love," said Don Quixote.

"Well, it wasn't what you're probably thinking. I fell in love with a big basket full of fine linen, which didn't happen to belong to me."

The second man was too depressed and miserable to answer Don Quixote. The first man explained for him. "He's a singer," he said.

"Surely it's not a crime to sing," said Don Quixote.

"What I mean is that he confessed under torture to being a horse thief. We don't like people who confess, so we give him a hard time and that's why he's so miserable."

The third man explained that he was there for the want of some money – ten ducats to be precise.

"I'll gladly give you twenty to free you from this misery," said Don Quixote.

"It's no use now," replied the man. "I needed the money to bribe the judge at my trial."

At the very end of the chain gang was a handsome man of around thirty, with a slight squint. He was chained up even more tightly than the others, so that he couldn't move his arms at all. Don Quixote asked one of the guards who he was and why he was bound like that. The guard answered that his name was Ginés de Pasamonte and that he was the most dangerous criminal of the lot, having committed more crimes than all the others put together.

Ginés de Pasamonte told Don Quixote to stop asking questions and said if he wanted to know more about him, he could read his autobiography.

"It's true," said the guard. "He wrote his own life story in prison; it's called *The Life of Ginés de Pasamonte*."

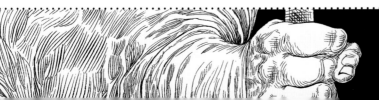

"Is it finished?" Don Quixote asked Pasamonte.

"How can it be, when my life isn't over yet?" he responded.

He and the guard then started arguing. The guard got exasperated and raised his staff to hit Pasamonte, but Don Quixote put himself between the two of them. Turning to the chain gang, he began speaking.

"Dear comrades," he said, "I know that you are being punished for your crimes, but I can see that you do not like your punishments, and are unwilling to accept them. As a knight errant I have been sent to help the needy and oppressed. I am therefore requesting your guards to let you go in peace."

Turning to the guards he said, "None of these men have done any harm to you personally, so it is your duty to let them go. I am asking you this politely, but am prepared to use force if necessary."

"That's a good joke," said one of the guards. "Now just be off and leave us in peace, or you'll get yourself in trouble."

"You're the one that's in trouble," fumed Don Quixote, and thumped the man with his pikestaff.

The man fell to the ground, dropping his pistol. The other guards rushed up and the convicts, seizing their chance, and with a bit of help from Sancho, quickly freed themselves from their shackles. Ginés de Pasamonte picked up the pistol lying on the ground and pointed it at the other guards, who turned and fled, followed by a hail of stones thrown by the rest of the convicts.

≈ DON QUIXOTE'S FOURTH AND SANCHO'S FIFTH BEATING AT THE HANDS OF THE UNGRATEFUL SOULS WHOM DON QUIXOTE HAD RELEASED FROM THEIR CHAINS

The convicts began stripping the clothes off the fallen guard, but Don Quixote called them to him. "It is normal for well-born people to give thanks to those that do them favours," he said. "I would therefore like you all to go immediately to the city of El Toboso, carrying the chain I have just freed you from. There you shall present yourselves to the lady Dulcinea del Toboso and tell her that her devoted servant, the Knight with the Face in a Sorry State, was responsible for giving you your liberty."

Ginés de Pasamonte said that this was not possible. "We'll be splitting up to avoid the Holy Brotherhood," he explained, "but tell you what, we'll all say a few prayers on your behalf while we're on the road."

"You ungrateful guttersnipe!" roared Don Quixote. "You can go to El Toboso by yourself, carrying the whole chain on your back."

But Pasamonte wasn't in the mood for arguing, and winked at his companions. They all started raining stones down on Don Quixote, who toppled over. One of the prisoners then snatched up the shaving basin and smashed it down on Don Quixote's back. Sancho tried to shelter behind his donkey, with little success. The men took the tunic Don Quixote was wearing, Sancho's topcoat and anything else they could, and made off.

Lying there all battered next to Rocinante, who had also been felled by the shower of stones, Don Quixote turned to his squire and said, "I had always heard that doing good to low-born ruffians was a waste of time. I should have listened to you, Sancho, but what's done is done. Let it be a lesson for the future."

"If you've learnt any lessons from this, I'm a Dutchman's uncle," retorted Sancho. "But you'd better listen to me now when I say that if we don't keep out of the way of the Holy Brotherhood for a while, we'll be in even worse trouble. They don't give a fig for any chivalric stuff."

"I know you're a born coward," said Don Quixote, "but on this occasion I'll take your advice. Though, mark my words, if you ever tell anyone that I did this because I was frightened, you'll be lying, and I'll make sure everyone knows it."

"We're not running away; we're just being sensible," replied Sancho. "Now just see if you can get on Rocinante and follow me."

Sancho mounted his donkey and they headed for the Sierra Morena mountains, where Sancho thought they could hide out for a few days.

≈ THE START OF DON QUIXOTE'S GREAT ADVENTURE IN THE SIERRA MORENA, WHICH GETS VERY COMPLICATED AND INVOLVES A LOT OF DIFFERENT CHARACTERS

Don Quixote was delighted when they reached the mountains. Here was a place for real adventures! Meanwhile, Sancho was too busy stuffing himself with food from his donkey's saddlebags to care about adventuring.

Soon Don Quixote spotted something lying on the ground. It was a half-rotted travelling bag attached to part of a saddle. Sancho went over and picked it up. Inside were some fine linen clothing, a number of gold coins wrapped in a handkerchief, and a notebook. Don Quixote took the notebook but told Sancho to keep the money for himself.

"Someone must have been attacked by robbers and brought here by them to be buried," said Don Quixote.

"That can't be right," said Sancho. "If they were robbers they would have taken the money."

"True," said Don Quixote. "Perhaps we'll find a clue to what happened inside this notebook."

The first thing he found in the book was a poem, written in a very fine hand, lamenting the cruelty of love. Further on he found a paragraph bitterly attacking a woman for rejecting the writer. The rest of the notebook was filled with similar stuff.

While Don Quixote was reading the notebook, Sancho was rifling through the remains of the bag to see if there was any more money hidden. Suddenly all the awful things he had been through – the beatings, the blanket-tossing, the horrible balsam of Fierabras – seemed worth it. There was no more treasure hidden in the bag, but Sancho was quite content.

Don Quixote was burning with curiosity to find out who the owner of the saddlebag was. A little later, as they wandered through the mountains, he spotted a wild-looking man wearing little more than a pair of tattered trousers, leaping nimbly from rock to rock on the hillside above them. It immediately struck Don Quixote that this must be the bag's owner. He ordered Sancho to dismount and cut across the hillside to try to find him.

Sancho bluntly refused. "As soon as I leave your side I'll be completely terrified," he said. "And besides, it'd be better not to try too hard to track him down – if he is the owner of the saddlebag, then I'll have to give him his money back."

They continued on their track around the hill, where they came across a long-dead mule, still with its bridle and saddle. They quickly concluded that this must have belonged to the same man.

Just then they heard a whistle and looked up to see an old man tending a flock of goats.

"I see you've found that mule," said the goatherd as he drew near. "Have you come across its owner?"

"No," replied Don Quixote, "but we did find a travel bag."

"Ah, I found that too, but refused to go near it – I was sure I'd be accused of stealing if I touched it," said the old man.

"Of course, we left it alone too," said Sancho.

"Tell me, my good man, do you know anything about the owner of these things?" asked Don Quixote.

"Well," said the old man, "about six months ago, not far from here, a very polite and well-bred young gentleman appeared on that mule, and asked us where the most rugged and remote part of the mountain range was. We told him, and he immediately headed off in that direction. We heard nothing more until a few days later, when he suddenly appeared and, without a word, attacked one of us goatherds, punching and kicking like crazy. He then took a load of bread and cheese and raced away.

"A few of us set off to track him down, and eventually we found him hiding in a hollow tree. He was very polite, and explained that he was performing a penance for his sins. We told him that if he ever needed food he should just ask us; he certainly didn't have to take it by force. He said he was sorry for his earlier attack, and would humbly beg for his food from now on. He then started weeping noisily.

"Suddenly he stopped and slumped to the ground, staring down with a strange expression on his face. Without any warning he jumped up and began to attack the man standing nearest him, calling him Fernando and shouting, 'You traitor, I will rip out your heart in revenge for the wrong you've done me!' We pulled him off and he disappeared into the bushes without another word.

"We've seen him several times since then; when he's sane he asks politely for food, and is calm and reasonable, but when he's out of his mind he just attacks us and steals the food, even though we'd gladly give it to him."

Just then, the man himself appeared and politely greeted them in a hoarse voice. Don Quixote replied equally politely and, dismounting from Rocinante, embraced him as if he were an old friend.

"Good sir," said Don Quixote, "I see that you have suffered grave misfortune. I have decided that my duty as a knight errant is to serve you as well as I can, either by finding a remedy for your troubles or, if there is no such remedy, at least by sharing your woes with you. So, I beg you to tell us who you are and what has brought you to this."

The young man looked Don Quixote up and down in silence for a while, and then said, "I'm starving. If any of you has anything to eat, please let me have it, and then I'll tell you my story. But I must ask you not to interrupt me once I've started telling it, because if you do, I'll stop that instant."

The man's statement brought to Don Quixote's mind the goats in Sancho's story, but he said nothing.

Some food was found for the man, which he stuffed down with incredible speed. Once he'd eaten, he led the others into a grassy glade. They all stretched out on the ground and the man started speaking.

≈ Cardenio's story

"My name is Cardenio, and my father is a rich nobleman from one of the finest cities in Andalusia. Growing up there, I fell in love with a young maiden called Luscinda, who loved me in return. As we grew older, her father decided it would be improper for me to visit their house, but we were allowed to write to each other. I finally decided to ask for her hand, but Luscinda's father thought that the request should come from my father, as he was still alive.

"I immediately went to my father, and found him with a letter in his hand. It was from an important aristocrat, Duke Ricardo, who lived some distance away, asking me to become a companion to his elder son. I had no choice but to accept. Before leaving for the duke's, I went to Luscinda's father asking him to wait a few days before the marriage was settled, so that I could find out what the duke expected of me.

"I was very well received at the duke's. The person who was most pleased at my arrival was the duke's younger son, Don Fernando, and we soon became firm friends. Soon afterwards, Don Fernando had a fling with a wealthy farmer's daughter – Dorothea was her name – and even went as far as promising to marry her. He wasn't really serious about her, however, and quickly decided he'd be better off out of the way for a while until things cooled down. The duke gave permission for us both to visit my family.

"Foolishly I had told Don Fernando all about Luscinda, and when we got back to my home city, he saw her at a window in her father's house. He immediately fell deeply in love with her. From then on he couldn't stop singing her praises, and insisted on reading all my letters to her, and hers to me. Then one day, Luscinda wrote asking me to get hold of a book on chivalry for her, one that she was very fond of, called *Amadís of Gaul.*"

On hearing these words, Don Quixote broke in. "If you'd mentioned at the start that the lady Luscinda liked books on chivalry, I would immediately have known how marvellous she was. By the way, you should also have sent her the book *Don Rugel of Greece*, as I know she would have enjoyed that too." He then apologized to Cardenio for interrupting his story and asked him to continue.

But Cardenio stayed silent, and stood with his head sunk down, deep in thought. Eventually he looked up and said, "There is one thing about *Amadís of Gaul* which seems obvious to me, however much people deny it, and that is that Master Elisabat was carrying on with Queen Madásima."

"Outrageous!" exploded Don Quixote. "Anyone who says such a thing is an utter scoundrel and should be made to take it back."

≈ Sancho's sixth beating

Hearing himself referred to as a scoundrel, Cardenio had a fit of madness, seized a rock and flung it at Don Quixote, hitting him in the chest. Sancho leapt up and attacked Cardenio in turn, but Cardenio felled him with a punch and then jumped up and down on him, bruising his ribs terribly. The goatherd tried to defend Sancho but was also soundly thrashed by Cardenio, who then straightened himself up and, perfectly composed, strolled off into the woods.

Sancho got up and, furious at being beaten, started to take it out on the goatherd, blaming him for not having warned them how dangerous Cardenio was. The goatherd retorted that he had warned them, and the two of them set to, pulling each other's beards and punching wildly, until Don Quixote calmed them down.

Don Quixote was determined to track down Cardenio, and, remounting Rocinante, headed into the wildest part of the Sierra Morena, with Sancho reluctantly in tow.

Sancho was dying to talk but knew that he was not supposed to speak without first getting permission. Finally, though, he could bear it no longer and burst out, "Don Quixote, sir, please give me my discharge and let me return to my wife and children. It's bad enough here getting beaten up every five minutes, without having to stay silent as well. At least at home I'll be able to chatter away to my heart's content."

"I understand," said Don Quixote, "and I lift the ban for the time being. You can talk as much as you like, but only while we're in these mountains."

"Fine," said Sancho. "Well, what I want to know is, what on earth made you stick up for that Queen what's-her-name – you know, the Mad Screamer or something? If you hadn't said anything, I'm sure that crazy man would have just gone on with his story and we'd have been spared a beating."

"If you knew what a pure and noble woman Queen Madásima was, you wouldn't say such a thing," replied Don Quixote. "It was my duty to defend her reputation."

"I'm not saying one thing or the other," said Sancho. "They'll get their just deserts. As for me, fiddle-de-dee – what I say is, if you lie when you buy, it's your purse that will sigh. And there's many who think they'll find bacon where there isn't even a hook. And you can't make a door into a field."

"What are you talking about?" asked Don Quixote. "I don't see what all those sayings have got to do with anything. Do shut up, and remember that everything I do is in strict accordance with the rules of chivalry."

"I don't see what wandering around in these mountains looking for a madman has got to do with chivalry," muttered Sancho.

"Enough!" said Don Quixote. "If you must know, we are here not just to find the madman, but for me to perform a deed which will make me famous for ever."

"Is it dangerous?" asked Sancho.

"No, but much depends on you," replied Don Quixote.

"On me?"

"Yes, because if you come back quickly from where I'm about to send you, my suffering will rapidly end and my glory begin. I am going to stay here and imitate Amadís of Gaul, the finest knight errant that ever existed. You may recall that, spurned by the lady Oriana, Amadís changed his name to Beltenebros and retreated to Ragged Rock mountain to do penance. I am going to follow suit and stay here, behaving like a rejected lover and ranting and raving."

"But no one's rejected you," said Sancho, "or have you heard that the lady Dulcinea del Toboso has been up to no good?"

"Good heavens, no," replied Don Quixote, "but that's the whole point. It's dull and pointless going mad for a good reason – it's much more impressive going mad for no cause at all. I am mad now and I'm going to stay mad until you come back from my lady Dulcinea del Toboso, whom I'm sending you to with a letter. If she says the right things in her reply, my penance will end and I will become normal again; and if she does not, I will go truly mad and be quite happy in my madness. Oh, and by the way, are you looking after Mambrino's helmet properly?"

"Good grief," replied Sancho, "I'm getting sick and tired of some of the stuff you come out with about chivalry, and winning islands and everything. Anyone who heard you going on about that barber's basin as if it were a magic helmet would think you'd gone soft in the head."

"Well," said Don Quixote, "it's obvious to me you're the most stupid squire that ever attended a knight. Haven't you realized yet that wherever we knights errant go, we have magicians following us who can transform things at their will? One of these magicians has made Mambrino's helmet look like an ordinary barber's basin so that no one will steal it."

≈ Don Quixote's penance

While they were talking, Don Quixote and Sancho had come out into a meadow at the foot of a rocky peak.

"This is the spot where I will carry out my penance," declaimed Don Quixote, and he launched into a long speech, imploring his lady Dulcinea to take note of his actions. He then dismounted Rocinante, took off the horse's saddle and bridle and slapped him on the rump saying, "Noble steed, I release you to go where you will!"

But Sancho said, "Now that my donkey seems to have gone, it may be a good idea to saddle Rocinante and let him take the donkey's place – I'll get to the lady Dulcinea and back again much quicker than if I have to walk."

"That is not a bad plan," replied Don Quixote, "but first you must stay and witness my penance so that you can report it all to the lady Dulcinea."

"What else do I have to see?" asked Sancho.

"Don't you know anything? I have to throw off my armour, tear my clothes and hit my head against these rocks. There'll be plenty more after that as well."

"Do mind what you hit your head against," said Sancho. "It would be much better if you knocked it against something soft, like cotton. I'll make sure to tell the lady Dulcinea that it was against really hard rocks."

"That is a kind thought," said Don Quixote, "but I must do everything properly. As a knight errant, I cannot possibly encourage anyone to tell lies on my behalf. You could, though, leave some bandages for me."

"They've all gone with the donkey," replied Sancho. "Now, I think it would be much better if I left for El Toboso as soon as possible, rather than hanging around for days watching you do all that penance. The sooner I'm back to rescue you the better."

"True, but how are we going to write the letter to the lady Dulcinea?" asked the Knight with the Face in a Sorry State.

"And the note you promised to write handing three of your donkeys over to me," added Sancho.

"We could use a sheet from Cardenio's notebook," said Don Quixote, "but be sure to get it copied out neatly by a schoolmaster or someone in the first village you come to."

"What about the signature?" asked Sancho.

"Just make sure that whoever copies it out writes 'yours until death, the Knight with the Face in a Sorry State' at the bottom," replied Don Quixote. "It doesn't really matter about the writing because, if I remember rightly, Dulcinea can neither read nor write, and has never seen any letters written by me. In fact, she's been kept in such seclusion by her father, Lorenzo Corchuelo, and her mother, Aldonza Nogales, that I've only seen her myself four times. I doubt if she's ever noticed me."

"You don't mean to tell me that Lorenzo Corchuelo's daughter, known as Aldonza Lorenzo, is the lady Dulcinea del Toboso?" asked Sancho incredulously.

"Indeed she is," said Don Quixote, "and she's worthy to be mistress of the whole universe."

"My," chuckled Sancho, "she's a strapping lass. She's got a fine pair of lungs on her too. But honestly, sir, I thought you were talking about some fine lady, not some village girl who spends most of her time working in the fields."

"I've told you many times," said Don Quixote, "that you talk too much, and are dim-witted as well. Do you really think that all those maidens that fill poetry books actually existed? Of course they didn't. The poets made most of them up to have someone to write about. It's just the same with me. It's enough that I have decided that Aldonza Lorenzo is beautiful and virtuous, without having to worry if she really comes from a noble family. You see, beauty and virtue are the only qualities that count when deciding if someone is worth being in love with. I've decided in my imagination that the lady Dulcinea has these in plenty, and as far as I'm concerned she outshines any woman who's ever existed. People can say what they like – it doesn't matter to me."

"I'm sure you're right," said Sancho. "Now let's get on with that letter and I'll be off."

Don Quixote took out the notebook and carefully wrote his letter to Dulcinea. He said he would read it out so that Sancho could learn it by heart in case he lost the notebook on his journey. Sancho said he couldn't possibly memorize anything as complicated as a letter, but asked Don Quixote to read it out anyway.

"Here it is," he said.

Most noble lady,

O lovely lady Dulcinea del Toboso, one gravely wounded by your absence wishes you the good health he does not himself enjoy.

If you spurn me, patient as I am, I will not be able to bear it. My good squire Sancho will bring you tidings of the suffering I am undergoing on your behalf.

If you wish to comfort me, I am yours. If not, I shall end my life to satisfy your cruelty.

Yours until death,

The Knight with the
Face in a Sorry State

"That's the most wonderful thing I've ever heard," said Sancho. "Now can you write on the back the note about giving me the donkeys?"

"Certainly," said Don Quixote, and he did so. "But before you go, you've got to wait while I take my clothes off and perform a couple of dozen mad deeds for you to report to the lady Dulcinea. It won't take very long – only half an hour or so."

"I really don't think that's necessary," said Sancho. "And if you must carry out any mad deeds, then I beg you to do so with your clothes on; and then just a few, you know, the most important ones. And mark my words, if the lady Dulcinea doesn't believe me when I tell her, I'll give her what for."

Then Sancho started worrying about what Don Quixote would eat, but Don Quixote said that going without his normal food was part of his penance, and he would survive on wild herbs and fruit. Reassured, Sancho agreed to go.

After a tearful farewell, he and Rocinante set off, but they soon turned back and Sancho said to Don Quixote, "I think you're right, sir: if I'm to report your mad deeds with a clear conscience, I'd better see one of them at least."

Quick as a flash Don Quixote took off his trousers and, standing there dressed only in his shirt, leapt high in the air twice and then turned two somersaults. Sancho looked aghast and quickly turned Rocinante away, deciding that he'd seen quite enough to convince anyone that his master was truly mad.

≈ SANCHO MEETS THE PRIEST AND
MASTER NICOLÁS THE BARBER

While Don Quixote was carrying out his penance – which chiefly consisted of wandering about writing woeful poems in the sand and carving them on the trunks of trees – Sancho was making his way to El Toboso. On the second day, he arrived at the inn where he'd suffered his unfortunate adventure in the blanket. He couldn't bring himself to go in, although he was dying for a good hot meal. As he was hanging about outside, two men came out. They were none other than the priest and Master Nicolás the barber from Don Quixote's own village.

"Isn't that Sancho Panza, who's supposed to have gone off with Don Quixote?" said the barber.

"Indeed it is," replied the priest, "and that's Don Quixote's horse."

They were very keen to hear news of Don Quixote.

"Friend Sancho," the priest said. "Where is your master?"

Sancho was reluctant to tell them. "He's doing something frightfully important somewhere," he said, "but I can't tell you what or where."

"If you don't tell us," said the barber, "we'll think you murdered him and made off with his horse."

"I'm no murderer," retorted Sancho. "If you must know, he's in the mountains doing penance." And he then told them all about the state his master was in, and the letter he was carrying.

The priest and the barber were amazed at all this and wanted to see the letter. Sancho put his hand inside his shirt, looking for the notebook. But it wasn't there, because he had forgotten to ask for it, and Don Quixote had never given it to him.

When Sancho realized that he didn't have the notebook, he turned horribly pale, yanked out half his beard and punched himself in the face until he was bleeding profusely. The priest and the barber asked what on earth the problem was.

"Oh, nothing important," replied Sancho bitterly. "It's only that I've gone and lost three whole donkeys just like that." He then explained about the loss of his donkey, and the note Don Quixote had written.

"Don't worry," said the priest. "We'll have your master write out the order again when we find him."

Sancho immediately felt much better and said he wasn't too worried about losing the letter to Dulcinea, as he almost knew it by heart.

"Tell it to us," said the barber, "and we'll copy it down."

"It went something like this," said Sancho. "'Most nobbled lady'."

"Surely you mean 'Most noble lady'?" corrected the barber.

"That's right," said Sancho. "Then it went on: 'Oh blubbery lady Dulcinea, in gravy I'm winded something something something, in thickness and in stealth'; and then it was signed: 'yours until death, the Knight with the Face in a Sorry State'."

The two men were very amused by Sancho's wonderful memory and asked him to repeat the letter a couple more times. Each time, Sancho garbled it more and more. He then recounted many of his and Don Quixote's adventures, including the incident of the chain gang, although carefully leaving out any mention of blanket-tossing. He explained how his master was going to become an emperor and set Sancho up with a lady-in-waiting as a wife (as he'd be a widower by then) and give him a fine estate, though certainly not any islands as he wasn't interested in them any more.

The priest and the barber were amazed at how Sancho had been taken in by Don Quixote's madness, but decided that it was harmless enough for him to believe all this, and very entertaining as well. They told him to pray for his master, and said that it was extremely likely that in time Don Quixote would become an emperor, or at least an archbishop. Sancho was very anxious to know what kinds of favours archbishops might bestow on their faithful squires.

"Usually they make them sextons or priests," replied the priest.

"Oh dear," said Sancho, "that wouldn't suit at all, as you have to be single to be one of those, and I'm married."

The barber told Sancho not to worry, and said that they'd sort it all out when they found his master. The priest and the barber then decided that they ought to try to rescue Don Quixote from his pointless penance. They suggested that all three of them go into the inn to eat while they thought of a plan. However, Sancho said he'd rather stay outside, and asked them to bring out some hot food for him and some oats for Rocinante.

≈The plan to rescue Don Quixote, and the rest of Cardenio's story

The priest and the barber decided they would disguise themselves as a damsel in distress and a squire and seek out Don Quixote, asking him to come to the damsel's aid. Being a knight errant he could not possibly refuse, and they could then find a way of tricking him back to his own village, where they might cure him of his madness.

They asked the innkeeper's wife if they could borrow some clothes and explained why they needed them. She immediately realized that the man they were talking about had stayed at the inn, and she told them all that had happened at the time, including Sancho's adventure with the blanket. Then she gleefully kitted out the priest in a green velvet bodice and old woollen skirt trimmed with velvet bands. The priest covered his head with his cotton nightcap and wound black ribbon around his face and beard. He pulled an enormous hat on over the cap, wrapped himself in his cloak and mounted his mule side-saddle. The barber disguised himself with a reddish-coloured oxtail as a beard that dangled down to his waist. They said goodbye to everyone, including Maritornes, who promised to say a prayer for them, and set off.

It soon struck the priest that it wasn't very fitting for a holy man to be dressed in this way, and he said to the barber that they should swap disguises. They were just debating this, when Sancho appeared and immediately fell about laughing. The barber agreed to the priest's request, but did not want to dress up until they were near to Don Quixote, so they folded up the dress and bodice and put the oxtail beard away.

The next day, they reached the foot of the mountain where Don Quixote was. They discussed what to do next and decided that Sancho should go on ahead and tell Don Quixote that he'd delivered the letter to Dulcinea, who had not written a reply, as she couldn't write, but had instead told Sancho to order his master to pay her a visit immediately.

Sancho headed off to where he expected to find Don Quixote, leaving the priest and the barber in a shady spot by a cool stream. They were relaxing there, when they were astonished

to hear a clear, sweet voice singing a beautiful song. The voice sang a second song, and then sighed deeply. The priest and the barber got up and walked towards the sound. Rounding a rock, they came across a man. They immediately recognized him as Cardenio, whom Sancho had described to them earlier.

At that moment, Cardenio was quite sane. "Gentlemen," he said, "I am sure you have come to try to persuade me to abandon this life and take up a better one. But, I assure you, if I leave here I will be worse off. You probably think me mad, and I know that sometimes I am seized by fits, during which I'm told I do awful things. But before you judge me, I beg you to hear my tale. I'm sure that then you'll understand."

He then told the story that he'd begun to tell to Don Quixote and the others earlier, and soon reached the part where he was back in his town with Don Fernando.

"I told Don Fernando that I was determined to ask for Luscinda's hand," he continued, "but also that Luscinda's father thought the request should come from my father rather than from me. I explained to him that I was afraid to bring this up with my father as I suspected that he didn't want me to marry yet. Don Fernando said that he himself would speak to my father and persuade him to let me marry. He then found an excuse to send me back to his home. Luscinda was very upset at my departure and I had a sense of foreboding, though I wasn't quite sure why.

"Four days later, a letter arrived for me from Luscinda: instead of speaking on my behalf, Don Fernando had asked permission from Luscinda's father to marry her himself! Luscinda's father, deciding that Don Fernando was a better match than me, had granted permission and declared that the wedding should take place in two days' time.

"Imagine my horror. I immediately rushed back to my home town. I was lucky enough to find Luscinda gazing out of the window where we had often talked in secret.

"She whispered to me, 'Cardenio, at this very minute the treacherous Don Fernando and my greedy father are waiting in the hall downstairs for the wedding ceremony to begin. Do not worry, but make sure you're watching. If I can't persuade them to stop the wedding, I have a dagger hidden in my dress with which I will end my life, to show how true my love for you is.'

"'And I, my lady, have a sword waiting to defend you, or kill myself, as the need arises,' I replied.

"Because there was so much activity in the house I was able to sneak in unnoticed, and I hid behind a curtain in the hall. The ceremony started and the priest reached the point where he said, 'Do you, Luscinda, take Don Fernando to be your lawful wedded husband?' I craned forward to see what would happen next – oh, if only I had burst out and interrupted the ceremony! But I did nothing.

"Luscinda said nothing for ages, and then I heard her whisper, 'I will.' Don Fernando said the same and gave her a ring.

"That was it. All my dreams were shattered. I had no idea what to do. Then Luscinda suddenly fainted and collapsed into her mother's arms. Her mother loosened her bodice to help her breathe, and a piece of paper was discovered hidden there. Don Fernando took it and read it and then sat in a chair brooding in silence.

"I left the house in a daze, found my mule and rode out of the city not knowing where to go. Eventually I found myself here, and you know the rest of my story. I'm sure you realize now that nothing can console me for the treachery of my best friend and my beloved, and that the only peace I will find is in death."

Just as he was finishing, a voice interrupted him. What it said will be revealed in the fourth part of this story, because this is where the wise historian Cide Hamete Benengeli ends the third.

PART FOUR ≈ WHICH BEGINS WITH AN AMAZING COINCIDENCE

≈ THE VOICE THAT broke in just as Cardenio was finishing his story said, "Can it be true that at last I have found a place where I can lay my weary body down and end it all?"

The priest, the barber and Cardenio followed the sound and, turning a corner, saw what they thought was a young shepherd boy sitting bathing his feet in a stream. The three men crouched behind some rocks and watched.

After a while the boy took off his cap and a great shock of fair hair tumbled down – it wasn't a boy at all, but an incredibly beautiful woman. The men decided to reveal themselves, and stood up. As soon as the woman saw them, she snatched up a bundle lying beside her and made to run away, but tripped and fell.

"Please stop, lady, whoever you are," said the priest. "We only wish to help you."

The woman looked dazed and remained silent, but after some more reassuring words from the priest she began to speak.

"I see, gentlemen, that you mean me no harm, and so I will tell you my story, although I assure you that there is no cure

for my grief. I come from a town in Andalusia, where there is an important duke, with two sons. My parents are tenant farmers of this duke. They are of humble origins but are very wealthy. I was their only child and they doted on me. I managed the farm for my father, and in my spare time would read improving books or play the harp. In short, I lived a very happy if secluded life. But then, as bad luck would have it, the duke's younger son, Don Fernando, laid eyes on me."

As soon as the woman spoke the name Don Fernando, Cardenio broke into a terrible sweat and began trembling uncontrollably. The woman didn't notice, and went on with her story.

"The minute he saw me, Don Fernando fell passionately in love with me. He kept the whole household awake with his serenades and bombarded me with love letters. I confess I was flattered by all the attention, but my parents pointed out that I would be considered too lowly to be an acceptable wife to him. I kept my distance from him but my coolness only made him all the keener. One night, with the help of a maid whom he'd bribed, he stole into my room and declared that we should become husband and wife there and then. He was so earnest that he finally persuaded me, and my maid acted as witness.

"The next day, he left early, but not before giving me a ring as a token of our marriage. After that he only came to visit me once more, although I knew he was still in town. I was becoming more and more upset, when, about a month later, I heard news that in another city Don Fernando had married a beautiful woman called Luscinda from a noble family."

At the mention of Luscinda's name, Cardenio hunched his shoulders and bit his lips. Tears started streaming from his eyes, but the woman continued regardless.

"When I heard this, I fell into an uncontrollable rage. I calmed down and decided to make my way to the city and confront Don Fernando. I disguised myself as a shepherd boy, packed some things in a pillowcase, and set off with one of my father's shepherds, whom I had confided in, as my servant. After two and a half days I arrived at the city and asked someone the way to Luscinda's parents' house. I learnt that the wedding was the talk of the town, and was immediately given all the gossip.

"It seems that as soon as Luscinda had said 'I will' she fainted, and a note was found hidden in her bodice. In it she said that she was already the wife of a nobleman called Cardenio and so couldn't be Don Fernando's wife. She'd only agreed to go through with the wedding ceremony so as not to disobey her parents, and she intended to kill herself as soon as it was over – apparently they found a dagger hidden in her dress.

"When Don Fernando read the note, he decided that Luscinda had deceived him, and tried to stab her with the selfsame dagger, but was prevented from doing so by the others. Luscinda recovered the next day and told her parents that she was indeed married to Cardenio. I was also told that Cardenio had been at the wedding and had left the city in despair, though not before writing a letter setting out the wrongs that Luscinda had done him. Luscinda herself had then gone missing, driving her parents to distraction.

"I was trying to work out what to do, when I heard a town crier giving a description of me and offering a large reward for anyone who found me. I immediately left the city with my servant, still in disguise. That night, we took shelter in a wild part of the mountains. Unfortunately my servant then tried to take advantage of me, so I pushed him over a cliff, where I left him – whether dead or alive I don't know. I moved on and eventually found a herdsman who agreed to take me on as his servant, but after some months he too found out that I wasn't a boy. I fled from him and that is why you find me here. I am too ashamed to return to my parents, even though I know they love me dearly."

She fell silent. Cardenio stepped forward and said, "So you must be the lovely Dorothea, the daughter of the wealthy Clenardo."

Dorothea was amazed to hear her and her father's name spoken by someone dressed in rags. "And who are you?" she asked.

"I, madam, am that unlucky Cardenio of whom you have spoken. I came up here intending to die, but instead have gone half crazy. But perhaps there is hope for both of us, for if what you say is true – as I am sure it is – then Don Fernando could not marry Luscinda, since he is already married to you; and Luscinda could not marry him, as she is already mine. Whatever happens, I swear that I shall not rest until I see you rightfully reunited with Don Fernando, or have avenged with my sword the wrongs he has done you."

Dorothea was overwhelmed by Cardenio's offer, and fell at his feet. The priest suggested that they all return to his village, where they could decide what to do next. The barber offered to help in whatever way he could, and then briefly told them why they were in the mountains, of Don Quixote's madness and how they were waiting for Don Quixote's squire. Cardenio recalled, as if from a dream, his row with Don Quixote, but could not explain the reason for the argument.

Just then they heard Sancho calling out. They went to meet him and he told them that he'd found Don Quixote, thin, pale, starving hungry and dressed only in his shirt, moaning and sighing for his lady Dulcinea. Although Sancho had reported that Dulcinea had summoned Don Quixote, Don Quixote refused to go until he had performed deeds worthy of her name.

"Frankly," went on Sancho, "if all this goes on much longer, he's never going to become an emperor, or even an archbishop. So we'd all better find a way of getting him down from this mountain."

≈ How Don Quixote was tricked into coming down from the Sierra Morena

The priest told Sancho not to worry, and then explained the plan they had hatched to Cardenio and Dorothea. On hearing it, Dorothea said that she would be much better than the barber at playing a damsel in distress, especially as she'd read lots of books on chivalry. She got a fine dress, a shawl and some jewels out of her pillowcase and quickly changed. Sancho was amazed at the sight of her and asked the priest who this beautiful woman was.

"This lady is none other than Princess Micomicona of the kingdom of Micomicón. She has come all the way from Guinea to beg a great favour from your master, to revenge a wrong done to her by a wicked giant."

"Well, she's certainly in luck," said Sancho. "My master is sure to kill that scumbag of a giant – as long as he's not a ghost,

that is, as he's not very good at dealing with ghosts. And then I hope, sir, that you'll encourage him to marry the princess straight away. Then he won't be able to become an archbishop, which would be a great relief to me."

Dorothea mounted the priest's mule and the barber stuck the oxtail beard on his face and mounted his own mule. Sancho then led them to where he had last seen Don Quixote, leaving Cardenio and the priest behind. They soon found the knight, now wearing his clothes but not his armour. The barber helped Dorothea dismount and she fell at Don Quixote's feet, saying that she would not rise until Don Quixote swore to carry out an immensely important favour for her.

"Rest assured, madam," he replied, "I will do whatever you ask, as long as it does not dishonour my king, my country or the lady whom I adore."

Sancho whispered to his master, "Don't worry, sir; it's nothing very important: just kill some tiresome giant. Oh, and by the way, she's the terribly royal Princess Micomicona of the kingdom of Micomicón in Ethiopia."

Don Quixote turned to Dorothea and said, "Do not fear, Princess, I will soon restore you to your kingdom." He ordered Sancho to help him into his armour and to saddle Rocinante. They all started back down the mountain.

Meanwhile, Cardenio and the priest had crept up and were watching from behind some bushes. The priest then quickly disguised Cardenio by cutting off his beard and giving him his own brown cape and black cloak to wear. The two of them made their way to the base of the mountain, arriving before the others.

As soon as Don Quixote and his companions appeared, the priest rushed over and cried, "Greetings, esteemed knight and neighbour, Don Quixote de la Mancha."

Don Quixote was astonished but then recognized the man as the priest from his own village. He tried to dismount, saying that it was improper for him to be on horseback while a holy person was forced to walk, but the priest refused, telling Don Quixote that he should stay on the horse on which he had carried out the greatest exploits of the age. "Perhaps," he said, "I could sit on the saddle behind one of these other gentlemen."

Master Nicolás alighted and offered his seat to the priest, but, just as he was about to remount, the mule bucked, kicking its back legs in the air. The barber fell to the ground and his oxtail beard promptly came off. He quickly held his hands to his face and cried that his teeth had been kicked in.

Don Quixote was amazed. "A miracle!" he declared. "The mule has plucked this man's beard clean from his face without a trace of blood or bruising."

The priest snatched up the beard and rushed over to where Master Nicolás lay. Muttering some words which he said were a beard reattachment spell, he fixed the oxtail back on the barber's chin. Don Quixote looked on fascinated.

"You must teach me that spell," he said. "I'm sure it will come in useful some day."

Don Quixote asked the princess where she wished to go. Before she could answer, the priest broke in. "Unless I'm much mistaken, your highness wishes to direct us to the kingdom of Micomicón. I believe it to be about nine years' journey from here."

"Actually I only left it about two years ago," replied Dorothea, "but I am happy in that I have succeeded in what I set out to do – to meet the marvellous knight Don Quixote de la Mancha, whose fame has spread to the four corners of the earth."

"Please, no flattery," said Don Quixote. He then turned to the priest and asked, "Pray, sir, what brings you to these parts, without even a cloak or cape to wear?"

"Well," replied the priest, "I and my good friend Master Nicolás the barber were heading to Seville to collect some money. Yesterday we were set on by highwaymen, who stripped us of everything. They left this young man" – he pointed to Cardenio – "in a similar state. Everyone says that the men who attacked us were criminals in a chain gang who had been released by some lunatic. I hope he's truly sorry, whoever he is."

Don Quixote turned bright scarlet but said nothing. However, Sancho piped up, "If you must know, the man who did it was my master, even though I warned him not to."

"Idiot!" fumed Don Quixote. "Anyway, it's not up to knights errant to find out whether those in distress are good or bad. I was simply doing my duty when I let those men go."

Dorothea tried to calm him down. "Good knight," she said, "I am sure if the priest had known it was you he would not have said anything. Now, let me tell you about myself. My name is Princess Micomicona. My father, Tinacrio the Sage, was a very wise man, who prophesied that he and my mother, Queen Jaramilla, were about to die, leaving me an orphan. Once they were dead, a giant called Pandafilando of the Horrid Face, lord of a neighbouring island, would invade with his armies and demand to marry me. My father said that I should travel to Spain, where I would find a knight errant to rescue me from my troubles, called Don Cupoftee or some such."

"He must have said Don Quixote," put in Sancho, "also known as the Knight with the Face in a Sorry State."

"Yes, that's right," said Dorothea, "and my father also said that once this knight had killed Pandafilando, I must agree to marry him if he so desired."

"I knew it!" whooped Sancho. "My master's going to get married and become an emperor." He grabbed the reins of Dorothea's mule and knelt down in front of her, trying to kiss her hands, to the great amusement of the others.

Don Quixote replied to Dorothea, "Oh, worthy lady, I will of course rescue you from the wicked Pandafilando, but I'm afraid I cannot possibly contemplate marrying you."

Sancho was furious. "What do you mean?" he stormed. "How can you refuse? Is your precious Dulcinea better looking by any chance? Don't you see that I am never going to become a lord if you go on behaving like this?"

≈Sancho's seventh beating

The insult to the lady Dulcinea was too much. Don Quixote grabbed his pikestaff and began thumping Sancho. If Dorothea hadn't begged him to stop, who knows where it would have ended.

"You guttersnipe!" Don Quixote roared at Sancho. "Do you think you can go on with your impertinence like this? Don't you understand that it is only thanks to the lady Dulcinea that I can carry out my valiant deeds?"

To which Sancho said, "All I'm worried about is that if you don't marry this lady, you won't become an emperor. And then how will I get my reward? Why don't you marry her and then go back to Dulcinea? As for which one's more beautiful, they both seem fine enough to me, although I've never clapped eyes on the lady Dulcinea."

"How can you say you've never seen the lady Dulcinea when you've just brought back a message from her, you liar?" demanded Don Quixote.

"Er, what I mean is I didn't have the chance to check her out in detail. Overall, though, she seemed fine to me," replied Sancho hastily.

"Then I forgive you," said Don Quixote.

Sancho was still indignant at the beating he'd received, but with a bit of encouragement from Dorothea, he and Don Quixote made their peace. Don Quixote then whispered to Sancho that he had some matters to discuss, so the two of them moved on ahead of the others.

"And now, Sancho," said Don Quixote, "tell me everything that happened when you gave my letter to Dulcinea. How did she react? Who copied it out for you?"

"To be honest," said Sancho, "no one copied it out, because I didn't have it with me."

"You're quite right," said Don Quixote. "I found the notebook after you'd gone. So what did you do?"

"Luckily I'd learnt it by heart," replied Sancho, "so I repeated it to a clerk, who wrote it out. He said it was the loveliest letter he'd ever heard."

"And when you found the lady Dulcinea, was she sitting in luxury, stringing pearls or embroidering in gold thread?" asked Don Quixote.

"Actually she was sieving wheat in the yard," replied Sancho. "I went over to give her the letter, and she said, 'Pop it on that sack over there, dearie; I'll read it when I've finished.'"

"Did you notice an exquisite scent when you approached her?"

"Well, there was a pretty strong smell, but I wouldn't really call it exquisite," replied Sancho. "I've noticed I sometimes smell similar myself."

"You must have been mistaken, or had a cold in the head," said Don Quixote. "Now tell me, did she read my letter?"

"No," said Sancho. "She said she couldn't read or write. Instead she tore the letter into little pieces so that no one else in the village would get hold of it. I told her about your penance, and she said I should tell you to leave this godforsaken place and start for El Toboso straight away. I asked if the Basque knight had visited, and she said he had, and seemed an OK sort of bloke, but she hadn't seen any convicts yet."

They went on talking, with Sancho trying to persuade Don Quixote to go away with Princess Micomicona before visiting El Toboso. He was getting rather anxious that his lies about seeing Dulcinea would be discovered, and was very relieved when Master Nicolás shouted out from behind that the party had decided to stop at a spring.

The priest had brought some food along with him, and they were eating this and drinking from the spring when they saw a boy coming along the road towards them. As soon as the boy caught sight of Don Quixote, he burst into tears and, running up, clasped Don Quixote round the legs.

"Don't you recognize me?" he whimpered.

Don Quixote did indeed recognize him – it was Andrés, the boy he'd rescued when he was first setting out on his adventures. Don Quixote turned to the others and described how he'd found Andrés tied to a tree being beaten by his master, and how he'd forced the boy's master to free him.

"It's all true," said Andrés, "except it didn't turn out the way you thought it would."

"What, did your master not pay you then?" asked Don Quixote.

"No, he didn't, and as soon as you'd gone he flogged me some more, until I was half dead," said Andrés. "I've spent the whole time since then in hospital. It's all your fault. If you hadn't interfered he would have just hit me a dozen or two times, paid me and let me go. But you drove him wild with all your insults, and then left, so he took his anger out on me. I don't think I'll ever be the same again."

Don Quixote leapt to his feet, determined to find Andrés's master and make him pay up for what he'd done; but Dorothea stopped him, saying that he was already duty-bound to carry out her orders.

"It's true," agreed Don Quixote. "Andrés will have to wait."

"I don't want vengeance," said Andrés. "I just want some food and anything else you can spare to help me on my way. I'm off to Seville."

They gave him some bread and cheese; and, as he was leaving, he turned to Don Quixote and said, "Damn you and all other knights errant. If you ever come across me again, whatever trouble I'm in, for heaven's sake leave me alone, as I know you'll just make things worse."

Don Quixote jumped up to chase him, but Andrés ran off, leaving Don Quixote thoroughly embarrassed and all the others desperately trying to stifle their laughter.

121

≈ Back at the inn

The following day, they reached the inn where Sancho had suffered his blanket-tossing. Don Quixote was exhausted, and a bed was made up for him in the attic where he'd slept on his first visit. After supper, when everyone except Don Quixote and Sancho was sitting around the dining table, the conversation turned to the mad knight and his strange adventures.

The innkeeper's wife related what had happened last time Don Quixote and Sancho had stayed, including the part about Sancho and the blanket. They all laughed heartily. The priest then said that it was books on chivalry which had turned Don Quixote mad.

The innkeeper said, "I don't see how you can think that. We've got several here, and I must say they're the most entertaining things you can imagine. At harvest time you'll find twenty or thirty farm workers in here of an evening, while someone reads one of them out. Myself, I could listen to them night and day."

"Let's see these books," said the priest.

The innkeeper fetched a case from his room. In it were some loose sheets of paper and three books: *Don Cirongilio of Thrace*, *Felixmarte of Hyrcania* and *The History of the Great Captain Gonzalo Fernández de Córdoba together with the Life of Diego García de Paredes*.

"We need Don Quixote's housekeeper here," said the priest.

"I'm just as good as her at dealing with books," said the barber, indicating the fire burning in the hearth.

"What, are my books sinners that you're going to burn them?" asked the innkeeper.

"Only these two," said the priest, indicating *Don Cirongilio* and *Felixmarte*.

"I'd rather burn one of my children than either of those," said the innkeeper. "If you must destroy any, then make it the other one."

"My friend," said the priest, "those two books are full of nonsense, while the third is a true history. It tells of two great generals. One, Diego García de Paredes, was so strong that with one finger he could stop a millstone turning at full speed. He also managed single-handedly to defend a bridge against a great army."

"Is that all?" scoffed the innkeeper. "Those other books tell of much more impressive deeds."

However much the priest tried to persuade the innkeeper that Don Cirongilio and Felixmarte were just inventions and their stories fiction, the innkeeper refused to believe it. Dorothea whispered to Cardenio that the man was almost as gullible as Don Quixote.

The innkeeper was packing the books up again when the priest spotted the loose sheets of paper. He asked to see them and then said to the others, "This looks much more interesting. If you agree, I'll read it out to you. It's a story called *The Tale of Inappropriate Curiosity*."

The priest read out the story, which was about a man called Anselmo; his wife, Camilla; and his best friend, Lothario. Anselmo foolishly decided to test the faithfulness of his wife by throwing her together with Lothario. Of course it all ended in tears.

≈ Don Quixote fights a giant

The priest was coming to the end of the tale when Sancho burst in.

"Quick!" he said. "You've got to come and help my master. He's been fighting that giant enemy of Princess Micomicona. He's chopped the giant's head off and the place is swimming in blood."

"The idiot!" yelled the innkeeper. "He's attacked the skins full of wine that I store behind the bed in the attic."

They heard Don Quixote shouting and rushed up to the attic. They found him dressed only in his shirt, with a filthy red nightcap belonging to the innkeeper on his head. He had a blanket wrapped around his left arm and in his right he held his sword, with which he was madly slashing the air, although his eyes were tight shut. He was in fact asleep and dreaming that he was in Micomicón, fighting the giant Pandafilando. The wineskins were all cut through and the attic was flooded with wine. The innkeeper was furious and began raining punches down on Don Quixote, until he was dragged off by Cardenio and the priest. The barber then tried to wake Don Quixote up by flinging a bucket of cold water over him.

Meanwhile, Sancho was looking on the floor for the giant's head. "Now I know that this place is enchanted," he said. "Last time I was here, I was beaten up by I don't know who or what; and this time, the giant's head I saw cut off has vanished. If I don't find it, all my plans to become a duke will be ruined."

Don Quixote, dripping wet and only half awake, was standing in front of the priest, whom he took to be Princess Micomicona. He fell to his knees and said, "Fear not, lady, no more harm can come to you, as I have just destroyed the evil giant who was plaguing you."

Sancho was overjoyed. "Didn't I say it was true," he shouted. "Now I'm going to get my reward!"

The others were all very amused at Don Quixote's delusions and the credulity of Sancho. All of them, that is, except the innkeeper, who was furious at the loss of his wine.

Downstairs his wife was also enraged. "Last time they were here they left without paying a cent," she fumed, "and this time that madman's hacked all my wineskins to bits. I tell you, I'm not letting them get away with it!"

The priest tried to calm everyone down, promising the innkeeper and his wife that he'd make good their losses as best he could.

≈ MYSTERIOUS STRANGERS APPEAR

A party of travellers arrived at the inn. There were four men on horseback, finely dressed and with their faces covered in black travelling masks; a woman in white also on a horse, and with her face covered; and two servants on foot.

Dorothea quickly covered her face with a veil and Cardenio went into another room. The four men on horseback dismounted and helped the woman off her horse. One of them took her into the inn and helped her into a chair, where she sat sighing heavily.

Dorothea went up to her and said kindly, "What is the matter, my lady? Perhaps I can help."

But the woman remained silent. Dorothea repeated her question, but the man accompanying the woman said, "Don't waste your time trying to help this ungrateful woman, and don't ask her to talk, unless you want to hear lies spoken."

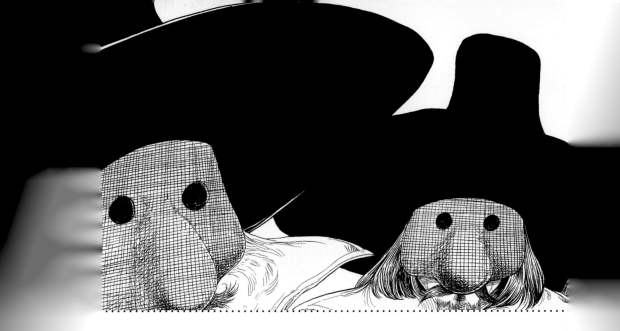

At this the mysterious woman burst out, "I have never told lies. It is precisely because of my honesty that I find myself in this terrible state."

Cardenio, who had been listening from the other room, shouted out, "What! Whose voice do I hear?"

The woman jumped up and began looking around wildly, trying to find whoever it was had spoken. In her agitation she let her mask slip, revealing an astonishingly beautiful face. The man with her grabbed her by the shoulders. His own mask then fell off and Dorothea, who was trying to help the woman, looked up and swooned. She had recognized her husband, Don Fernando.

The priest ran over and removed Dorothea's veil to sprinkle water on her face. Don Fernando recognized her in turn, but kept his grip on the other woman, who was struggling to free herself. Cardenio rushed in, and the first thing he saw was Luscinda – for it was she – in Don Fernando's arms. Don Fernando recognized Cardenio and they all stood staring at each other in amazement.

Luscinda was the first to break the silence. "Don Fernando," she said, "you can see how heaven has reunited me with my true husband. If you cannot accept our being together, then at least let me kill myself to prove to him that I have remained faithful."

Meanwhile, Dorothea had come round. She knelt at Don Fernando's feet, weeping piteously. "My lord," she said, "this is indeed your beloved Dorothea. I beg you to take me back. I know that I am only a humble farmer's daughter, and cannot compete in beauty or nobility with Luscinda, but I love you and she does not. And remember that, whether you deny it or not, we are already married. You will have to live with your conscience if you reject me now."

Everyone was moved by Dorothea's pleas.

Don Fernando stood still, holding on to Luscinda and staring at Dorothea. After a while he said, "You have won, lovely Dorothea. I cannot resist your arguments." He released Luscinda, who at once fell into Cardenio's arms. They embraced, each declaring their love for the other.

Seeing this, Don Fernando started to become angry again, and put his hand on his sword as if about to attack Cardenio.

But Dorothea clasped him by the knees and said, "I beg you, my lord, not to do anything rash. Surely you can find it in your noble heart to let these two people live in peace."

The others all crowded round, adding their voices to Dorothea's. Eventually Don Fernando relented. He bent down and raised Dorothea up, saying, "It is not right for my beloved to kneel at my feet. I hope you will forgive me for my bad behaviour."

Turning to Cardenio and Luscinda, he said, "I wish you many happy years together, and I pray that Dorothea and I will be allowed the same."

They were all overjoyed. Even Sancho shed a tear, although he later maintained it was only because he'd realized that Dorothea wasn't Princess Micomicona, and he wouldn't be getting the favours he'd expected.

Don Fernando then explained how he happened to be travelling with Luscinda. After the wedding and his failed attempt to kill Luscinda, he'd gone off in a fury. Some months later, he'd learnt that Luscinda was in a convent. He and three companions had immediately gone there and kidnapped her. She'd fallen into a dead faint, and even once she'd recovered she had said nothing, but only sighed and wept. In this way they'd made their way to the inn, where they had met the others.

After hearing all this, Sancho went up to his master. Don Quixote had just woken up and Sancho said to him glumly, "Don't bother about getting up. All that stuff about killing giants and rescuing princesses is over and done with."

"You're quite right," said Don Quixote. "I've just been fighting that dreadful giant. I managed to cut his head off with one stroke of my sword. You should have seen the blood!"

"Wine, more like," said Sancho. "You should know that your so-called dead giant is just a burst-open wineskin."

"You madman, what are you talking about?"

"It's all true. And Princess Micomicona has turned into an ordinary person called Dorothea," said Sancho.

"I told you this place was enchanted," said Don Quixote. "Now, help me get dressed."

Downstairs the priest was telling Don Fernando and the others all about Don Quixote's adventures. He ended by saying that now Dorothea had been reunited with Don Fernando, their play-acting would have to stop and they'd have to find another way of persuading Don Quixote back to his village. Cardenio said that Luscinda could play Princess Micomicona instead of Dorothea, but Don Fernando said that he was quite happy for Dorothea to continue with the impersonation, as it was all in a good cause.

Don Quixote then appeared, in full armour and with Mambrino's helmet perched on his head. He turned to Dorothea and said gravely, "Madam, I am informed by my squire that your highness has ceased to be, and has turned into an ordinary person. I hope this is not because your father believes I will let you down. I have already dealt with that paltry giant and am quite up to any other challenges that lie ahead."

"Rest assured," replied the quick-witted Dorothea, "although some changes have taken place which have made me happier than I ever thought I could be, I am still the same person I was. It is too late tonight, but tomorrow we must continue on our journey."

Don Quixote turned to Sancho. "See, you dunderhead," he said, "all those things you told me about Princess Micomicona being turned into someone called Dorothea, and the giant not being a giant at all, were nonsense. I've a good mind to beat some sense into you."

"Calm down, sir," replied Sancho. "I may have been mistaken about Princess Micomicona, but as for the giant being a wineskin, I swear that's absolutely true. You'll find out yourself when the innkeeper presents you with the bill for the damage."

"You're obviously a fool," muttered Don Quixote.

"That's enough arguing," broke in Don Fernando. "Let's all settle down."

≈ More mysterious strangers appear

At that moment, a man arrived leading a donkey on which was seated a woman. The man and woman were both dressed in Moorish style. Dorothea, seeing that they both looked rather uncomfortable at finding so many people present, said that the woman was welcome to share a room with her and Luscinda. The man thanked Dorothea and explained that the woman did not speak Spanish and only understood a little. The woman sat down and Dorothea asked if they could see her face. The man translated and she took off her veil. Dorothea thought that the woman was more beautiful than Luscinda, and Luscinda thought she was more beautiful than Dorothea. The others just thought she was beautiful.

Don Fernando asked the man what the woman's name was, and he replied "Lela Zoraida"; but the woman, obviously understanding, broke in and insisted that her name was María.

The innkeeper prepared a meal, and all the guests sat at a large table, with Don Quixote at its head. When Don Quixote had finished eating, he launched into a long speech in which he compared writing and soldiering as different professions. He started by declaring that he believed his chosen profession of knight-errantry was the best in the world.

"Anyone who thinks that writing is more important than soldiering is wrong," he declared. People argued that brainwork was superior to physical work but, Don Quixote pointed out, soldiering required brains as well as brawn. Moreover, while it was true that many writers deserved to be admired because they were poor, soldiers were often also poor and in addition had to face physical dangers and discomfort. Not only that, but soldiers had no guarantee that they would be rewarded for their efforts – indeed, far more of them died in battles than gained from them.

The others were all amazed at how clearly and wisely Don Quixote spoke, and agreed that it was impossible to tell from this speech that he was mad.

Once Don Quixote had ended his speech, the company turned to the man who had just arrived and asked him to tell his story. He began by explaining that he came from León in northern Spain.

"I was one of three sons," he continued. "My father was quite well off compared with most other people in the region, but he was also extravagant and generous, having learnt these habits when he had been a soldier in his youth. He feared that if he continued in these ways he would leave his whole family destitute, so he decided to share his money out equally, giving a quarter to each of his three sons, and keeping a quarter for himself to live on. He urged us each to choose a profession. I, as the eldest, got to choose first and decided to become a soldier. The middle brother said he would use the money to buy goods and sail to America to trade. My youngest brother thought he would go into the Church, and to the University of Salamanca to finish his studies.

"The day we all departed, we insisted on giving my father back some of the money he had shared out, as we all thought he would need it more than we did. It is now twenty-two years since I left home, and in that time I have had no news of my father or brothers, although I have written letters to them."

The man then described the adventures that had befallen him in that time. He had served in Flanders under the duke of Alba and had then joined Don John of Austria to fight against the Ottomans in the Mediterranean. At the famous Battle of Lepanto he had been captured by the Ottomans and taken to Constantinople as a slave. His first master had been Alouk Ali Fartach, admiral of the Ottoman fleet. He had been an honourable man, and kind to his captives, of which he had three thousand. But Alouk Ali had died, and the man had passed to the cruel Hassan Aga, a Venetian who had gone over to the Ottoman side and become the king of Algiers. The man had been taken to Algiers and kept prisoner there by Hassan Aga.

Next to the prison was the house of a rich Moor, whose daughter was Lela Zoraida. When she was a little girl, Lela Zoraida had had a Christian maidservant and had decided that she wanted to become a Christian herself. She had found a way of communicating with the prisoner through a window overlooking the jail. As well as exchanging letters, she had secretly handed over money to allow the man and some of his companions to ransom themselves.

When he was out of the prison, the man had managed to meet Lela; and they had fallen in love and decided to marry as soon as they could. He and his companions had then escaped in a boat, taking Lela with them. She had come willingly, although she had been upset at deceiving her father, who was not an unkind man and who loved her dearly.

While they were crossing to Spain, they had been set upon by French pirates, who had taken almost all the money and jewels that Lela had brought with her. However, the pirates had not harmed them, and had left them with just enough money to buy a donkey. They had landed safely in Spain, where the man's companions had all gone their separate ways. He and Lela Zoraida were trying to make their way back to his home to discover what had happened to his father and brothers.

Everyone was fascinated by the man's story, and they all offered to help in any way they could.

≈ YET MORE MYSTERIOUS STRANGERS APPEAR

As night fell, a coach drew up, accompanied by some men on horseback. The innkeeper's wife went out to explain that the inn was completely full, but one of the men on horseback said, "Even so, we must find some room for his honour the judge."

On hearing this, the innkeeper's wife quickly said, "Oh, what I mean is that there isn't a single free bed. If his honour has a travelling bed in his possession, my husband and I will gladly give up our own room for him."

This was agreed, and the judge got down from the coach, leading by the hand a beautiful girl of about sixteen years old.

Don Quixote addressed the judge in courteous tones. "Good sir," he said, "you may safely enter this castle, although it is small and uncomfortable. Within its walls you will find both beauty and bravery unmatched in all the land."

They went into the inn. The judge was so amazed at Don Quixote's appearance and at his speech that he could not think of a reply. Fortunately the others then came in to greet the new guests.

The man with Lela Zoraida was sure he recognized the judge, and took one of the men who had arrived with him to one side to ask who he was.

"He's Juan Pérez de Viedma," replied the man. "He's from the mountains of León and he's on his way to Mexico to take up an important post in the supreme court there. The girl with him is his daughter. Her mother died in childbirth and left her a great deal of money."

The man was convinced that the judge was his long-lost youngest brother. He called Don Fernando, Cardenio and the priest over and told them. He asked their advice as to how to make himself known to the judge, as he was not sure what kind of welcome he might receive when the judge realized how poor he was.

"Don't worry," said the priest, "I am sure your brother is an honourable man, but I will arrange it, if you need convincing."

By this time, supper was ready. All the men except for the former captive sat round the table while the ladies ate in their own room. As the men were eating, the priest began.

"Strange to say, your worship, but a companion of mine in Constantinople, where I was held captive for some years, had the same surname as you. He was called Ruy Pérez de Viedma and was from a village in the mountains of León." The priest then retold the tale of the captive and Lela Zoraida up to the point where their boat had been attacked by French pirates. "I have no idea what happened to them after that," he ended.

When the priest had finished, there were tears in the judge's eyes. "The man you are talking about is my eldest brother," he said, "and everything he told you about our family is true. My father is still alive and desperate to hear news of his missing son, and our other brother is a rich merchant in Peru. Oh, if only I could see Ruy Pérez again, and thank Lela Zoraida for all she has done for him!"

The priest got up from the table and soon returned, leading both Lela Zoraida and Ruy Pérez by the hand. "You can stop crying now, Judge," he said, "for here are your beloved brother and your sister-in-law to be."

The judge was overjoyed. It was quickly decided that Lela Zoraida and Ruy Pérez would go with the judge to Seville, where news would be sent to the brothers' father to come and attend Lela Zoraida's baptism and the wedding. Don Quixote was amazed by all these events, which he put down to the mysteries of knight-errantry.

It was very late by now and it was agreed that everyone should try to get some rest. Don Quixote offered to stand guard to protect the castle and its inhabitants from any passing giants or other wicked characters.

Some time before dawn the silence was broken by a young man's voice singing beautifully outside the inn. Dorothea, who was already awake, woke up Doña Clara, the judge's daughter, so that she could hear it too. Clara listened for a while and then started to tremble violently.

"What's the matter?" asked Dorothea. "Surely it's just some servant singing."

"Oh no," replied Clara. "He's no servant; he's a rich nobleman's son."

Clara explained that the boy lived across the road from her father's house in their home town. He had fallen in love with her and indicated that he wanted to marry her. Clara thought she was falling in love with him, but, having no mother, didn't have anyone to advise her what to do. She had left the town with her father without saying goodbye. Two days after they'd set out, she had seen the boy standing by the door of an inn dressed as a footman. "He's been following us ever since," she went on, "but always manages to keep out of my father's sight."

"Don't worry," said Dorothea, "I am sure we can sort all this out."

Clara was not convinced. She believed her origins were too humble to allow the boy's father to agree to their being married. Dorothea repeated her assurance that some solution could be found, and they settled back down to sleep.

By now the only two awake inside the inn were the innkeeper's daughter and Maritornes, who decided to play a trick on Don Quixote. At the front of the inn was a hole for taking hay into the hayloft. The two girls settled themselves down behind the hole and looked out at Don Quixote, who was sitting on Rocinante, leaning on his pikestaff and sighing heavily for his beloved Dulcinea.

The innkeeper's daughter whispered to Don Quixote, "Mister Knight, sir, please come over here."

Don Quixote recalled his last stay at the inn – or castle, as he thought. He convinced himself that the beautiful daughter of the lord of the castle was in love with him and was calling to him from a window with golden bars. He rode over and, looking up, said, "Most lovely lady, I am afraid I cannot love you, as I am sworn to another, but I am otherwise at your bidding."

"All my lady wants is one of your hands," said Maritornes.

So as not to appear rude, Don Quixote agreed. The hole into the loft was high enough that Don Quixote had to stand on Rocinante's saddle and stretch his arm up to reach it. Meanwhile, Maritornes had hurried downstairs and taken the halter off Sancho's donkey. She returned to the loft and quickly tied one end of the halter around Don Quixote's outstretched wrist and the other to the bolt on the hayloft door. She and the innkeeper's daughter then scurried off, leaving Don Quixote trapped. He didn't dare budge, just in case Rocinante moved and he was left hanging by his arm in mid-air. Fortunately Rocinante was a patient soul, and simply stood there.

Don Quixote was sure that his entrapment was the result of a magic spell. He yearned for Amadís's sword, and called out for help from the magicians Lirgandeo and Alquife, but nobody heard him. Dawn started breaking and, convinced he would never be freed, he began bellowing like a bull.

≈Even more mysterious strangers appear

Don Quixote was still suspended there, when four horsemen pulled into the yard and began knocking loudly at the inn door. Don Quixote shouted to them, "Sir Knights, or whoever you are, you have no business disturbing this castle at this hour."

"Castle? What castle?" asked one of the men. "Look, if you're the keeper of this inn, then open up now. We're in a hurry and all we want to do is feed our horses."

Don Quixote protested that it was a castle, not an inn, but the men ignored him and renewed their banging, waking the innkeeper, who opened the inn door. At this moment, one of

the men's horses trotted over to Rocinante, who moved forward a pace or two to greet the newcomer. Don Quixote's feet slipped off Rocinante's saddle and he found himself dangling in excruciating agony. He made so much noise that even Maritornes woke up. She quickly sneaked into the hayloft and untied the halter, letting Don Quixote tumble to the ground. Without a word, he picked himself up and, grabbing his shield and pikestaff, remounted Rocinante. He rode off some way and then came cantering back.

"If anyone says it was right for me to be put under that evil spell, I challenge them to a duel now," he declared.

The newly arrived travellers looked astonished at this behaviour.

"Don't worry about him – he's mad," said the innkeeper.

The men then asked the innkeeper if he had seen a young man of about fifteen dressed as a footman, and proceeded to describe Doña Clara's admirer. The innkeeper replied that there were far too many people staying at the inn for him to remember them all.

Just then one of the men spotted the judge's coach. "That's the coach we think he's been following – he must be here," he said.

The men split up to find the boy, leaving Don Quixote fuming that his challenge had been ignored.

One of the men soon found the boy asleep and shook him awake saying, "Really, Don Luis, I don't think those clothes are fitting for someone of your background."

Don Luis immediately recognized the man as one of his father's servants. The servant explained that Don Luis's father had discovered where his son had gone from a fellow student.

"You're coming home with us, young man," said the servant, who had been joined by his three companions.

"Not if I can help it," replied Don Luis.

Don Fernando, Cardenio and the others had heard what was going on and all crowded round, while Don Luis and his father's servants argued. Eventually the judge came up. He recognized Don Luis and took him to one side to question him.

Meanwhile, a great commotion had broken out inside the inn doorway. Two of the other guests, seeing how distracted everyone was, had tried to sneak off without paying their bill. The innkeeper had spotted them and was demanding payment, but the two men had started beating him up. The innkeeper's wife and daughter and Maritornes rushed out looking for someone who could help. They spotted Don Quixote, and the daughter begged him to come quickly.

Don Quixote replied in a leisurely fashion, "Lovely lady, it is my desire to assist you, but before I can do so I must ask permission of Princess Micomicona, under whose command I currently serve. Until I have done this, I must ask your father to defend himself as well as he can."

"It'll be too late by then," wailed Maritornes.

Don Quixote found Dorothea and went down on his knees, begging her highness to give him leave to assist the lord of the castle, who was in something of a pickle. The princess graciously agreed and Don Quixote returned to the inn door. But then he stopped, horrified.

"I cannot attack those men," he said. "They are common people and not knights errant. This is a task for my squire, Sancho Panza. I must summon him."

The men went on beating up the innkeeper, while the innkeeper's wife and daughter and Maritornes ranted at Don Quixote for being a coward.

While all this was happening, Don Luis was talking to the judge. The boy explained that he had fallen in love with Doña Clara and wanted to marry her. The judge was very impressed by his sincerity. He suggested that Don Luis persuade his father's servants to let him stay another day so that they could think more about what was to be done.

≈ How the barber's donkey's packsaddle caused a riot

Using fine words rather than violence, Don Quixote finally convinced the two men to pay the innkeeper. Everything calmed down. And then, who should turn up but the barber from whom Don Quixote had taken Mambrino's helmet and Sancho the donkey's packsaddle.

Sancho was at that moment adjusting something on the packsaddle. The barber spotted him and cried out, "Thief! Give that back to me." He made a grab for the packsaddle but Sancho snatched it back with one hand and punched the barber squarely on the jaw with the other.

"Help! Help!" cried the barber. "This man's not just a thief but a murderer too."

"Liar," replied Sancho. "I'm no murderer, and my master won these fair and square."

Don Quixote arrived and was delighted to see how well his squire was defending himself. He decided he would knight him at the first opportunity. The barber continued furiously demanding his possessions back.

"It's not just the packsaddle, but a new brass basin," he declared.

Don Quixote separated the two and put the packsaddle on the floor in the middle of the room. He said, "This man is obviously mistaken. The object he is referring to is not a basin, but Mambrino's helmet. As for the rest of it, my squire did ask for the trappings of this man's horse after I had defeated him. I gave them to him, and if they have since been turned into a donkey's packsaddle, all I can say is that these things happen in chivalric adventures." He turned to Sancho and said, "Now hurry and fetch Mambrino's helmet."

Sancho fetched the basin and gave it to Don Quixote, who held it up to everyone present and declared that it was obviously a helmet. The barber, exasperated, appealed to them all to confirm that it was a basin.

The other barber, Master Nicolás, then decided to join in the fun. "I am a practising barber myself," he said, "and was a soldier in my youth, so I know all about armour; and I declare that this is a helmet, with a bit missing."

"That's exactly right," said Don Quixote.

The priest, who had guessed what his friend was up to, quickly agreed with Don Quixote, as did Don Fernando and Cardenio.

The poor barber was dumbfounded. "Good grief," he said, "if all these people say that it isn't a basin but a helmet, then I suppose this here must be a horse's trappings and not a donkey's packsaddle."

"Actually, it looks just like a packsaddle to me," said Don Quixote. "But we are in a strange, enchanted place," he continued, "so I wouldn't be sure of anything."

"Don Quixote is quite right to be uncertain," said Don Fernando. "In order to decide what this thing is, I will take a secret vote of all the ladies and gentlemen present." And he started to go round collecting votes and whispering in people's ears. Those in the know thought it was all hilarious, but Don Luis's four servants, who had only just arrived, didn't understand what was going on, and nor did three other newcomers, who were members of the Holy Brotherhood.

Don Fernando stopped going round and said, "Everyone I ask says it's obvious that it's the trappings from a fine horse, and not a donkey's packsaddle."

The barber was in despair. "You're all wrong. I swear it looks just like a packsaddle to me, and I'm stone-cold sober."

One of Don Luis's servants said, "I don't understand this, unless it's some kind of joke. It's obvious that this is a barber's basin, and that is a donkey's packsaddle."

One of the Holy Brotherhood then chipped in. "I agree. Anyone who says this isn't a packsaddle must have been drinking."

"You lying scoundrel," roared Don Quixote, and he swung his pikestaff at the man, who ducked just in time. The other members of the Holy Brotherhood called for help, and the innkeeper, who was also an officer of the law, rushed to get his staff of office and his sword.

The place was suddenly in uproar. Don Luis's father's servants surrounded Don Luis to make sure he didn't escape; the barber tried to grab the packsaddle, and so did Sancho; Don Quixote was attacking the members of the Holy Brotherhood with his sword; Cardenio and Don Fernando were rushing to Don Quixote's assistance; Don Luis was yelling at his servants to help Don Quixote too. The priest was shouting; the inn- keeper's wife was screaming; the innkeeper's daughter was weeping; Maritornes wailing; Dorothea looking bemused; Luscinda astonished; and Doña Clara fainting away. The barber was punching Sancho, who was punching the barber. One of the servants was grabbing Don Luis by the arm and Don Luis was smacking him on the jaw; the judge was trying to defend the servant; Don Fernando had one of the Holy Brotherhood under his feet and was trampling up and down on him; and the innkeeper was roaring for help.

Suddenly, in the middle of all this commotion, Don Quixote cried out in a loud voice, "Stop, everyone, and sheathe your weapons, if you value your lives! I told you this place was enchanted. Some demons have cast a spell and made us all start fighting each other."

Peace was restored, although the innkeeper and the members of the Holy Brotherhood weren't at all happy. Continuing the discussion that had been interrupted by the mêlée, it was decided that Don Luis would go with Don Fernando to Andalusia, rather than home to his father. Three of the servants would return to Don Luis's father to find out what his orders were, while the fourth would stay with Don Luis.

One of the officers of the Holy Brotherhood then remembered that he had on him an arrest warrant for someone who had freed a load of convicts. He got out the warrant and peered closely at it and then at Don Quixote. Convinced that this was the man in question, he seized Don Quixote by the collar and called out, "Assist me in the arrest of this highwayman!"

Don Quixote was livid at finding himself manhandled, and grabbed the officer by the throat. The other members of the Holy Brotherhood and the innkeeper ran to help their comrade; the innkeeper's wife and daughter and Maritornes immediately set up a chorus of cries and yells.

"Good grief!" said Sancho. "My master is right when he says this place is enchanted. It's impossible to get five minutes' peace around here."

Don Fernando prised Don Quixote and the officer apart, and Don Quixote launched into a great tirade at the Holy Brotherhood. "You ruffians! You guttersnipes!" he yelled. "Do none of you idiots know that knights errant are not bound by your silly little laws?"

Meanwhile, the priest was trying to convince the peace officers that Don Quixote was mad and that there was no point in arresting him. Reluctantly, they finally agreed and turned their attention to sorting things out between Sancho and the hard-done-by barber. It was agreed that the pack-saddles would be exchanged, but Sancho could keep the rest of the trappings he had taken from the barber's donkey. Both men were reasonably satisfied.

The priest took the barber aside and quietly paid him a handsome sum for the basin, so that Don Quixote could not now be accused of having stolen it. The innkeeper spotted this and demanded payment in his turn for Don Quixote's board and lodging, and compensation for the wine and the wineskins.

The priest calmed the innkeeper down, and Don Fernando paid the bill, although the judge also offered to contribute.

Don Quixote then went over to Dorothea, knelt before her and said, "Gracious lady, I think we must now leave this castle and continue on our adventure."

Dorothea agreed, and Don Quixote turned to Sancho and told him to saddle Rocinante and prepare for their departure.

"Actually, sir, I don't think we have to be in any hurry," said Sancho, "because I don't see how this lady can be a real queen. If she was, she wouldn't be carrying on with one of this lot here every chance she gets. And if she's not a queen, there's no adventure to be had and we may as well stop and have something to eat."

Dorothea blushed but said nothing – it was true that she had been snatching kisses from Don Fernando whenever she had thought no one was looking.

Don Quixote's fury knew no bounds. "You ignorant peasant!" he roared. "You vile-mouthed, slandering idiot! How dare you speak of one of these ladies like that in my presence!"

Sancho was quaking in his boots, but the quick-witted Dorothea intervened. "Do not be angry, Sir Knight with the Face in a Sorry State. You yourself have said that this place is enchanted, and it is possible that some trick made Sancho see these things."

The others agreed that this was the most likely explanation, and Don Quixote was finally persuaded to forgive Sancho.

≈ Don Quixote begins his journey home

Those at the inn then came up with a plan to get Don Quixote home without having to continue with the story of Princess Micomicona. They built a stout wooden cage and hired a man with an ox cart. Then, under instructions from the priest, Don Fernando and his companions, Don Luis's servants, the members of the Holy Brotherhood, Master Nicolás the barber and the innkeeper disguised themselves and crept into Don Quixote's room when he was sound asleep. They grabbed him and tied him hand and foot. He awoke bewildered but quickly decided that all this was the result of another magic spell. Sancho could see through the men's disguises but decided not to say anything.

The men brought in the cage and shut Don Quixote in it. As they did so, Master Nicolás the barber intoned in a strange voice, "O Knight with the Face in a Sorry State, be not downcast at your imprisonment, for it is prophesied that soon the famous Lion of La Mancha will be reunited with the White Dove of El Toboso. And you, noble squire, do not fear for your master. Accompany him on his journey and you will receive the rewards that have been promised you."

Don Quixote thought the prophecy meant that he would soon be married to Dulcinea, and he resigned himself to his captivity. He said, "Rest assured that my faithful squire will be well paid for his service, even if he doesn't get his island, as I have left him money in my will."

Sancho bowed and kissed Don Quixote's hands.

The cage was carried outside and hoisted onto the ox cart. Don Fernando and Cardenio decided not to accompany it, in case Don Quixote recognized them. The innkeeper's wife and daughter and Maritornes came out to say their goodbyes, pretending to weep bitterly at Don Quixote's departure.

A strange procession set out. At its head was the ox cart, led by its owner. On the cart sat Don Quixote in the cage, with his hands tied and his legs stretched out. On either side were the members of the Holy Brotherhood, carrying guns. Behind the cart came Sancho on his donkey, leading Rocinante by the reins. Bringing up the rear were Master Nicolás the barber and the priest, astride their mules and with masks over their faces.

They had not gone very far when they were overtaken by a party of well-dressed men, also on mules. The leader of the group was a churchman – a canon from the city of Toledo. He stopped and asked the members of the Holy Brotherhood why they were transporting a man in this way.

"We haven't got a clue," one of them replied.

Don Quixote overheard and said, "Good sir, if you are perchance familiar with the ways of knight-errantry, then I can explain to you."

The canon replied that he knew a great deal about the subject as he had read many books on chivalry. Don Quixote then explained that he was travelling in a cage because he had been put under a spell by evil magicians. The priest, who had ridden up, confirmed what Don Quixote had said, adding that the man in the cage was the renowned Knight with the Face in a Sorry State, whose deeds were famous throughout the world.

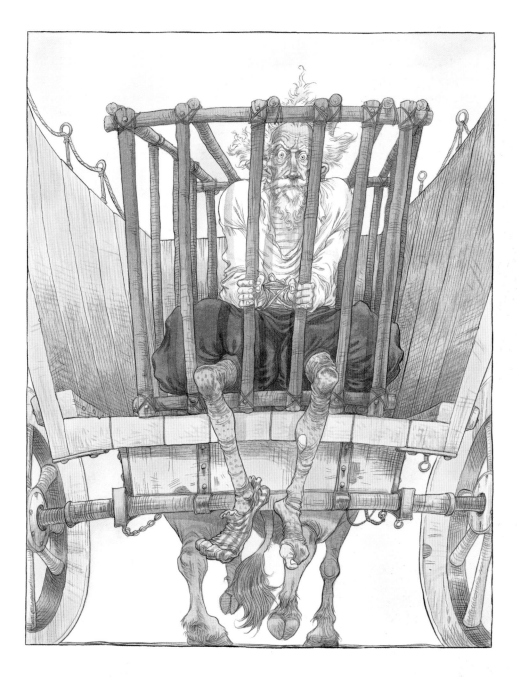

Sancho could bear it no longer and broke in. "Look, I'm sorry to have to say this, but Don Quixote is about as enchanted as my mother. He's perfectly sane and eats and drinks like a normal person." Turning to the priest he said, "And I know who you are too, so there's no point in carrying on with your disguise. It's not fair – if you hadn't interfered, my master would be married to Princess Micomicona by now, and I would be a count at the very least. Now what am I going to tell my wife and children when I come back home with nothing?"

"Good grief," said the barber, "you're as full of crazy ideas as your master. You'll soon be keeping him company in that cage."

The priest, meanwhile, had decided that he had better inform the canon what was going on. The two rode on ahead a little, and the priest explained about Don Quixote's madness and his various exploits.

The canon then said, "I can see that those books on chivalry are not such a good idea, though I confess I've read quite a few myself. At least, I've started many, but can't recall ever having finished one – they all seem to end up the same. I even began writing one myself once. People said it was quite good, but I never got beyond the first hundred pages."

The priest and the canon continued chatting away, about books and how terrible most modern plays were, and other interesting things.

The barber rode up and said that they had decided to stop to rest the oxen for a while. The canon sent his servants on ahead to a nearby inn, telling one of them to come back with food and drink.

Sancho took the chance to have a quiet word with his master. "I think you should know, sir," he said, "that those two over there are the priest and the barber from our own village. I'm sure they've decided to carry you off like this because they can't stand the fact that you're so famous."

"They may look like the priest and the barber to you," replied Don Quixote, "but they are clearly not them – no ordinary mortals could possibly have imprisoned me in this cage. As I have told you, there is enchantment afoot."

"Good grief," retorted Sancho, "how can you be so thick-skulled that you can't see what's obvious? It's not magic; it's just dirty tricks that have led to you being trapped in there."

At this point, Don Quixote needed to answer the call of nature. The priest agreed that he could be let out of the cage as long as Sancho ensured that he did not try to run away. Don Quixote pointed out that he couldn't possibly escape as he was under an enchantment.

≈ Don Quixote discusses chivalry with the canon, gets into a fight with a goatherd, tries to set free a statue and suffers his sixth beating before finally returning home

Once Don Quixote had relieved himself he sat on the grass and started talking to the canon, who was amazed at how intelligent and reasonable he was until he got on to the subject of chivalry.

"My dear sir," said the canon, "how can you possibly believe all the nonsense that's written in those romantic books? They've brought you nothing but trouble; they've addled your wits and led to you being shut up in a cage like a wild animal. You should give them up and read true histories about real people such as Caesar, Hannibal and Alexander the Great."

But Don Quixote would not be swayed. "You say the books I read are full of lies, but I say that is a lie. How could anyone deny that people like Amadís of Gaul and Fierabras really existed? If they didn't exist, then nor did Caesar, nor Achilles, nor Hector. And besides, these books can cheer up the saddest soul."

With that he launched into a fantastical description of a scene from a chivalric tale, with a vast lake of black pitch swimming with monsters, a gold and diamond castle inhabited by beautiful damsels, and – of course – a brave knight errant. "What could be more delightful to read about than that?" he asked. "For my part," he continued, "since I myself became a knight errant I have been generous, patient, polite and brave.

What's more, once I free myself from my unlucky imprisonment, I intend to become the king of some great kingdom. Then I'll be able to do real good for my friends, especially my faithful squire, Sancho, whom I would love to make a duke or some such, although I'm not sure he's really up to the job of governing a dukedom."

Sancho heard the last bit of this conversation and said, "Don't worry, sir, I'm sure I could manage a dukedom; and if it's any problem, I'll just rent it out to someone and live on the rent money."

By this time, the canon's servants had returned from the inn and laid out a picnic under the shade of some trees. They were all sitting around eating and drinking, when a she-goat trotted up, closely followed by a goatherd who was well dressed and much better spoken than a normal goatherd.

He sat down and told them a story of how he and his friend Anselmo, both wealthy young men from a nearby village, had been in love with a beautiful girl called Leandra, the daughter of a rich farmer. Unfortunately Leandra had become very taken with a returning soldier, Vicente de la Rosa, and had run away with him. He had robbed her and left her languishing in a cave, where she'd been found three days later. Her father had sent her to a convent, and the goatherd and his friend had come to this valley to try to get over her.

On hearing the story, Don Quixote said, "If I were not under a spell, I would immediately set out to rescue Leandra from the convent, where I'm sure she's being held against her will. I would of course further assist you in any way I could, as is required by my profession."

"Who is this man?" asked the goatherd.

"Why," replied the barber, "have you not heard of the famous Don Quixote de la Mancha, righter of wrongs, saviour of damsels, destroyer of giants?"

"That's the kind of thing you read in books about knight-errantry," said the goatherd. "Either you're pulling my leg, or that man has a screw or two loose."

"You scoundrel," shouted Don Quixote, and he picked up a loaf of bread and hurled it at the goatherd, hitting him full in the face.

The goatherd launched himself at Don Quixote, scattering dishes and glasses everywhere, and the two men laid into each other, to the great amusement of everyone else except Sancho, who tried to go to his master's rescue but was held back by one of the canon's servants.

In the middle of all this, a trumpet was heard in the distance.

Don Quixote said to the goatherd, "Brother demon, for you must be some kind of devil to be beating me like this, I suggest we call a truce, as that trumpet sound is summoning me to a new adventure."

The goatherd quickly agreed. At that moment, a procession came into view, with a number of men dressed in white penitents' costumes carrying a statue of the Virgin Mary.

The procession had been organized by the local village to encourage the rains to fall, as the whole region had been suffering from drought. Forgetting that he had seen processions of penitents many times, Don Quixote thought that the statue was an important lady being kidnapped by some ruffians. He grabbed his shield, hastily mounted Rocinante and cantered towards the procession, with the priest, the barber, Sancho and everyone else shouting at him to come back.

The procession stopped and one of the priests leading it turned to Don Quixote and said, "Now, sir, what is it you want? Be quick, as we haven't got all day."

"I command that at this instant you set free that beautiful lady, whose sad face shows she is being carried off against her will," said Don Quixote.

At this, they all burst out laughing, enraging Don Quixote, who drew his sword and charged. He swiped at one of the men supporting the statue, who used the prop he was carrying to fend off the blow. The prop was chopped in half, and with the half left in his hand the man thumped Don Quixote as hard as he could on the shoulder. Don Quixote toppled off Rocinante and lay on the ground, quite still. Thinking that he had killed him, the man dropped the prop, hoisted up his tunic

and fled. Sancho rushed up and threw himself on his master's body, weeping and wailing, and crying that he was only a poor enchanted knight who had never hurt anyone.

The priest, the barber and the others ran up, and the men in the procession thought they were about to have a battle on their hands. Fortunately one of the priests in the procession recognized the priest from Don Quixote's village, who quickly explained about Don Quixote, and everyone calmed down.

Sancho's cries roused the fallen knight.

"Oh, lovely Dulcinea, see what terrible things happen to me when I am away from you," he said. "Now, friend Sancho, help me onto the magic cart. My shoulder is smashed and I can no longer ride Rocinante."

"Certainly, sir," responded Sancho. "Let's go back to our village with these gentlemen, who only want to help you. When we're there we'll work out how to set out on another adventure. Perhaps the next one will be a bit more profitable."

"I agree," said Don Quixote. "We must wait for the bad magic that's plaguing us to pass."

The procession moved on and the canon, the peace officers and the goatherd went their separate ways. The priest, the barber and Sancho Panza loaded Don Quixote onto the ox cart, this time resting on a mound of hay rather than locked in a cage, and they started the journey back to their home village.

Six days later they arrived, on a Sunday at midday, when the village square was thronging with people. A boy ran off to Don Quixote's house to tell the housekeeper and his niece that he was back. When he came through the door, the two women cried out in distress at the state he was in, and cursed all books on chivalry more than ever.

Hearing of their return, Sancho's wife, Juana Panza, hurried up and immediately asked Sancho how the donkey was.

"Better than me," replied Sancho.

"Thank goodness for that," said Juana. "Now, what have you managed to bring back from all your squiring? Shoes for the children? A new skirt for me?"

"I'll tell you later," said Sancho.

Don Quixote was put to bed and the priest told the niece to look after him and make sure he didn't escape again. Whether she succeeded or not will be found out in the second volume of this history.

VOLUME TWO

CIDE HAMETE
BENENGELI

In which many more mysterious characters are encountered...

TERESA PANZA

SANCHICA
PANZA

SANSÓN
CARRASCO

TOMÉ CECIAL

DULCINEA
DEL TOBOSO

ALDONZA
LORENZO

THE DUCHESS AND THE DUKE

MONTESINOS

GINÉS DE
PASAMONTE

ALTISADORA

RICOTE

ROQUE GUINART

ANA FÉLIX

CERVANTES THE AUTHOR

≈ WHICH BEGINS WITH DON QUIXOTE WHERE WE LEFT HIM, TUCKED UP IN BED AT HOME

ACCORDING TO Cide Hamete Benengeli, after Don Quixote had been brought back in the ox cart, the priest and the barber went a whole month without seeing him, because they did not want him to be reminded of what had happened. Don Quixote's niece and housekeeper looked after him, and eventually began to think that he might be recovering his sanity. The priest and the barber were delighted and decided to pay him a visit. They found him propped up in bed, as thin and shrivelled as a mummy, but otherwise well. The three men talked, first about Don Quixote's state of health, and then about matters of government. The priest and the barber were amazed at how sensible Don Quixote seemed.

The priest then thought he should make sure that Don Quixote really was cured of his mania for knight-errantry.

"I hear," he said, "that the Turkish fleet is planning to attack. His majesty has made arrangements to fortify the kingdom, but I do not know if this will be enough."

"It is obvious," said Don Quixote, "that what the king needs to do is summon to Madrid all the knights errant wandering around Spain. It would only take half a dozen to defeat the Turks – after all, a single one can easily overcome an army of two hundred thousand men. And even if none of the knights errant of old are available, all I can say is, there is one living who matches them in courage. I'm sure you know who I mean."

"Oh no, it seems my master is at it again," groaned the niece.

"Yes, I shall be a knight errant until I die," said Don Quixote stoutly.

The priest was busy trying to convince Don Quixote that the knights errant he was so obsessed with had never existed, when they heard shouts from downstairs. Sancho Panza was trying to get into the house, and the housekeeper and niece were trying to stop him.

"Clear off," they yelled. "You're the one who keeps leading our master astray."

"Liars," replied Sancho. "I'm the one who's been led astray. Your master promised me an island, and I'm still waiting for it."

"What's one of them? Something you eat, you greedy pig?" demanded the niece.

"Something you govern, actually," said Sancho.

"I don't care what one is," said the housekeeper. "Go and govern your own home and stop bothering us."

Don Quixote, overhearing this, began to worry that if the argument went on, Sancho would reveal things about their adventures that might prove rather embarrassing; so he called out to the women to let him in. The priest and the barber left, convinced that Don Quixote was as mad as ever.

≈ Thanks to the graduate Sansón Carrasco, Don Quixote discovers that a book has been written about his adventures

As soon as they were alone, Don Quixote said to Sancho, "I am very sad that you should think I lured you away. We shared all our adventures, and even if I wasn't tossed in a blanket, I endured a hundred other batterings."

"And that's fair and proper," said Sancho, "because, according to you, knights errant are supposed to suffer more than their squires."

"I'm not sure about that," said Don Quixote. "Now, friend Sancho, tell me what everyone in the village is saying about me. Don't make anything up – I promise not to shout at you."

"Well," said Sancho, "the common people say you're mad and I'm stupid. The posher people don't approve of you calling yourself Don like a nobleman, and the noblemen think you're getting ideas above your station. As for the rest of it, some people call you 'brave but unlucky', others 'polite but interfering' and others 'bonkers but entertaining'."

"Virtuous people have always been slandered," said Don Quixote. "If that's all they're saying, it's not too bad."

"Oh, it's worse than that," said Sancho. "If you want to know more, I'll bring along Sansón Carrasco, who's just got back from the University of Salamanca. Apparently, he says, there's a whole book about you and your adventures called *The Ingenious Gentleman Don Quixote de la Mancha*. It mentions me by name, and Dulcinea del Toboso, and it has stuff in it that only happened when you and I were alone together. I don't understand it – how could the person who wrote it know about those things?"

"He must be some wise magician," said Don Quixote.

"Then how come his name, according to Sansón Carrasco, is Cide Hamete Benenjeree?" asked Sancho.

"That's a Moorish name," said Don Quixote.

"It must be," said Sancho, "as I've heard the Moors are very fond of ice cream."

Don Quixote was extremely curious about this book, and sent Sancho off to find Sansón Carrasco. When Sansón arrived, he threw himself at Don Quixote's feet and said, "Pray, give me your hands, esteemed Don Quixote de la Mancha, one of the most famous knights errant that ever existed, or ever will exist. Blessed be Cide Hamete Benengeli for having written your history, and doubly blessed be the person who translated it so that we can all read it."

"So it's really true that my story has been written by a Moor?" asked Don Quixote.

"Oh yes," replied Sansón, "and more than twelve thousand copies have been printed. Soon every country in the world will have its own translation."

"That's very gratifying," said Don Quixote, "as long as the story is complimentary."

"Rest assured that it is," said Sansón. "It tells of your courage, gallantry and patience, as well as your pure love for my lady Doña Dulcinea del Toboso."

"I've never heard her referred to as Doña," said Sancho, "so the story's obviously wrong."

"That's a minor detail," said Sansón.

"Which of my deeds do people praise most?" asked Don Quixote.

"It varies," said Sansón. "There's those who like best the windmills that you thought were giants. Others consider the story of the mill hammers the finest bit, and others the part when the armies turn out to be two flocks of sheep. Some people do think, though, that the author could have left out some of the beatings that you received."

"I rather agree," said Don Quixote.

"And what about me?" asked Sancho.

"Oh, you're the second most important character in the story," replied Sansón. "A lot of people would rather read about you than anyone else, but there's also those who believe you must be really dim if you think you could ever become the governor of an island."

They continued talking about the book, which Sansón Carrasco said was being read throughout the land. "There are one or two places where the author appears to have slipped up," he said. "There's a part where Sancho seems to have lost his donkey, although we aren't told how, and then a while later he's suddenly riding it again with no explanation of how it came back. And the author forgets to tell us what Sancho did with the gold coins he found in the travelling bag in the Sierra Morena – lots of people would like to know the answer to that."

"I'm afraid, sir, that I can't tell you right now; I'm much too hungry," said Sancho. "I'm off home for a meal, but then I'll come back and explain."

≈ The mysterious disappearance of Sancho Panza's donkey in the Sierra Morena explained

Don Quixote invited Sansón Carrasco to eat with him. They discussed chivalry over the dining table and then had a siesta.

Sancho returned. "About the donkey," he said. "It was like this: we were running away from the Holy Brotherhood after we'd released all the prisoners in the chain gang. We were really tired, and I had fallen asleep for the night on my packsaddle on top of the donkey. Some thief came and propped up the packsaddle with four sticks and then took my donkey away without me noticing. Dawn came, I moved and the sticks gave way, so I crashed to the ground and discovered what had happened. I was distraught and I confess I bawled my eyes out.

"And then, a few days later, while we were travelling with Princess Micomicona I caught sight of my donkey. Riding him was that thief Ginés de Pasamonte, dressed as a Gypsy. He scarpered and I got the donkey back. As for the money, I spent it on stuff for myself, my wife and my children – it's the only reason my wife puts up with me wandering off with my master, Don Quixote."

"Is that all that needed correcting?" asked Don Quixote.

"Oh, I'm sure there's more," replied Sansón, "but those are the most important parts."

"And has the author said there'll be a second volume?" said Don Quixote.

"Yes, he has," said Sansón, "but he says he hasn't found it and doesn't know where it is. What's more, people are saying that sequels are never as good as the original, and that quite enough has already been written about Don Quixote, so there's doubts about whether it'll appear or not. But others are clamouring for it, saying they can't get enough of quixotic adventures. And the author himself says he's going to publish it as soon as he finds it, whatever it's like, as all he's interested in is making as much money as possible."

"So that's all he wants, is it?" said Sancho. "If he tries to do anything in too much of a hurry, he certainly won't succeed. He'd do better keeping an eye on us – we'll soon give him plenty to write about. If my master took my advice, we'd be out on the road righting wrongs right now."

≈ Sancho Panza has an interesting conversation with his wife, Don Quixote plans his third expedition, and his niece and housekeeper plan to stop him leaving

Just as Sancho had finished speaking, Rocinante neighed loudly, which Don Quixote took as a good omen. He decided they would set off on a third expedition in three or four days and asked Sansón Carrasco's advice as to which direction they should head in. Sansón replied that a jousting tournament was soon to be held in the city of Zaragoza in the kingdom of Aragón, and suggested that they go there, as Don Quixote could undoubtedly win fame by defeating all the Aragonese knights. Don Quixote then asked Sansón Carrasco to write a poem of farewell to Dulcinea on his behalf. He also asked him to keep their plans secret.

Now, the translator of this story is convinced that this next part can't be true, as Sancho sounds far too intelligent in it, but he's left it in anyway.

Sancho walked home grinning delightedly.

"What are you looking so happy about?" asked his wife, Teresa.

"I'd be happy to be a bit less happy than I seem."

"What?" said his wife.

"I'm happy because I'm setting off again with my master, to try to find more treasure like those gold coins; but I'm a bit sad because I'm leaving you and the children. I'd be even happier if I could find money without having to leave home, so I'm happy not to be totally happy."

"Ever since you became a knight's squire I've had no idea what you're talking about," said Teresa. "If you do go off, I hope it's not for long."

"I'm sure it won't be," said Sancho, "as I'm bound to become the governor of an island soon."

"It doesn't matter one way or the other," replied Teresa. "Lots of people get by without ever being governors. But if you do become one, don't forget about me and the children. Sanchico is now fifteen and ought to be in school if his uncle the priest is going to get him into the Church. And Mari Sancha, our daughter, is quite ready to get married."

"Mark my words," said Sancho, "if I get a bit of something to govern, I'll marry Mari Sancha to someone so high up that no one will go near her without calling her 'my lady'."

"There's no need for that," said Teresa. "It'd be much more sensible to marry her to someone who's her equal. She won't have a clue what to do if she has to act all posh. That nice lad Lope Tocho, Juan Tocho's son, will do nicely."

"Stupid woman!" said Sancho. "Why on earth shouldn't I marry Mari Sancha to someone who'll give me grandchildren called Lord and Lady? Everyone knows that you have to take your good fortune when you find it. What's wrong with me taking on a governorship and us stopping being poor? I tell you, Mari Sancha is going to become a countess, and that's that."

"But people always gossip nastily about rich people who were once poor," said Teresa. "They can make life horrible for you."

"Nonsense," said Sancho, "everyone ends up being respectful towards those who are finely dressed and have loads of servants, no matter where they first came from."

"Have it your own way," sighed Teresa, "if you're revolved to go off..."

"You mean *resolved*."

"Don't you start correcting me," said Teresa. "I'll speak as I like. If you must go, at least take Sanchico with you so that he too can learn how to be a governor."

"As soon as I'm a governor I'll send for him," said Sancho. "And we're agreed that our daughter will marry a count?"

"The day Mari Sancha marries a count is the day I'll bury her," said Teresa, and she burst into tears at the thought of her daughter dead. Sancho consoled her by saying he'd put the marriage off as long as he could, and went to find Don Quixote.

Meanwhile, Don Quixote's niece and housekeeper were talking to the knight, trying to persuade him not to embark on more dangerous adventures.

"If you insist on going off, I'll complain to the king," said the housekeeper.

"I'm sure he's too busy to be bothered with my affairs," replied Don Quixote.

"Tell me," the housekeeper went on, "aren't there knights at the king's court? If there are, couldn't you go and be one of them?"

Don Quixote patiently explained the difference between knights at court, who sat about at their ease, doing nothing; and knights errant, who braved hardship and danger and would take on any foe, however fearsome.

"Oh, sir," said the niece, "isn't it time you admitted that everything you tell us about knight-errantry is made up?"

Don Quixote was outraged. "If you weren't my own sister's daughter, I'd punish you so severely that you'd never forget it," he fumed. "What would Amadis of Gaul say if he heard you uttering such nonsense?"

"I think it's you talking nonsense, dear Uncle," replied his niece.

They went on arguing until Sancho arrived, whereupon the two men shut themselves in Don Quixote's room.

The housekeeper guessed they were planning their next expedition, and was in despair. She decided to see if Sansón Carrasco could dissuade her master from leaving.

She found Sansón and explained the problem. Sansón replied, "Do not worry. Now go home and prepare a hot meal for me. I'll soon be along to sort things out. And on the way be sure to say a prayer to St Apollonia."

"But that's a cure for toothache," said the housekeeper.

"I'm a university graduate, so I should know what I'm talking about," retorted Sansón.

≈ Don Quixote and Sancho debate the question of Sancho's wages

The housekeeper returned to Don Quixote's house, where Don Quixote and Sancho were deep in conversation.

"I've evinced my wife to let me go," said Sancho.

"Surely you mean *convinced*," said Don Quixote.

"Sir," said Sancho, "I think I've asked you before kindly not to correct my speech if you can help it. If you don't understand me, just say: 'Sancho, you devil, I don't understand you.' If I can't think of another way of putting it, then you can correct me. I'm so treasonable..."

"*Reasonable,*" said Don Quixote.

"There you go again," said Sancho. "You're just trying to get me all muddled."

"Maybe so," said Don Quixote. "Now tell me, what does Teresa say?"

"She says I'm to keep an eye on you," replied Sancho, "and that he who shuffles the pack doesn't cut it, and a bird in the hand is worth two in the bush, and the lamb goes to the slaughter as quickly as the sheep."

"You're certainly coming up with some gems today, friend Sancho," said Don Quixote, "but I don't see where this is leading us."

"Where it's leading, sir," said Sancho, "is that I would like a salary for serving you, if that's OK."

"If I knew of any account in any history of knight-errantry of a squire being paid wages, then I would gladly oblige. But no, squires always went without pay and were given rewards for their service when things went well and when they least expected it. If you are prepared to serve me under these conditions, then you are welcome to do so. But first, you had better return home and clear this with your wife. If she does not agree, then we must part company now, although we can still remain friends. I will easily find another squire, one who is less clumsy, more obedient and less talkative than you."

Sancho was very downcast when he heard this, as he had been convinced that his master would not dream of setting out without him. He was musing silently when Sansón Carrasco came in.

Sansón, who was a famous wag, embraced Don Quixote, loudly declaiming, "O flower of knight-errantry! O shining light of chivalry! O honour and hope of the Spanish nation! May nothing prevent you from setting out on your third expedition. There are many poor souls out there in dire need of your services. If I may assist you in any way, even perchance by serving you as squire, pray command me forthwith."

Don Quixote turned to Sancho. "Did I not tell you I would have no trouble finding a replacement squire? Here is this fine young graduate offering me his services. But no, I must not put this paragon of the arts at risk. I will find some other squire, as Sancho here does not deign to come with me."

"I do deign, I do," said Sancho, weeping with remorse. "Don't let anyone say I'm ungrateful. If I tried to find out what my pay might be, it was only to please my wife. All that's needed is for my master to change his will so that it can't be repoked, and we'll be off."

When Sansón heard Sancho say *repoked* instead of *revoked* he realized that everything he'd read about him in the first volume of *Don Quixote* was true. At that moment, he truly believed that there had never existed two such lunatics as the knight and his squire.

≈Don Quixote and Sancho set out for El Toboso

Don Quixote then declared that they would definitely set out in three days. The niece and housekeeper were appalled at Sansón Carrasco's treacherous behaviour, and wailed and moaned louder than ever at their master's decision. Eventually Don Quixote calmed them down, and Sancho placated his wife, and they were ready to go. They departed at dusk, accompanied for a short way by Sansón. Their first destination was the great city of El Toboso, where Don Quixote intended to seek a blessing from his beloved Dulcinea.

As they made their way, they talked of fame and fortune. Sancho said that if they wished to become truly famous, they should try to become saints, as there were far more famous saints than famous knights errant. Don Quixote said that although this was true, not everyone could be a saint, and each person had to follow their own path to glory. Theirs was that of knight-errantry. They discussed this all that night and most of the following day until, at dusk, they reached the outskirts of El Toboso. Don Quixote decided they would enter the city at night, so they waited in a nearby oak wood while it grew dark.

At around midnight they rode into El Toboso. It was a moonlit night, and the village lay in silence, apart from the barking of dogs, grunting of pigs, miaowing of cats and braying of donkeys.

"Now, Sancho," said Don Quixote, "lead me to Dulcinea's palace."

"What palace?" asked Sancho. "The place I saw her was a tiny house."

"She must have retired temporarily to a small apartment," said Don Quixote. "But look," he continued, pointing at a dark shape, "I am sure that must be her palace over there."

Don Quixote led the way and after a couple of hundred paces came out at the foot of a large building. He looked up and realized he'd made a mistake.

"We've come to the church, Sancho," he said.

"I can see that," said Sancho. "Please may we not have to walk through the cemetery, as it's not a good idea at this time of night. And if I remember rightly, the lady's house is in some little dead-end alleyway."

"Fool!" fumed Don Quixote. "Have you ever heard of castles and royal palaces in dead-end alleyways?"

"Everywhere's different," replied Sancho. "But I don't know how I'm expected to find the place when I've only seen it once and you must have been there a thousand times."

"Haven't I told you that I have never set eyes on the lovely Dulcinea, and certainly never entered her palace – it's the fame of her beauty that has made me fall in love with her," said Don Quixote.

"Well, if you haven't seen her, nor have I," said Sancho.

"What do you mean?" asked Don Quixote. "You told me you saw her sieving wheat when you took her my letter."

"I only heard about her doing that; I didn't actually see her," said Sancho.

"This is no time for jokes," said Don Quixote.

Don Quixote was getting ever more bad-tempered, when Sancho had an idea. "Sir," he said, "it's nearly daybreak and it wouldn't be good for us to be found wandering around the city like this. Why don't we leave and you can rest up in some nearby woods. I'll come back later, track down Dulcinea and let her know where you are. Then she can fix up a meeting."

Don Quixote agreed, and they left the town and made their way to a forested glade. Sancho started back towards El Toboso and left Don Quixote sitting on Rocinante, propped up on his lance and sighing deeply. As soon as he was out of sight, Sancho dismounted and sat down under a tree.

"So how are you going to get yourself out of this one?" he said. "You've absolutely no idea where to find Dulcinea, and you'll probably get beaten up trying to find her. What a disaster! You've said a thousand times that your master is mad, and you must be even madder to be following him. Still," he mused, "if he's that mad, always thinking that black is white and white is black, and that windmills are giants and flocks of sheep armies, perhaps it won't be too hard to persuade him that he has seen the lady Dulcinea."

185
≈

≈ Sancho Panza's cunning plan

Sancho settled down for a few hours to make Don Quixote think he'd had enough time to go into El Toboso and back again. It was late afternoon and he had just got back on his donkey, when three peasant girls, also on donkeys, appeared.

Sancho quickly returned to Don Quixote and said, "Please, sir, follow me. The lady Dulcinea and two of her servants are coming out to meet you."

Don Quixote was delighted. As soon as he came out of the wood he looked eagerly around. "Where is she?" he asked. "All I can see is three peasant girls on donkeys."

"Gracious heavens!" said Sancho. "Is it really true that those magnificent snow-white mares look like donkeys to you?"

"They do," said Don Quixote.

"Clear the mist from your eyes, sir, and come and greet your beloved lady," said Sancho.

He rode forward towards the three girls and, dismounting from his donkey, fell to his knees before one of them, saying, "O queen and princess of beauty, pray receive your admiring knight, who is struck dumb with awe by your presence. I am Sancho Panza, his trusty squire; and he is the famous Don Quixote de la Mancha, also known as the Knight with the Face in a Sorry State."

Don Quixote had by now joined Sancho, but all he could see was a moon-faced peasant girl with a pug nose. He dared not open his mouth.

The girl took one look at the strange pair kneeling in front of her and said, "Move yourselves; we're in a hurry."

"Precious lady of El Toboso," said Sancho, "is your heart not melted by the sight of this brave knight?"

One of the other girls said, "Look here, I don't know what your game is, but I'm warning you – we can give as good as we get. Now clear off!"

"Friend Sancho," said Don Quixote, "let us go. Some evil enchantment has prevented me from seeing my lady as she really is."

The girl who was supposed to be Dulcinea goaded her donkey and galloped off across the fields. Unfortunately her goading irritated the donkey so much that it bucked her off. Don Quixote and Sancho rushed over to help. Sancho was adjusting the packsaddle and Don Quixote was trying to help the girl up, but before he could do so she had sprung to her feet, taken a couple of steps back and vaulted onto the donkey from behind. Without looking back, she and her two companions raced away.

Don Quixote was heartbroken. "What have I done to make those enchanters so angry that they should turn my Dulcinea into a coarse and ugly peasant girl? Not only that, but when I tried to help her I was nearly knocked out by the stench of raw garlic."

"Curse you, you villainous wizards! I hope you're pleased with yourselves," shouted Sancho, trying to keep a straight face.

≈ Don Quixote and Sancho meet some strange characters in a cart, and Sancho briefly loses his donkey

Don Quixote and Sancho continued towards Zaragoza, Don Quixote gloomy and lost in thought and Sancho trying to cheer him up. They were near the outskirts of a small town, when a cart pulled out into the road in front of them, drawn by mules and laden with the most remarkable characters.

Driving the cart was a ghastly demon. Behind him was Death, with Cupid at his feet and an angel with multicoloured wings sitting next to him. There was also an emperor, a knight in armour wearing a hat stuck with feathers instead of a helmet, and several others.

Sancho was overcome with fear and even Don Quixote was startled by the sudden appearance of the strange cart. However, he immediately took it as an opportunity for a new adventure. Placing himself in front of the mules, he said, "Stop, driver or devil, and tell me who you are and where you are going."

"We're actors," replied the driver, "and we're heading to that town there to perform a play. We've already performed it once today, at another town, and we couldn't be bothered to change out of our costumes."

"Ah, I understand," said Don Quixote. "I wish you good people well."

But just then one of the members of the troupe dressed as a clown came prancing up. He was carrying a stick with three cow bladders attached to it and began leaping about, jangling bells and thumping the stick on the ground. Rocinante took fright and bolted. Sancho leapt off his donkey and started running after Rocinante, who had by now tripped and fallen, leaving Don Quixote sprawling in the dust. The clown jumped onto Sancho's donkey and began to hit him with the bladders, causing him too to bolt.

Sancho couldn't decide whether to go and help his master or chase after his donkey, but his loyalty won out and he went to Don Quixote's aid. Helping Don Quixote up, he said, "Sir, that devil has stolen my donkey."

"Don't worry," said Don Quixote. "We'll take the mules from the cart to replace him."

"Actually, I don't think that will be necessary," said Sancho.

Sure enough, the donkey had dumped the clown on the ground and was trotting back to his owner, leaving the clown to walk to the town where the play was to take place.

"These characters should be punished for that devil's impertinence," said Don Quixote.

"I don't think, sir, that that would be a good idea," said Sancho. "Everyone knows that actors can get away with murder, so we'd better not provoke them."

But Don Quixote was determined. He shouted at the players in the cart to stop. They could see that he was angry, and they all dismounted and picked up stones ready to hurl at him if he approached.

"Sir," said Sancho again, "I really don't think you should go on with this. It would be madness to attack a group that has Death on its side. And in any case, there doesn't seem to be a single proper knight errant among them."

"You have a point there, Sancho. As you know, I cannot take up arms against anyone who has not been made a knight. If you wish to extract revenge for the beating your donkey received, then you may."

"There's no need for that," said Sancho. "All I'm interested in is peace and quiet."

And so they left the troupe of actors and continued on their way.

≈ DON QUIXOTE AND SANCHO ENCOUNTER THE MYSTERIOUS KNIGHT OF THE WOODS, ALSO KNOWN AS THE KNIGHT OF THE MIRRORS, AND HIS SQUIRE

That evening, Don Quixote and Sancho Panza stopped for the night in a shady grove of trees. They ate and then had a long discussion about actors and other interesting matters. Finally they both dozed off, but Don Quixote was soon awakened by a noise behind him. Turning, he could make out two men on horseback.

One of them dismounted and, sighing, said to the other, "This is the perfect spot, my friend. There is grass for the horses, and peace and quiet for me to think of love." The man then stretched out on the grass with a noise that Don Quixote recognized as the creaking of armour.

Don Quixote crawled over to Sancho and shook him awake. "We have an adventure," he whispered. "There's a knight errant over there, and not a very happy one by the sound of it. But listen, he seems to be tuning a lute or something and getting ready to sing."

The unknown knight then sang a song to his lady love. When he had finished, he added mournfully, "Oh, most ungrateful lady Casildea de Vandalia, what do you want of me? Is it not enough that I have made all the knights in Navarra, and León, and Castille, and even La Mancha, acknowledge that you are the most beautiful woman in the world?"

"That's not true," murmured Don Quixote to Sancho. "I am from La Mancha and I have never acknowledged any such thing. The fellow is clearly raving."

The Knight of the Woods evidently heard something, for he immediately got up and called out, "Who's there? Are you a happy soul or an unhappy one?"

"Unhappy," replied Don Quixote.

"Then come and join me," said the Knight of the Woods. "For in me you will find unhappiness itself."

Don Quixote and Sancho went over and the knight greeted Don Quixote warmly. "Pray, sir, are you in love?" he asked.

"I am, unfortunately," replied Don Quixote.

"I understand," said the Knight of the Woods. "It's terrible when we are disdained."

"My lady love has never disdained me," retorted Don Quixote.

"She certainly hasn't," chipped in Sancho. "She's as meek as a lamb and softer than butter."

"Is this your squire?" asked the knight.

"Yes," said Don Quixote.

"Well, I've never come across a knight's squire who's allowed to interrupt his master," said the knight. "My own squire here wouldn't dream of doing such a thing."

"Look here," said Sancho, "I can speak when I like, in front of any old—"

"That's enough. Let's get out of here," said the other knight's squire, grabbing Sancho by the arm. "We can have a squirely chat about whatever we like and leave our masters to talk about their lady loves until dawn."

≈ Sancho Panza and the Squire of the Woods discuss many interesting matters, including the trials of being a squire, islands and wine

The story now relates how the two squires sat some distance from their masters and began to talk.

"It's a hard life we lead," began the Squire of the Woods.

"True," said Sancho. "Out in the cold and rain, and often with nothing to eat from one day to the next."

"But at least if our masters are fortunate, we can hope to be rewarded with a nice little countship or governorship of an island," said the Squire of the Woods.

"I've told my master I'll be happy with an island governorship," said Sancho. "He's promised me one lots of times."

"Me, I'm going to become a canon," said the Squire of the Woods. "My master's already chosen a canonship for me."

They went on in this vein for a while, and then the Squire of the Woods said, "Actually, I'm thinking of giving up all this squiring and going back to my wife and children – I've got three."

"I've got two," said Sancho. "My daughter I'm bringing up to be a countess, although her mother isn't. I pray I get to see them all again. It's really only greed that's got me back into this adventuring – I found a purse full of gold coins in the Sierra Morena and I keep dreaming that I might find another. It's why I go on following my master, even though I know he's more of a madman than a knight."

"My master's pretty crazy too. He's pretending to be mad to help some other knight who's lost his wits."

"Is he in love?" asked Sancho.

"Yes," replied the Squire of the Woods, "with Casildea de Vandalia, the cruellest lady in the world."

"It's a comfort to me that you're serving someone as mad as my master," said Sancho.

"Mad, but brave, and a scoundrel to boot," said the Squire of the Woods.

"Mine's no scoundrel," said Sancho. "He's innocence itself, and only wants to do good for people. A child could convince him it was midnight in the middle of the day. It's because he's so simple that I'm so fond of him and couldn't leave him, however ridiculous the things he does."

At this point they broke off their conversation to eat and drink, the Squire of the Woods having brought along some fine provisions. Sancho took a swig from a flask. "This wine is from Ciudad Real, isn't it?" he asked.

"Good grief, how did you know that?" said the Squire of the Woods.

"Don't assume that someone like me is ignorant of things like that," said Sancho. "Actually, I have a great talent for identifying wine. It runs in the family."

"A gift like that shouldn't be wasted," said the Squire of the Woods. "That's why I think we should both give up this adventuring and go back to our own homes."

"I'll serve my master until he reaches Zaragoza, and then we'll see," said Sancho.

≈ The Challenge

Meanwhile, Don Quixote and the Knight of the Woods were having their own conversation.

"In conclusion, sir," the Knight of the Woods was saying, "I fell in love with the glorious Casildea de Vandalia. She forced me to prove my love for her by performing a series of difficult and dangerous tasks. I carried them all out, but I am most proud of the fact that I defeated the famous knight Don Quixote de la Mancha in single combat and forced him to admit that Casildea was more beautiful than Dulcinea del Toboso."

Don Quixote was amazed to hear this and nearly burst out with the dreadful words "You liar!" Fortunately he managed to control himself and calmly said, "I do not know about your other adventures, sir, but as to defeating Don Quixote de la Mancha, I have my doubts. It might have been someone who looked like him, although not many people do."

"What do you mean? Of course it was Don Quixote – tall and thin, with greying hair, a hooked nose and a long black drooping moustache. He calls himself the Knight with the Face in a Sorry State, rides a horse called Rocinante and has a peasant called Sancho Panza as his squire. His lady love is Dulcinea del Toboso, formerly known as Aldonza Lorenzo. If that is not enough to convince you, I am prepared to justify myself with my sword."

"Know, sir," said Don Quixote, "that Don Quixote is the dearest friend I have in the world. You could even say I value him as much as I do myself. I know that it is impossible for him to be the one you defeated, and yet I also know that your description is accurate and that Don Quixote is plagued by evil magicians. Only two days ago they transformed Dulcinea del Toboso into a hideous coarse peasant girl. They must have transformed Don Quixote in a similar fashion. If that is not enough to convince you, here is Don Quixote himself, who will justify himself with arms, on foot or on horseback, however you prefer."

"He who could defeat you transformed can certainly defeat you as you truly are," said the Knight of the Woods. "But, sir, let us wait until daybreak to fight. And let us agree that the loser is at the command of the winner as long as he is not made to do anything dishonourable."

"I agree," said Don Quixote, and the two of them went off and woke their squires, who were by now fast asleep, to get them to prepare their horses.

The squires were making their way through the gloom, when the Squire of the Woods said to Sancho, "I should tell you that it's our custom in Andalusia that when two knights fight, their squires have to fight too."

"I've never heard my master mention anything of that sort," said Sancho, "and he knows all the rules of knight-errantry by heart. Even if it was true, I wouldn't do it. I don't believe in fighting, and anyway I can't – I haven't got a sword and I've never worn one in my life."

"We could hit each other with sacks," said the Squire of the Woods.

"That would be better," said Sancho, "but I still can't bring myself to fight someone I've just shared a meal with."

"I could slap you on the face two or three times first to make you really cross," said the Squire of the Woods.

"Even better, I could thump you on the head with a stick so hard that you'd never wake up," said Sancho, "then we wouldn't have to fight at all."

By now the birds were twittering and day was breaking. The first thing that Sancho laid eyes on as the sun came up was the nose of the Squire of the Woods. It was enormous, swollen and hooked in the middle, covered in warts and purple in colour like an aubergine. It filled Sancho with such fear that he vowed not to fight its possessor under any circumstances.

Now that it was light, Don Quixote could also get a good look at his opponent. He was not very tall but well built. His visor was already down and over his armour he wore a kind of frock coat, on which were many small mirrors shaped like crescent moons. His lance was thick and long, and tipped with iron. Don Quixote concluded that the knight must be very strong, but unlike Sancho he was not daunted. He was backing off to prepare his attack, when he happened to catch sight of the squire's remarkable proboscis and quickly concluded that this was some new species of human.

Just then, Sancho grabbed Rocinante's reins and begged Don Quixote to help him into a tree, so that he could get a better view of the fight.

"I think," said Don Quixote, "that what you really want is to get out of the way of that nose. I don't blame you: if I were not me, I'd be scared of it too."

≈ Don Quixote's magnificent defeat of the Knight of the Mirrors, whose true identity is revealed

While all this was going on, the Knight of the Mirrors had assumed that Don Quixote was getting ready to charge. Without checking, he had taken his horse off some distance and, wheeling it round, was heading towards Don Quixote, at more of an amble than a gallop if the truth be told, as his horse was almost as ancient and ragged as Rocinante. When he saw that Don Quixote was in fact busy helping Sancho into a cork oak tree, he reined in his horse, which stopped dead.

Don Quixote, thinking that his enemy was bearing down on him, spurred Rocinante and galloped full pelt at the Knight of the Mirrors, whose horse now refused to budge, and whose lance was not ready. With the greatest of ease Don Quixote landed an almighty blow on his opponent's chest, knocking him backwards off his horse.

The fallen knight lay on the ground so still that he might have been dead. Don Quixote strode over to loosen his helmet. And whose face should be staring back up at him but ... Sansón Carrasco's.

"Come here quickly, Sancho!" he called. "You will never believe what strange enchantment has been at work."

Sancho dropped from his perch in the tree and dashed over. He too was amazed. "It might be one of those magicians who's been plaguing you," he said. "I'd run him through if I were you."

"Good idea," said Don Quixote, drawing his sword.

Just then the knight's squire came running up, without the nose that had made him so hideous, and cried, "Don Quixote, sir, take care! That is your friend Sansón Carrasco."

"Where's your nose?" asked Sancho.

"Here," said the squire, reaching into his pocket and pulling out a varnished papier mâché monstrosity.

Sancho peered more closely at the man. "Good heavens!" he cried. "Is this Tomé Cecial, my neighbour and good chum?"

"Of course it is," said the denosed man. "I'll tell you all about it later; but for now, please make sure your master doesn't kill or injure the Knight of the Mirrors, who is indeed the brave but misguided Sansón Carrasco."

At this point, the Knight of the Mirrors came to. Don Quixote held the tip of his sword to his face and said, "Sir Knight, if you do not wish to die, admit that the lovely Dulcinea del Toboso is more beautiful than your Casildea de Vandalia. Furthermore, admit that the knight you claim to have defeated was not Don Quixote de la Mancha, but some other, just as I believe that you are not Sansón Carrasco, but one who has been made to resemble him."

"I confess everything and agree with everything," said the prostrate knight. "Now please let me get up if I can."

Don Quixote and the knight's squire helped the knight to his feet. So convinced was Don Quixote that sorcery was afoot that he even made Sancho doubt that the men in front of them were Tomé Cecial and Sansón Carrasco.

Leaving the two of them behind, whoever they were, Don Quixote and Sancho continued towards Zaragoza, Don Quixote excessively proud of himself on account of his great victory over the Knight of the Mirrors.

According to Cide Hamete Benengeli, the explanation for all this is as follows. Sansón Carrasco had encouraged Don Quixote to set off on his third adventure following a discussion he had had with the priest and the barber. They had all decided that Don Quixote could not be persuaded by reason to stay at home. Instead, Sansón Carrasco would disguise himself as a knight errant and track down Don Quixote on the road. He would challenge him to a combat in which the loser would be at the mercy of the winner. He would easily win and command Don Quixote to return home and not leave his village for at least two years. Don Quixote would obey because he would not break the rules of chivalry, and during this period they might have a chance of curing him of his madness.

This had seemed an excellent plan, and Tomé Cecial, a cheery and rather impetuous man, had volunteered to act as Sansón's squire. Unfortunately, things had not turned out in quite the way they'd hoped.

≈Sansón Carrasco plots revenge for his humiliating defeat, while Don Quixote embarks on his adventure with the lions

With Don Quixote and Sancho gone, Sansón and Tomé tried to find a village where Sansón's back could be put right.

"Well, we got what we deserved," said Tomé. "I've had enough of this mad game-playing; I think I'll go home now."

"You can do what you like," responded Sansón, "but I'm not resting until I've had my revenge on Don Quixote."

Meanwhile, Sancho and Don Quixote were deep in conversation about magicians and enchantments, when a distinguished-looking man of about fifty, dressed in green and riding a very fine dappled mare, caught up with them. They exchanged greetings and rode on in silence for a while.

Don Quixote saw that the man was looking at him with some astonishment and said, "It seems, sir, that you have noticed my unusual appearance. I should explain that I am a knight errant, Don Quixote de la Mancha, also known as the Knight with the Face in a Sorry State. My many valiant deeds have been written about in a book, of which thirty thousand copies have been printed. I know that one should not praise oneself, but there is no one else around here to do it for me."

"I'm afraid I'm even more bemused than before," said the man. "I find it hard to believe that there can be a knight errant alive today. Still, it means that your story should ensure that those nonsensical tales of imaginary knights errant are quickly forgotten, and not a moment too soon."

"There is much to be said about whether those tales are fiction or not," said Don Quixote.

The man began to suspect that Don Quixote might be a fool or a simpleton, but said no more on the subject. Instead, he briefly told them something of himself.

"My name is Don Diego de Miranda, and I live in a nearby village, where I spend my time with my family and friends. My pastimes are hunting and fishing. I own some six dozen books, in Spanish and Latin, although none concern chivalry. I entertain often. I don't like gossip and don't interfere in other people's lives. I go to church regularly and I give money to the poor but never boast about it."

Sancho listened to all this and decided that the man must be a saint. He dismounted from his donkey and proceeded to kiss his feet. "You're the first saint I've seen in my life riding with short stirrups," he said.

Don Quixote laughed and the man said, "I'm no saint, but a poor sinner."

Don Diego then told them about his son, who was eighteen. "He's spent the last six years studying Latin and Greek at Salamanca University. He's obsessed with ancient poetry and refuses to study anything else, however much I try to persuade him."

Don Quixote came to the boy's defence. "If he has found his subject," he said, "you should allow him to pursue it. The study of poetry is a fine and worthy thing." And he proceeded to hold forth in a most intelligent way on the subject of ancient poetry.

Don Diego was astonished, and began to revise his opinion of Don Quixote as a simpleton. Sancho, meanwhile, had grown rather bored and wandered off the road to buy some cheese curds from a group of shepherds who were milking their sheep near by.

Just at that moment, Don Quixote saw coming towards them on the road a wagon sporting royal banners. He was sure this signalled an exciting new adventure and called to Sancho to bring him his helmet, which was slung across the pommel of Sancho's saddle.

Sancho became flustered, and could not think what to do with the curds he had just bought, so he put them in the helmet. He rode over to Don Quixote, who immediately asked for the helmet. Sancho had no choice but to hand it over as it was. Don Quixote put it on his head without looking inside it, and soon whey from the curds began trickling down his head.

"What is this, Sancho?" he asked. "Are my brains melting, or is my head turning to putty? Hand me a cloth – I can't see a thing."

Sancho said nothing, but gave his master a cloth. Don Quixote wiped his face and then took off the helmet. He peered inside and sniffed at the contents. "By the life of my lady Dulcinea, these are curds, you vile wretch," he said.

To which Sancho replied, "If they are curds, sir, you should give them to me and I'll eat them. They must have been put there by one of those swinish enchanters who pursue you. I, of course, would never dream of dirtying your helmet in such a way."

"Anything is possible," said Don Quixote as he carefully cleaned himself up. He then placed himself in front of the wagon and said to the driver, "Whose wagon is this, and what are you carrying in it?"

"It is my wagon," said the driver, "and I am carrying two lions to his majesty the king. They are a present from the general of Oran."

"Are they large lions?" asked Don Quixote.

"They are," said a second man, sitting next to the driver. "There's a male and a female, and they're both hungry because they haven't eaten yet today."

"Well," said Don Quixote, "I'll show the magicians who sent them who's afraid of itsy-witsy little lions. Come, my man, open the cages and turn the animals out."

Hearing this, Sancho rushed over to Don Diego and said, "Please, sir, do something to stop my master fighting those lions. They'll tear him to pieces."

"Is he mad then?" asked Don Diego.

"Not mad, just reckless," replied Sancho.

"I'll soon put a stop to this," said Don Diego, and he rode up to Don Quixote saying, "Sir Knight, this adventure is hopeless, not to say insane. Furthermore, the lions have not come here to attack anyone, and are a present for his majesty. You should leave them in peace."

"I know what I'm doing, sir," said Don Quixote. "Stand aside." And turning to the lion keeper he said, "If you don't want to be impaled on this lance, open the cages at once."

Seeing that this crazy apparition was in earnest, the mule driver said, "If you must go ahead, please let me first unyoke the mules and take them away to safety – they and the cart are the only things I own."

The keeper then turned to the others and declaimed, "All of you are witnesses that I am being forced to do this against my will. I say now that any damage caused by the animals is this here gentleman's responsibility."

Sancho and Don Diego redoubled their efforts to stop Don Quixote, but to no avail. Giving up, they and the mule driver rode off as fast as they could. The keeper made one last attempt to dissuade Don Quixote and then resigned himself to obeying him.

Don Quixote dismounted from Rocinante, tossed away his lance and drew his sword. He approached the cart and the keeper opened the first cage. In it was the male lion, a huge and fearsome beast. The lion got up and slowly turned round to face the outside world; then he unsheathed his claws and stretched; then he opened his mouth and yawned very slowly; then he stuck out his enormous tongue and washed his face very carefully; and only then did he stick his head out of the cage and look around, with eyes like burning coals. Standing in front of him was Don Quixote, willing him to come out so that they could fight. But the lion was having none of it. Instead, he slowly turned round, showing Don Quixote his backside, and calmly lay down again.

Don Quixote tried to make the keeper hit the lion to provoke him into coming out, but the keeper refused. "You should be satisfied," he said. "The animal had his chance to come out, and did not. You have demonstrated your bravery and it would be foolish to go on tempting fate."

Don Quixote agreed and signalled to the others, who were still fleeing while glancing anxiously back at every step. When they saw that it was Don Quixote waving at them, they cautiously returned to the cart. The lion keeper recounted the adventure in great detail, praising Don Quixote's bravery to the skies. Don Quixote told Sancho to pay the keeper and the mule driver two gold coins in recompense for the delay in their journey. The keeper promised to tell the king the whole story.

"If he asks who carried out the deed," said Don Quixote, "tell him it was the Knight of the Lions – I have decided I shall no longer be called the Knight with the Face in a Sorry State."

The mule cart went on its way, and Sancho, Don Quixote and Don Diego de Miranda went on theirs. Don Diego was musing over what he had witnessed, when Don Quixote said to him,

"I am sure, Don Diego, that you think me both foolish and mad, but I am only behaving as a true knight errant should. True bravery lies between the wicked extremes of cowardice and recklessness, but it is better to err on the side of rashness than of cowardice."

"It is clear," said Don Diego, "that you understand the laws of chivalry completely. Now, let us hurry to my village, where I invite you to rest from your labours."

≈ Don Quixote and Sancho pass a pleasant few days at the home of the country gentleman Don Diego de Miranda and then set off to attend a country wedding, which does not turn out exactly as planned

At Don Diego's house Don Quixote and Sancho were treated to a hospitable welcome by Don Diego's wife, Señora Doña Cristina; and his son, Don Lorenzo. Over the next few days, Don Quixote and Don Lorenzo spent many hours discussing poetry, and Don Lorenzo read out some of the poems he had written. Don Quixote was extremely complimentary and made many intelligent comments. Both Don Lorenzo and his father continued to be amazed by Don Quixote, whose conversation was a strange mixture of madness and sanity.

After four days, Don Quixote and Sancho reluctantly took their leave, laden with provisions from the generous Don Diego. They were still intending to go to Zaragoza, but Don Quixote wanted to visit the mysterious Cave of Montesinos on the way.

They had not gone far, when they met a group of four men riding donkeys. There were two students and two farmers. Don Quixote greeted them and they began talking.

"If you are not in a hurry, Sir Knight," said one of the students, "you should join us at the wedding we're heading for. It's between the richest farmer in the region, young Camacho, and the most beautiful woman, a farmer's daughter called Quiteria. Camacho is extremely generous and it promises to be a magnificent event. But the thing we're most excited about is seeing what our friend the shepherd Basilio will get up to. He and Quiteria have been in love since they were children, and he's been distraught ever since Quiteria's father decided to marry her off to the rich Camacho. He declares that the day Quiteria and Camacho marry is the day he will die."

"It sounds like Quiteria and Basilio should be the ones getting married," said Sancho.

"Not necessarily," said Don Quixote. "If people were only to marry those they were in love with, then parents could not marry off their children as they saw fit and there would be many bad matches that led to misery for husband or wife, or both."

With this and other observations they rode on. The two students had an argument and ended up in a fencing match, refereed by Don Quixote, after which they were better friends than ever. Just as night was falling, the party reached the outskirts of the village where the wedding was to be held. Don Quixote refused to enter the village, and went off to find a place to rest in the countryside, accompanied by a very reluctant Sancho, who remembered well the comfort of Don Diego's house.

Don Quixote woke as dawn was breaking, and called out to Sancho, who went on snoring heavily. "Slumber on!" said Don Quixote. "I am sure it is right and fair that the servant should sleep without a care in the world while his master lies awake, worrying about how he will sustain him."

Sancho did not wake up until Don Quixote prodded him with his lance. He stretched and smelt the air. "My," he said, "this is going to be a fine wedding."

"That's enough of that, you glutton," said Don Quixote. "Now let's go and find out what Basilio is going to do."

"I don't care," said Sancho. "He shouldn't have been poor if he wanted to marry Quiteria. It's all very well being a fine fencer and athlete and all those other things they say he is, but none of those will buy you a pitcher of wine in an inn. If he's going to get on he needs one thing, and that's money."

"For heaven's sake," said Don Quixote, "do stop your chatter. It's a wonder you find time to eat or sleep, the way you go on."

"You may recall, sir," said Sancho, "that before we set out this time it was put in the agreement between us that I could talk as much as I liked, as long as I wasn't rude to anyone or went against your authority."

"I'm not sure I remember any such thing," said Don Quixote. "In any case, let us be off, as the celebrations are sure to start soon."

They reached the field where the wedding was to be held and found a gargantuan feast being prepared. Sancho took one look and nearly swooned. A cook handed him a vast pot holding three chickens and two geese and told him to be getting on with that until it was time for the proper meal.

Meanwhile, Don Quixote watched as twelve farmers in their finest clothes appeared on twelve beautiful horses. They rode around the field shouting, "Long live the rich Camacho and Quiteria, the fairest maiden in the world!"

"They wouldn't say that if they had seen Dulcinea del Toboso," said Don Quixote.

There then followed a rustic dance and a masquerade, in which two men dressed as Love and Wealth vied for the attentions of a beautiful woman.

"See how well the man who wrote the masquerade has shown the characters of Basilio and Camacho," said Don Quixote to Sancho.

"I'm backing Camacho," said Sancho.

"You're a typical peasant, always supporting the winner," said Don Quixote.

"I don't know about that," responded Sancho, "but I'm certainly in favour of the one with the fullest cooking pots. There's a lot to be said for having money. As my old grandmother used to say, there's just two different kinds of people in the world – the haves and the have-nots. She knew which side she was on. As for me, I can't see Basilio paying for all these geese and chickens and hares and rabbits. The way I see it—"

"Honestly, Sancho, it seems that Death is the only thing that will shut you up, and as I'm probably going to die before you, I doubt if I will ever have the privilege of hearing you stop talking."

"You can't rely on that bony old woman – Death, I mean," said Sancho. "She's as likely to carry off a lamb as a sheep. She's not fussy where she reaps. She's as hungry as a dog, and never satisfied."

"You should be a preacher," said Don Quixote.

"All I know of that is that he who lives well preaches well," replied Sancho, and he returned with gusto to his pot of fowl.

Don Quixote would have joined him had he not been distracted by the arrival of the wedding party. The bride herself looked extremely beautiful, though very pale. Sancho showered such praises on her that he made Don Quixote laugh, and even Don Quixote thought he'd never seen a lovelier woman – apart, of course, from Dulcinea.

The bride and groom were walking towards a platform on one side of the field, when they heard shouting behind them. Everyone turned to look. Standing there was a man dressed in a black coat trimmed with red flames, holding a long stick and wearing a wreath of funereal cypress on his head. It was Basilio.

He thrust the stick into the ground and then addressed Quiteria, saying, "You have turned your back on me, your true love, in favour of this rich man. I will not stand in your way. Long life and happiness to Camacho the Rich and Quiteria the Ungrateful, and death to Basilio!"

And so saying, he pulled at the stick he had thrust into the ground. The top half came away, leaving a sharp rapier sticking out of the ground. With great speed Basilio threw himself onto the rapier, which came out of his back all covered in blood.

Don Quixote dismounted and ran over. Basilio was still alive. He opened his eyes and said feebly, "O cruel Quiteria, if you were to wed me at the moment of my death, I would think that my rashness had not been entirely in vain."

The priest said that Basilio should be thinking of his final confession and not of marriage, but Don Quixote intervened and said that he thought Basilio's request was quite reasonable, and that as soon as he died and Quiteria became a widow, Señor Camacho could himself marry her.

Camacho was very uneasy about all this, but was finally persuaded. Quiteria, looking very shaken, agreed; and, with Basilio giving every indication that he was about to give up the ghost, the priest married the two of them.

No sooner had the pair said "I do" and been blessed by the priest than Basilio leapt to his feet and calmly pulled out the sword that had apparently run him through.

"It's a miracle!" shouted the onlookers.

"No miracle, just cunning," said Basilio, and showed them that the sword had not pierced him at all but had passed through a metal tube packed with fake blood hidden under his clothes.

Quiteria appeared to be very unsurprised by all this and everyone quickly concluded that she must have been in on the plan. Camacho and his companions were so enraged that they drew their swords and prepared to attack Basilio. In response, Basilio's companions drew their own swords, ready to defend their friend.

Sancho took refuge among the cooking pots while Don Quixote shouted, "Stop, my good men, stop! It is not right to take revenge for wrongs committed in the name of love. It is evident that Quiteria and Basilio belong to each other. Camacho is rich and can buy whatever he likes, while Basilio has only this little lamb, so leave them be."

Camacho calmed down and decided that perhaps he had had a lucky escape, for if Quiteria had been in love with Basilio before their marriage, she would probably have continued afterwards. He even decreed that the festivities could go on as before, but Basilio and Quiteria and their friends would not stay. They returned to their own village, taking Don Quixote and Sancho with them. Among the party, only Sancho was gloomy, at the thought of missing out on all the food that Camacho had laid on.

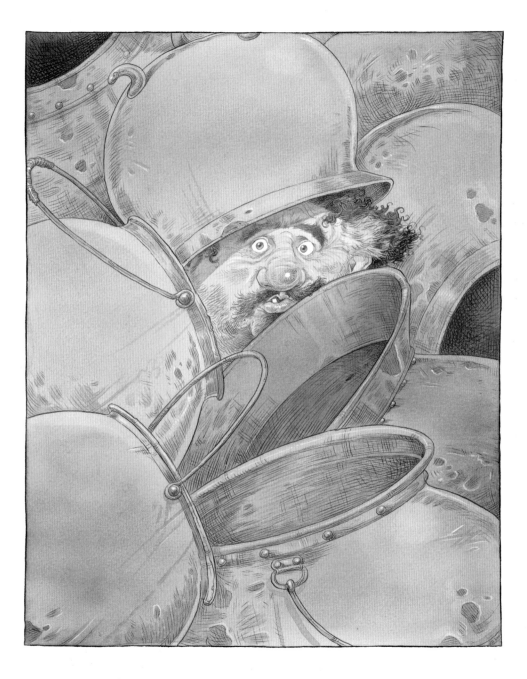

≈ The visit to the Cave of Montesinos

The bride and bridegroom were extremely grateful to Don Quixote for his intervention, and they lavished attention on him and Sancho. It turned out that Quiteria had known nothing of Basilio's plan, but was still very happy with its outcome.

After three days of hospitality, Don Quixote decided it was time to move on, as he was very anxious to visit the famous Cave of Montesinos. He asked one of the students they had first met up with for a guide. The student said that a cousin of his, who was very fond of reading books on chivalry, would be happy to accompany them. They loaded themselves up with provisions provided by Basilio and Quiteria and set off.

After a day and a half, they arrived at a village near the cave, where the cousin said they should equip themselves with rope. They bought nearly two hundred metres, as Don Quixote was determined to reach the bottom of the cave, however deep.

The following afternoon, they arrived at the entrance of the cave, which was all overgrown with fig trees and brambles. They dismounted and Sancho and the cousin began to wrap one end of the rope around Don Quixote's waist.

"You really shouldn't be doing this, sir," said Sancho. "You've no business exploring this horrible place."

"Tie the rope and shut up," said Don Quixote. "This is a job for me alone." Offering up a prayer to Dulcinea, he drew his sword and hacked his way through the vegetation to the cave mouth. The noise he made caused ravens and crows to pour out of the cave in such numbers that they knocked him to the ground. Undaunted he got to his feet and, when all the birds had gone, began to lower himself into the gaping hole, with Sancho and the cousin muttering prayers on his behalf.

As Don Quixote descended he kept calling for more rope. Eventually Sancho and the cousin could no longer hear his cries and all the rope had been paid out. After half an hour they decided they ought to bring him back up again and began hauling in the rope. At first it came up very easily, with no weight at all on it, causing them to believe that Don Quixote had remained behind in the cave. This made Sancho weep bitterly, and pull on the rope even faster. But when there was still about one hundred and fifty metres of rope to go they felt a weight, to their great relief. With twenty metres of rope to go, they could clearly see Don Quixote.

Sancho shouted out, "Welcome back, sir! We thought you were setting up home down there."

Don Quixote said nothing, and when they pulled him out they saw that he had his eyes tight shut and appeared to be asleep. They rolled him on the ground and shook him.

After some time he opened his eyes and stretched. Looking around, as if in alarm, he said, "May you be forgiven for taking me away from the most delightful sights that anyone has ever seen. O poor Montesinos! O wounded Durandarte! O weeping Guadiana!"

The other two begged him to explain himself, but Don Quixote said that he was very hungry, and first needed to eat. They spread provisions out on the ground and ate together.

When they had finished, Don Quixote said, "Now listen carefully to me, my good friends. Near the bottom of the cave, there is a big space set into the wall, dimly lit by light from cracks going right up to the surface. I decided to rest in there for a while and was suddenly overcome by sleep.

"I woke up and found myself in a delightful meadow. There then appeared before my eyes a castle with walls of clear crystal. Two large doors opened in the walls and out of them walked a distinguished old man with a long white beard, wearing a purple cloak. He came up and embraced me and said, 'We have been waiting many years for you, O valiant Don Quixote de la Mancha. I am Montesinos, guardian of this castle.'

"He led me into an alabaster room in which was a big marble tomb. Stretched out on the tomb was Montesinos's great friend, the knight Durandarte. Montesinos confirmed that it was true that he had cut out Durandarte's heart, at Durandarte's request when he was on the point of death at the Battle of Roncesvalles, so that he could carry it to his lady love, Belerma. Montesinos told me that he, Durandarte, Belerma and many others had been enchanted by Merlin, the French magician, and had been there for five hundred years.

"'I know Durandarte died in my arms,' said Montesinos to me, 'so I do not understand how it is that he often sighs and groans, as if he were living.' Just at that moment, Durandarte called out to his friend Montesinos. The old man knelt down in front of Durandarte with tears in his eyes. 'As I have told you many times, I did everything you asked,' he said. 'But this time, there is something new. The great knight Don Quixote de la Mancha, about whom Merlin has made so many prophecies, is here. Perhaps he can break the spell that enchants us.'

"Just then a procession of women, dressed in mourning and all weeping and wailing, filed in. At the back was a woman who Montesinos told me was Belerma. She was carrying Durandarte's heart, dried and salted, in a piece of cloth. She did not look as beautiful as I expected. Montesinos said that this was because she was so wrung out with mourning for her Durandarte.

'Otherwise,' he added, 'the famous Dulcinea del Toboso would hardly equal her in beauty.'

"'Sir Montesinos,' I said, 'there is no need for that kind of comparison. Dulcinea is Dulcinea, and Belerma is Belerma.' Montesinos apologized profusely."

"I'm surprised you didn't beat him up," said Sancho.

"That wouldn't have been right at all," said Don Quixote. "We must have respect for the old."

"Pardon me, sir," put in the cousin, "but how can all that have happened to you in such a short time – you've only been gone an hour."

"That's not possible," said Don Quixote. "Three days and three nights passed while I was down there."

"I hope you will forgive me, sir," said Sancho, "if I tell you I don't believe any of this happened."

"What," said the cousin, "would Señor Don Quixote lie?"

"No," replied Sancho, "but I believe Merlin may have enchanted him to make him believe it all."

"That could be true, Sancho, but it is not," said Don Quixote, "as I saw it all with my own eyes, and felt it with my own hands. One of the things Montesinos showed me was three peasant girls cavorting in the meadows, whom I immediately recognized as Dulcinea and her companions. Montesinos did not know who they were, but said he thought they must be fine ladies who had been enchanted, as they had only appeared a few days before."

When Sancho heard this he thought he might die laughing, and was finally convinced that his master was completely mad. "Oh, sir," he said, "it was a terrible day when you decided to go into that cave, because it's addled your brains."

"Because I know you well I will ignore that remark, Sancho," said Don Quixote.

"And I'll ignore yours," returned Sancho. "But tell me, how did you recognize Dulcinea?"

"By the clothes she was wearing, which were the same as when you showed her to me. I tried to speak to her, but she ran away. We were about to leave the place, when one of Dulcinea's companions came up and tearfully told me that her lady sent her regards and begged for the loan of six reals as she was short of money. I only had four reals on me – you gave them to me the other day, Sancho, to hand out as alms to any beggars we might meet – but I let her have those. The girl took them and, instead of curtsying, jumped a metre and a half straight up in the air."

"Sir, sir," said Sancho, "how can you believe this nonsense?"

"You only speak like this because you are so fond of me," replied Don Quixote. "There are many things in this world that you do not understand."

The translator of the original history says that when he got to this part, he found written in the margins of the manuscript, in Cide Hamete Benengeli's own hand, the statement: *I cannot believe that all this did indeed happen to Don Quixote, as it is too fantastical. However, I also cannot believe that the noble and truthful Don Quixote would ever tell a lie. I have therefore simply written it all down, and leave it to you, reader, to judge it for yourself.* He then continues with the story.

The cousin was amazed at Sancho's impertinence and Don Quixote's forbearance, and concluded that Don Quixote was in a good mood because he had just seen his beloved Dulcinea.

The three of them left the Cave of Montesinos. They had not been on the road for long, when they were overtaken by a man hurrying along with a mule laden with lances and halberds. The man said he could not stop, as the weapons he was carrying were to be used the next day. However, he would be staying at the inn on the road ahead, and if the others caught up with him there, he would explain what he was doing.

Shortly afterwards, they came across a boy of about eighteen, sauntering along and carrying a bundle of clothes on a sword slung over his shoulder. He told them he had served as a pageboy and was now going to enlist in the army. Don Quixote commended him on his decision, and held forth very eloquently about the virtues of military service. On hearing him speak so wisely, Sancho could not believe that this was the same man who had spouted such nonsense at the Cave of Montesinos.

≈ Don Quixote and Sancho hear the tale of the donkey village and come across the mysterious Master Pedro and his monkey

At nightfall the party reached the inn that the mule driver had spoken of. Sancho was pleased to see that his master recognized it as an inn and did not declare it to be a castle, as he usually did. They stabled Rocinante and the donkeys and found the mule driver. They all settled down and the mule driver began his explanation.

"The village I come from is some way from here," he said. "A while ago one of our village councillors lost a donkey. Two weeks later, one of the other councillors came up to him and said, 'You owe me a reward, friend, as I have found your donkey in a nearby wood. He looked half starved and ran off as soon as I saw him.' The two of them immediately went to the spot where the donkey had been seen, but there was no sign of him.

"'I know,' said the second councillor, 'I'm really good at braying, and if you can bray a little too, we'll walk round the wood in opposite directions, braying every now and again. Sooner or later, your donkey is bound to hear one of us and bray back.'

"'That's an excellent plan,' said the first councillor. 'As a matter of fact I'm a very fine brayer too.'

"They tried it out and each was amazed at how convincing the other's braying was. Indeed, they were so convincing that they kept thinking they'd found the donkey, when all they'd heard was each other. It wasn't surprising that the real donkey never responded, as he was by now lying dead and half eaten by wolves in the very heart of the wood. After a few hours, the councillors discovered this and returned, very disconsolate, to the village. They told everyone what had happened, each talking up the other's braying talents.

"News of this soon spread to all the surrounding villages; and now, every time someone from one of those villages sees one of us, they start braying, in mockery of our councilmen. Things have got so bad that fights keep breaking out. Tomorrow there's going to be a big battle between our village and the village that mocks us the most. That's why I've got all those weapons."

At that moment, a man appeared at the door dressed head to foot in chamois leather, with a green patch covering his left eye and half his left cheek.

"If it isn't Master Pedro!" declared the landlord of the inn. "We've certainly got a good evening ahead of us. Where are the monkey and the puppets, Master Pedro?"

"Waiting outside," said Master Pedro. "I'll bring them in."

While he was gone, the innkeeper explained that Master Pedro had a very intelligent monkey, which could answer questions through his owner. When Master Pedro came back, Don Quixote got out two reals and asked what was to become of him and Sancho. Master Pedro said that he would only take the money when the monkey had provided his service. He also explained that the monkey did not answer questions about the future, only about the past and the present.

"Then tell me what my wife, Teresa Panza, is up to right now," said Sancho.

Master Pedro gave a signal. The monkey leapt onto his shoulder, chattered rapidly into his ear and jumped down again. Master Pedro immediately ran over and fell to his knees in front of Don Quixote, saying, "O glorious Don Quixote de la Mancha, reviver of knight-errantry, comfort to the unfortunate, it is impossible to praise you highly enough!"

Don Quixote was dumbfounded; Sancho was dumbfounded; the cousin was dumbfounded. Even the mule driver and the pageboy were dumbfounded.

"As for you, Sancho Panza, the best squire in the world," Master Pedro continued, "your wife, Teresa, is well and is currently winding flax, with a jug of wine at her side to keep her cheerful while she works. And now I'm going to present my puppet show. Thanks to Don Quixote, in whose debt I am, I'm not going to charge anyone anything to see it."

He went off to set up the puppet theatre. Don Quixote took Sancho to one side and whispered, "I'm not happy about this, Sancho. I think that man must have made some pact with the devil to grant his monkey those powers."

"That's as may be, sir," said Sancho, "but all the same I'd like you to ask him whether what happened to you in the Cave of Montesinos was true, as I still think it was all lies or at the very least a dream."

"It's not impossible," said Don Quixote.

At that moment, Master Pedro came looking for Don Quixote to tell him that the puppet show was ready. Don Quixote repeated what Sancho had asked, and Master Pedro relayed it to the monkey. As before, the monkey leapt onto his master's shoulder and chattered away into his ear.

"He says that part of what you underwent in the cave was false and part of it was true," reported Master Pedro. "And that's all he can answer for now, as his powers are all used up for the time being, and won't return until next Friday."

≈ Don Quixote gets carried away

Don Quixote and Sancho made their way over to the puppet theatre. Master Pedro disappeared behind the theatre, leaving a servant boy standing in front. Don Quixote and Sancho joined the rest of the audience in time to hear the sound of trumpets, drums and gunfire.

As this died down, the servant boy began to speak in a loud voice. "You are about to witness the true history of the brave Don Gaiferos, who freed his wife, Melisendra, from the Moors in Spain, in the city of Sansueña, as Zaragoza was then called."

The puppets began to act out the story and the boy explained what was happening. His descriptions became increasingly complicated.

"Keep it simple, boy," called out Master Pedro, but the boy ignored him. They had reached the part where Melisendra and Don Gaiferos were escaping from Sansueña on a horse.

"See the hordes of Moors pouring out of the city!" cried the boy. "They're about to overtake the unhappy couple. I'm sure they're going to drag them back to the city tied to the tail of their own horse."

"Never!" shouted Don Quixote. "How dare you treat such a noble knight in that way, you rabble!" And so saying, he jumped up, unsheathed his sword and began laying into the Moorish puppets, beheading some and lopping the limbs off others.

"Stop, Señor Don Quixote, stop!" cried Master Pedro, who had to duck out of the way smartly to avoid losing his own head. "They're not real Moors, just papier mâché puppets. You're destroying everything I own."

But Don Quixote would not listen and continued until the whole theatre lay in tatters. The audience were in uproar, the monkey fled out of the window and took refuge on the roof, and even Sancho thought he had never seen his master so angry.

When he had finished, Don Quixote grew calmer and said, "See what good knights errant can do. Imagine the terrible things that would have befallen Don Gaiferos and Melisendra if I had not been present. Long live knight-errantry!"

Master Pedro was in tears. "Long life indeed, and death to me," he whimpered. "A while ago I was master of kings and emperors and had entire armies under my command. Now I have nothing, not even my monkey. I don't know what I'll do."

Sancho took pity on Master Pedro's plight. "Don't worry," he said, "my master is a good man and is sure to recompense you."

"But I've done nothing wrong," said Don Quixote.

"How can you say that when all these puppets lie smashed?" asked Master Pedro.

"But I thought they really were Don Gaiferos, Melisendra and all those others. I must have been tricked by those evil enchanters who pursue me. If I have caused damage, even if I didn't intend to, I will of course compensate Master Pedro."

It was agreed that the innkeeper and Sancho would arbitrate in deciding the sum to be paid to Master Pedro by Don Quixote. They began assessing the value of each damaged puppet. The first was Emperor Charlemagne, split in two.

"I ask five and a quarter reals for this one," said Master
Pedro.

"That's a bit steep," said Sancho.

"How about five reals?" said the innkeeper.

"No, give him the full amount," said Don Quixote, "and do
ask Master Pedro to be quick, as I'm getting hungry."

Master Pedro held up a second one. "This is the lovely
Melisendra. She's lost her nose and an eye, and I want two reals
and twelve maravedis for her."

"Don't be ridiculous; she can't be Melisendra," said Don
Quixote. "The speed that horse was going, she must be at the
French border by now. Stop trying to trick me."

Master Pedro could see that Don Quixote was starting to show
his madness again and quickly said, "My mistake, it's one of
Melisendra's serving girls. I only want eighty maravedis for her."

When they had totted up the cost of all the damaged puppets,
it was decided that Don Quixote owed Master Pedro forty and
three-quarter reals. Don Quixote paid this over, with an extra
two reals for the trouble of recapturing the monkey. Everyone
then settled down to supper, paid for by Don Quixote.

≈ Sancho demonstrates that he is very good at braying, and Don Quixote decides that sometimes discretion is the better part of valour

The next morning, everyone went their separate ways, Don Quixote giving the pageboy a dozen reals to help him on his journey. At this point, the great historian Cide Hamete Benengeli explains the secret of Master Pedro. It turns out that the puppeteer and monkey master was none other than the famous Ginés de Pasamonte, freed by Don Quixote from the chain gang in the first part of his adventures. He had recognized Don Quixote and Sancho as soon as they had come into the inn, and was able to amaze the audience by pretending that the monkey had identified them.

Don Quixote decided that before going to Zaragoza he would like to see the River Ebro. He travelled in that direction for two days without anything much happening. On the third day, as he was riding up a hill, he heard the noise of drums and trumpets. At first he thought it was a regiment of soldiers, but when he reached the top of the hill and looked down, he saw a rabble of some two hundred men armed with a great variety of weapons, waving banners. On one of the banners was a very lifelike portrayal of a small donkey with its head raised and mouth open, as if it was braying. He and Sancho quickly concluded that this was the village with the braying councillors, come out to do battle with a neighbouring village that had mocked them.

Much against Sancho's will, Don Quixote determined to address the men. He rode up to the banner with the donkey on it and, after first asking permission, launched into a long speech about honour and the taking up of arms. He said that there were only four important ways that men could justify fighting: in the cause of their religion; in self-defence; to defend their honour, family and possessions; and in serving their king in a just war. None of these applied in the present case.

"I'm afraid, gentlemen," he said, "that you are mistaken in considering yourselves insulted by these childish pranks. They are no reason to fight, and I therefore implore you to go in peace."

Don Quixote was about to continue, when Sancho intervened. "You should pay attention to my master, Don Quixote de la Mancha. He's very well educated, and always behaves like a good soldier and knows all the rules of duelling off by heart. He's quite right when he says it's silly to lose your temper over some braying. I mean, I used to bray a lot when I was a boy and nobody minded. Listen to this if you don't believe me."

He held his nose and brayed so loudly that the valleys all round echoed with the sound.

Unfortunately, a man standing next to Sancho decided that Sancho was mocking the donkey village and promptly knocked him out cold with the pole he was carrying. Don Quixote tried to go to Sancho's aid but found his path blocked by dozens of men pointing crossbows and muskets. A hail of stones poured down on him, and he beat a smart retreat, as fast as Rocinante's legs could carry him.

As soon as Sancho came to, the men slung him over his donkey's back and sent him on his way. The donkey plodded off, carefully following Rocinante's footsteps – the two of them were extremely firm friends and could not bear to be parted for long.

The donkey caught up with Rocinante, and Sancho slid off onto the ground. Don Quixote examined him and, finding that his wounds were not serious, said indignantly, "What possessed you to bray like that? It is not surprising that you ended up with a beating."

"I'm saying nothing," said Sancho, "except about knights errant running away leaving their squires at the mercy of their enemies."

"I did not run away," replied Don Quixote. "I staged a strategic withdrawal. Bravery that is not based on prudence is mere recklessness and is to be avoided. I was following the example of many brave men in history who have saved themselves for more opportune times."

When Sancho's aches and pains had abated a little, they continued on their journey. Sancho complained bitterly of his plight, and he had a long argument with Don Quixote about whether he should be paid a wage or not. Don Quixote finally agreed, but then Sancho also asked for compensation for not having been made governor of an island yet.

"And that should be calculated from the day you first made the promise," he said.

"When was that?" asked Don Quixote.

"Oh, around twenty years ago," said Sancho.

"Our adventures have barely lasted two months altogether, and you say twenty years," responded Don Quixote. "It's obvious you just want all the money I've put in your care for yourself. Very well then, have it. It'll be well spent if it means I'm rid of such a terrible squire. Ungrateful wretch. You're an ass now and will remain an ass until the end of your days."

Sancho listened to this outburst in horror, burst into tears and begged his master's forgiveness. Don Quixote pardoned him and told him to take courage, as he was sure he would soon receive his reward for all his service.

≈ The enchanted boat and the adventure of the mill wheels

Two days later, they arrived on the banks of the River Ebro. Don Quixote was thrilled by the sight of the magnificent river. As he rode along, he spotted a small boat tied up to a tree. He quickly dismounted, telling Sancho to do the same and tie Rocinante and the donkey to a nearby poplar or willow.

Sancho asked why and Don Quixote replied, "That boat is calling me to board it and go to the assistance of some knight or other important person."

"I'm pretty sure that boat's not one of the enchanted sort, but an ordinary fishing sort," said Sancho.

But Don Quixote would not be swayed. He jumped into the boat, making Sancho follow him, and then cut the rope, letting the boat drift off into the stream. Seeing them go, the donkey started braying and Rocinante began struggling to try to free himself. Sancho could not stop himself weeping at the state the animals were in, and Don Quixote berated him.

"Miserable cowardly wretch, what are you afraid of? Or do you believe you're in discomfort, when in fact you're sitting there like an archduke being carried along by this magic vessel? According to my calculations we've travelled three or four thousand kilometres already. We'll soon be over the equator – you'll know this for certain, because it's well known that all lice drop dead as soon as they cross it."

"I can't see any reason to put that to the test," said Sancho. "My eyes tell me we haven't moved eight metres from shore, and we've gone less than four metres downstream, because there are Rocinante and the donkey exactly where we left them."

"You obviously know nothing about navigation," said Don Quixote. "Now just test out what I told you."

Sancho slid his hand down the back of his left leg as far as the knee. He looked up. "Either that test doesn't work, or we haven't gone as far as you think, sir."

"Why, did you find something?" asked Don Quixote.

"Quite a few somethings," replied Sancho, hastily washing his hand in the river.

They drifted slowly along and came to some large watermills standing in the middle of the river.

"Look," said Don Quixote, "there is the fortress where they must be holding the knight or other important person prisoner."

"Those are just watermills for grinding wheat," said Sancho.

"Keep quiet, Sancho," said Don Quixote. "They might look like watermills, but they're not. They've been disguised by enchantments."

At this point, the boat entered the mill race and started picking up speed as it headed towards the mill wheels. Seeing it about to be sucked under the wheels, the millers came dashing out, armed with long poles to push it off. Their faces and clothes were all white with flour.

"You idiots, what are you doing?" they shouted.

"I told you, Sancho," said Don Quixote triumphantly. "Look at those ugly villains." And getting out his sword he yelled, "Miserable wretches, I am Don Quixote de la Mancha, also known as the Knight of the Lions, and I command you to set free whomever you are holding prisoner!"

Sancho got down on his knees and prayed for his life. The millers managed to keep the boat away from the wheels, but in doing so capsized it, pitching Don Quixote and Sancho into the water. Luckily Don Quixote could swim like a goose, but even so the weight of his armour would have done for him had the millers not jumped in and pulled him and Sancho out.

They were recovering on the bank when the fishermen whose boat it was appeared, in time to see it smashed to pieces by the mill wheels. They demanded payment for the boat, and Don Quixote calmly told them he would gladly pay on condition that they release the prisoner in the castle.

"What prisoner, you madman?" demanded one of the millers.

"Enough!" said Don Quixote to himself. "I am wasting my breath here. This rabble will never see sense." He told Sancho to hand over fifty reals for the boat, and as he left he raised his voice and said, "My friends, whoever you are, forgive me for not having rescued you. You must wait for some other knight."

Don Quixote and Sancho returned very downcast to their animals, Sancho particularly miserable at having had to hand over yet more money. He secretly made up his mind to leave his master as soon as possible. However, things didn't quite turn out that way.

≋ THE DUKE AND DUCHESS MAKE THEIR APPEARANCE

The following day, as the sun was setting, Don Quixote and Sancho were riding out of some woods when they spotted a group of falconers. The one in charge of the party was a fine lady dressed in green, carrying a goshawk and riding a snow-white mare.

"Sancho," said Don Quixote, "tell that lady that I, the Knight of the Lions, salute her beauty and seek permission to kiss her hands and serve her in any way her highness commands. Mind how you speak, and keep your proverbs out of it."

"I know how to talk to high and mighty ladies," said Sancho indignantly. He rode over, dismounted and knelt before the woman, saying, "Beautiful lady, my master, the Knight of the Lions, also known as the Knight with the Face in a Sorry State, has sent me, his squire, also known as Sancho, to ask you to give him permission to serve your loveliness."

"Well put, my dear squire," replied the lady. "Do tell me, is that master of yours the gentleman about whom a history has been published called *The Ingenious Gentleman Don Quixote de la Mancha*?"

"He is," said Sancho, "and I am the selfsame squire written about in the book."

"How splendid," said the lady. "Do tell your master that he is a welcome guest on my estates."

Sancho was delighted by this, and relayed the invitation to Don Quixote. Meanwhile, the lady had asked her husband, the duke, to be called, and had told him of their visitors. Both the duke and the duchess had read the first volume of Don Quixote's adventures and decided to treat him as a true knight errant for as long as he stayed with them.

Don Quixote and Sancho came up to the duke and duchess. Sancho made to get off his donkey to help his master dismount, but tangled one foot up in the ropes of his packsaddle and was left trapped, half on his donkey and half sprawled on the ground. Don Quixote, thinking that Sancho was holding his stirrup, swung off Rocinante, but the saddle slipped, depositing him and the saddle in a heap on the ground in front of the duke and duchess.

The duke ordered his huntsmen to help the fallen knight to his feet, and then himself dismounted and warmly embraced him, saying, "It is unfortunate, Sir Knight with the Face in a Sorry State, that your first visit here should start so badly, but the errors of squires may lead to worse outcomes than that."

"No meeting with you, valiant prince, could be unfortunate," replied Don Quixote. "As for my useless squire, it is true that he is better at loosening his tongue than at tightening up my saddle."

They remounted and headed for the duke and duchess's castle, the duchess insisting that Sancho ride with them, so that she could be entertained by his conversation. On arrival at the castle, they were greeted by two servants dressed in long crimson robes who helped Don Quixote off his horse. Next, two beautiful maidens appeared and draped a long scarlet robe around Don Quixote's shoulders.

At this, all the servants gathered round and shouted, "Welcome to the very flower and cream of knight-errantry!" They then sprinkled scented water on Don Quixote and the duke and duchess.

Don Quixote was amazed by all this, and for the first time in all his adventures believed that he was a real knight errant, as this was exactly how he'd read of them being treated in books.

≈ Sancho has an unfortunate encounter with a senior lady-in-waiting and Don Quixote is insulted by a pompous churchman

Determined to stick closely to the duchess, Sancho had left his donkey outside the castle. However, he was soon overcome with remorse at deserting his animal. He went up to a duenna, or senior lady-in-waiting, and said, "Señora González, or whatever your name is, be so good as to pop outside and see to my donkey; he's waiting at the castle gate."

"The name is Doña Rodríguez de Grijalba," replied the woman, "and I suggest you go and look after your donkey yourself."

Things quickly deteriorated after that. Sancho ended up calling Doña Rodríguez a wrinkled old fig, and she called him a garlic-stuffed oaf. Fortunately the duke and duchess overheard and calmed them both down, the duke reassuring Sancho that his donkey would be cared for as well as his master was.

Don Quixote was then taken upstairs. Some maidens helped him off with his armour, but he wouldn't let them change his shirt. Instead they gave the clean shirt to Sancho, and he and Don Quixote shut themselves in a fine bedchamber.

"You idiot," said Don Quixote as soon as they were alone. "Do you think that was sensible, insulting a duenna like that? For heaven's sake, keep your mouth shut and stop trying to play the court jester."

Don Quixote dressed, putting on the scarlet robe and a green satin cap that the maidens had given him, and with great pomp and ceremony they went down to dinner. The duke and duchess received Don Quixote at the door of the dining room. They were joined by a very serious churchman. The duke asked Don Quixote to take the head of the table. Don Quixote refused but the duke was so insistent that he was finally persuaded. Sancho watched in astonishment at the honours these nobles were bestowing on his master.

They'd no sooner sat down than Sancho started talking. "This reminds me of a story that took place in our village," he said.

Don Quixote was sure that Sancho was about to come out with more nonsense. "I think your honours would do well to throw this idiot out of here, before he really makes a fool of himself," he said.

"Good gracious, no," said the duchess. "He must stay here – he's so wise and entertaining."

Sancho then started telling the story in his rambling way. "There was this gentleman in our village. He was one of the Alamos of Medina del Campo and married Doña Mencía de Quiñones – you know, the daughter of Don Alonso de Marañon, the man who was drowned at La Herradura..."

"Do get on with it, my good man," said the churchman.

But Sancho continued rambling, to the delight of the duke and duchess and the growing impatience of the churchman. He finally came to the point of the story.

"So this gentleman invited a poor but honourable farmer to dine with him. The two were about to sit down, when the farmer insisted that the gentleman take the head of the table. The gentleman equally insisted that the farmer take the head, but the farmer kept refusing. Eventually the gentleman grew irritated and forced the farmer into the chair at the top of the table, saying, 'Sit down, you idiot; as far as you're concerned, wherever I sit will be the head of the table.'"

Don Quixote turned a lot of different colours at once, and the duke and duchess stifled their laughter so as not to embarrass him more, as they understood exactly what Sancho was getting at. To change the subject, the duchess asked Don Quixote what news there was of his lady Dulcinea. Don Quixote said that he had conquered giants on her behalf, and sent her villains to pay her homage.

"But how could they find her," he continued, "when some enchantment has turned her into an ugly peasant girl?"

This was too much for the churchman, who turned on the duke and berated him for encouraging the madman in his nonsense. "And you, sir, you simpleton," he added to Don Quixote, "who put it into your head that you are a knight errant? Go home and take care of your own business, and stop turning yourself into a laughing stock."

When he had finished, Don Quixote, quivering with rage, got to his feet and said, "My obligations to my hosts and my respect for your profession restrain me from responding as I might. Your harsh and public rebuke goes beyond the bounds of politeness, especially as you know nothing of me or my behaviour, bad or otherwise. A knight I am and a knight I shall die. I have performed brave deeds to the best of my abilities and my intentions have always been good. It is up to their honours the duke and duchess to decide whether someone who has lived their life in this way deserves to be called a fool."

"Bravo!" said Sancho. "And besides, this man says that knights errant never existed, so how can he know what he's talking about?"

"Are you, perchance, the same Sancho Panza of whom it's written in that book that your master has promised you an island?" asked the churchman.

"I am, and I deserve one too," said Sancho.

"And he will get it," put in the duke. "I have one to spare and, in the name of Don Quixote, I offer its governorship to Sancho Panza."

"Down on your knees, Sancho," said Don Quixote, "and thank his highness for this great favour."

This was all too much for the churchman, who jumped up declaring, "I believe your highness is as great a fool as these two sinners. You are welcome to them, and I shall keep away for as long as they stay in your house."

And he stormed out, to the great amusement of the duke and duchess.

≈ Don Quixote and Sancho are made the butt of some practical jokes

As soon as the churchman had left, the duke turned to Don Quixote and said, "You have answered very well for yourself, Knight of the Lions."

The table was cleared and four serving girls appeared, carrying towels and a silver bowl and jug. In silence they began to rub soap into Don Quixote's beard, building up so much lather that soon his whole face had disappeared. They then pretended to run out of water, and the one carrying the jug went out to get some more, leaving Don Quixote sitting there, looking quite ridiculous.

The duke and duchess had known nothing of this, and were torn between anger at the impertinence of the girls and amusement at the trick they had played on Don Quixote. Eventually the girl with the jug returned, and she and the others rinsed off Don Quixote and rubbed him dry.

They were about to leave, when, in order to stop Don Quixote realizing that it had been a joke, the duke called them over and said, "Now you must wash me, and don't run out of water this time."

They quickly obeyed, and in that way saved themselves from punishment by the duke.

Sancho said, "I've never seen that before, but I reckon my beard could do with a bit of a going-over."

The duchess called over the butler and said, "Take friend Sancho away and give him whatever he desires." She then asked Don Quixote to describe Dulcinea to her.

Don Quixote replied that sadly he could not, as terrible enchanters had turned her into an ugly peasant girl, and this had wiped out the memory of her true appearance. The duchess then reminded Don Quixote that, according to the history of his adventures, he had never actually seen Dulcinea, but had created her out of his own imagination. Don Quixote said that he had not created or given birth to her, but had invested her with all the qualities he thought she ought to have. The duchess then said that from now on she would make sure that everyone in her household believed in Dulcinea.

At this point a great racket was heard and Sancho burst in, wearing a piece of sackcloth as a bib and pursued by a throng of kitchen boys, one of whom was carrying a tub of filthy dishwater.

"What's going on?" demanded the duchess.

"This man won't let himself be washed," replied one of the kitchen boys.

"I will, but not with that filth," retorted Sancho.

The duchess thought that all this was hilarious, but Don Quixote was not so amused. Bowing deeply to the duke and duchess, he turned to the kitchen boys. "Gentlemen, I ask you to leave my squire be. He is as clean as any other squire and neither he nor I take kindly to mockery."

The duchess sent the kitchen boys away with a flea in their ear, much to their confusion as they did not know if she was being serious or not. Sancho fell to his knees to thank her for rescuing him. Don Quixote went to take his siesta and the duchess invited Sancho to while away the afternoon with her and her ladies-in-waiting in a shady apartment.

≈ Sancho is indiscreet, and he and Don Quixote are taken on a wild pig hunt

The duchess, her ladies-in-waiting and Sancho all settled down in the duchess's apartment.

The duchess began to speak. "In the first volume of Don Quixote's adventures," she said, "it describes how you made up your entire visit to Dulcinea. I ask you, Sancho, was this the behaviour of a true and faithful squire?"

Sancho got up and looked behind the curtains to make sure no one was eavesdropping. "The thing is, my lady," he said confidentially, "I'm sure my master's stark staring bonkers. Because of this, I've no problems making him believe all sorts of rot – why, I even made him think Dulcinea's been enchanted, although as that was only a week or so ago, you won't have read about it yet." Sancho then told the duchess and the ladies-in-waiting all about the three peasant girls, to their great amusement.

"Surely," said the duchess, "if Don Quixote is such a fool and a madman, anyone who follows him must be even more of an idiot. And if they're such an idiot, surely they're not fit to govern an island."

"You have a point, my lady," said Sancho. "If I'd any sense, I'd have left my master long ago; but the thing is, I'm very fond of him, I've eaten his bread, he's very grateful to me, he gave me his donkeys and, most of all, I'm a loyal kind of person, so I can't leave him. And if your highness doesn't think I should be given the island, then so be it. Though I must say I don't think I'd make a bad governor, even though I haven't been brought up to govern. I'm kind-hearted by nature, and good to the poor, and I'd probably get quite used to governing in a couple of weeks or so."

The duchess told Sancho not to worry. "My husband is an honourable man," she said, "and if he's promised you an island, an island you shall have. But to return to our conversation about Dulcinea. You should know that we have enchanters around here who keep us well informed of what's going on in the world. They tell us with complete confidence that the peasant girl you saw really was Dulcinea, who really had been enchanted, and that it is you who have been tricked, rather than you who tricked your master."

"That's perfectly possible," said Sancho. "After all, it was much too clever an idea for an idiot like me to come up with on the spur of the moment. Which means I can now believe what my master told me happened in the Cave of Montesinos."

The duchess asked about the Cave of Montesinos, and Sancho told her that part of their recent adventures. She then sent Sancho off to take his siesta and went to find the duke, to whom she related everything she had heard. She and the duke were both amazed that Sancho could so easily be made to believe that Dulcinea had truly been enchanted. They decided to play an elaborate joke in the knight-errantry style on their two guests.

Six days later, the duke and duchess took Don Quixote on a boar hunt. They offered him and Sancho hunting outfits. Don Quixote politely declined but Sancho cheerfully accepted his, a green suit, thinking he would sell it at the first opportunity.

They reached the woods where the hunt was to take place. Don Quixote, the duke and the duchess dismounted and took up position at the side of a boar track. Sancho hung back, and stayed firmly on his donkey, which he dared not desert in case something terrible happened to him. They were scarcely in place when a huge boar charged into view, closely pursued by baying hounds and huntsmen.

Sancho took one look and fled, abandoning his donkey and trying his best to scrabble up an oak tree. Unfortunately he slipped and ended up caught on a broken branch, dangling in the air with his new green coat starting to tear. He set up such a hullabaloo that those who heard him thought he was being eaten by some wild animal.

The boar was felled by a multitude of spears and carried off. Don Quixote turned round to see Sancho hanging from the oak tree, with his donkey close beside him – Cide Hamete tells us that he very rarely saw Sancho without his donkey, or the donkey without Sancho, so fond were the two of each other. Don Quixote went over and released Sancho and they made their way to the centre of the woods, where some tents had been put up and a sumptuous feast was being prepared with the boar as its centrepiece.

Sancho made it clear he did not approve of hunting as a sport. "I don't see how princes and lords can consider that sort of thing enjoyable," he said. "It's dangerous and it involves killing animals that haven't done any harm to anyone."

The duke said that Sancho was wrong, and that hunting was good preparation for the rigours of war. "You'll have to change your views when you're a governor, Sancho," he said.

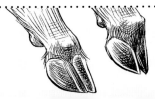

"Oh no," replied Sancho, "I'll have a broken leg and stay at home, and go on with my governing like a good governor should. I'll leave hunting and stuff like that to idle layabouts, although I'll probably treat myself to a game of bowls on high days and holidays."

≈ MERLIN THE MAGICIAN EXPLAINS HOW DULCINEA IS TO BE DISENCHANTED, LEAVING SANCHO VERY DISPLEASED

The party spent the rest of the afternoon in the woods. At nightfall the air became rather hazy and then, just before dark, lights suddenly sprang up all around them, accompanied by a deafening cacophony of trumpets, fifes and drums. A rider appeared in front of them, dressed as a demon and blowing on a huge hollow horn.

"Hey there, messenger!" cried the duke. "Who are you and where are you going?"

"I am the devil," replied the rider, in a strange, harsh voice, "and I am looking for Don Quixote de la Mancha. I bring with me six troops of enchanters, along with the exalted Dulcinea del Toboso and the brave Frenchman Montesinos, who will tell Don Quixote how Dulcinea is to be disenchanted."

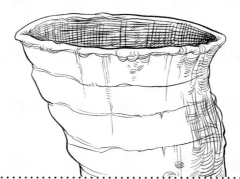

"If you really were the devil," said the duke, "you would know that Don Quixote stands in front of you."

"By God, so he does," said the devil. "I have so much on my mind that I failed to notice." Turning to Don Quixote he said, "Wait here, Sir Knight of the Lions. The brave but unfortunate knight Montesinos and Dulcinea will be along shortly." And then he rode off.

The noise of instruments began again, coupled with the sinister creaking of wheels. It reached such a pitch that even Don Quixote was hard pressed not to be scared. Sancho succumbed to fear, and fainted away on the duchess's skirts. She left him lying there but summoned a servant to throw cold water in his face.

Out of the gloom, there came a cart drawn by four oxen draped in black and with candles between their horns. On the cart was an old man with a long beard. "I am the sage Lirgandeo," he intoned, and the cart moved on.

Behind was another cart, bearing another old man. "I am the sage Alquife, the friend of Urganda the Unknown," he said.

A third cart appeared, bearing a younger man, who declared himself to be the enchanter Archelaus, the mortal enemy of Amadis of Gaul.

The three carts moved off and a coach appeared, drawn by six grey mules ridden by figures in penitents' costumes. On the coach were twelve more figures also in penitents' costumes. In the centre was a raised podium on which were seated a young woman and a robed figure both with veils over their heads. The robed figure stood up and drew back its veil, revealing the ghastly face of Death itself.

"I am Merlin the magician," he intoned, "and I have come to tell you, Don Quixote, O flower of knight-errantry, that there is only one way for Dulcinea del Toboso to be returned to her original beauty. And that is for your squire, Sancho, to give himself three thousand three hundred lashes of the whip on his ample backside."

"I don't see what my backside has to do with any enchantings," said Sancho, aghast. "If that is the only way for the lady Dulcinea to be disenchanted, then may she go to her grave enchanted."

"How dare you, you garlic-stuffed clown!" roared Don Quixote. "I'll tie you to a tree and give you six thousand six hundred lashes."

"That won't work," said Merlin. "Sancho has to give himself the lashes of his own free will."

"Neither me nor anyone else is going to lay a hand on me," declared Sancho. "If my master wants to whip himself for the sake of Dulcinea, he's welcome to. But not me!"

At this point, the maiden on the cart got up and took off her veil, revealing a beautiful face. Turning to Sancho, she said in a voice which sounded rather more like a man's than a maiden's, "You wretched squire, you impudent thief. Have you a heart of stone? If you were being asked to throw yourself off a tower, or murder your family, your reluctance would be understandable. But all that is needed to stop me looking like an ugly peasant girl is a paltry three thousand three hundred lashes, something that any workhouse orphan boy can expect in a month. Oh, and I should add that it's only thanks to the temporary kindness of Merlin that I don't look like a peasant girl now."

"I think the lady Dulcinea might think of a nicer way to ask," said Sancho. "No 'please', no 'thank you', no little presents to encourage me. My master's no better, abusing me like that. And they should both remember that it's not any old squire but a governor who's being asked to whip himself."

To which the duke said, "I'm afraid, Sancho, that unless you're prepared to comply, there won't be any governing for you."

"Can't I have a couple of days to think about it?" asked Sancho.

"No," said Merlin. "It has to be settled this instant."

"Go on, Sancho," said the duchess. "Show your gratitude for all that your master Don Quixote has done for you."

At this point, Sancho said to Merlin, quite irrelevantly, "The devil said that he had a message from Montesinos, but we haven't set eyes on him."

"The devil is a scoundrel and an idiot," replied Merlin. "The message was from me, not Montesinos, who is still waiting in his cave."

Finally, and reluctantly, Sancho agreed to the penance. As soon as this had happened, there was a great blast of trumpets and discharge of muskets. Don Quixote embraced Sancho and the coach moved off, with Dulcinea bowing to the duke and duchess and curtsying deeply to Sancho.

Dawn broke and the duke and duchess returned to their castle, very pleased with themselves for the way their joke had turned out, and determined to follow it up with more japes. The whole thing had been organized by one of the duke's stewards, who had himself played Merlin and found a pageboy to play Dulcinea.

≈ Sancho Panza writes to his wife, and the mysterious Distressed Duenna calls on Don Quixote for assistance

The next day, the duchess asked Sancho if he had started his penance.

"Oh yes," he replied, "I've given myself five lashes."

"With what?" asked the duchess.

"With my hand," replied Sancho.

"I'm not sure that really counts," said the duchess. "I think it has to be with a real whip." She promised to provide one that was not too harsh.

Then Sancho said, "I've got a letter here for my wife, Teresa Panza. I think it's in proper governor style, but I'd be very glad if your ladyship would look it over, just to check."

"Did you write it yourself?" asked the duchess.

"Oh no, I dictated it – I can't read or write," replied Sancho.

The duchess then read the letter, which went as follows:

> If I've got a good governorship, it's because I've had a good whipping.
> I think, Teresa, you ought to go about in a coach as you're now a
> governor's wife. People here think Don Quixote is mad. We've been in
> the Cave of Montesinos and I've got to give myself three thousand three
> hundred lashes minus five to disenchant Dulcinea.
> I'm leaving in a few days to be a governor. The donkey sends his regards.
> The duchess kisses your hands. I haven't found any more treasure.
>
> 20th July 1614
> Your husband the Governor,
> Sancho Panza

The duchess thought the letter was wonderful, and decided to show it to her husband at the first opportunity. She and Sancho joined Don Quixote and the duke in a garden where they were to eat. The duke chuckled over the letter, and after the meal he and the duchess allowed themselves to be entertained by Sancho's conversation. They were soon interrupted by the gloomy sound of a pipe and drum. Don Quixote jumped to his feet and Sancho, struck with fear, took refuge behind the duchess's skirts.

Three figures dressed in flowing black robes came towards them, two beating drums and one playing the pipe. Behind them, also dressed in black, and with a thin black veil over its head, came a fourth, enormously tall figure. It knelt before the duke and then rose, drawing back its veil to reveal the longest, thickest, whitest beard ever seen.

In a deep, grave voice the figure said, "I am Trifaldín of the White Beard, squire of the Countess Trifaldi or the Distressed Duenna as she is also known. I ask your highness to let her be admitted to tell you her woes. But first, she begs to know if the brave and never-conquered knight Don Quixote de la Mancha is present, for she has come all the way from the kingdom of Kandy on foot and without eating to find him."

"We have heard of this lady and her troubles," replied the duke. "Pray let her enter." And turning to Don Quixote he said, "See how your fame spreads – already damsels in distress are coming here to seek your help."

"Would that that spiteful and ill-mannered churchman could see this," said Don Quixote in reply.

"I hope this duenna isn't going to cause problems for my governorship; I have it on the authority of a chemist from Toledo that duennas are nothing but trouble," put in Sancho.

At this point, a dozen duennas, all dressed in mourning, filed into the garden in two lines. Bringing up the rear was the Countess Trifaldi herself. She and the other duennas all had thick black veils over their heads. Trifaldín took the Countess Trifaldi by the hand and led her up to the front of the procession.

She knelt in front of the duke, the duchess and Don Quixote and said in a rough, hoarse voice, "Before I tell you, high and mighty lord and lady, what a miserably miserable mess I'm in, pray inform me whether there are present that knightliest knight Don Quixote de la Manchissima and his squirissimus Panza."

"The Panza is present," butted in Sancho, "as is Don Quixotissimus, most Distressedest Duennissima."

Don Quixote rose and said gravely, "I am Don Quixote de la Mancha, madam, and I am at your service."

The Distressed Duenna then explained the cause of her distress. "I was the most senior duenna of the widowed Queen Doña Maguncia, ruler of the famous kingdom of Kandy. I was charged with looking after her daughter, Princess Antonomasia. The princess grew into a very beautiful girl and many people at court fell in love with her. Among them was a certain Don Clavijo, who was too low in rank ever to be thought of as a suitable match for the queen's daughter, but who was a fine poet and dancer. Showering me with little gifts, and using all his charms, he persuaded me to act as a go-between. He successfully wooed the girl and the two of them were married in secret. The queen was so overcome with grief when she discovered this that we buried her within three days."

"I hope she was dead," said Sancho.

"Of course she was; we don't bury living people in Kandy," said Trifaldín.

"It's been known for people who've fainted away to be buried by accident," said Sancho. "And if you ask me, Queen Maguncia would have been better off fainting rather than dropping dead – things often turn out OK in the end, and her daughter marrying Don Clavijo wasn't that awful."

"You are right," said Don Quixote, "but let the lady continue. I fear the worst part of her story is to come."

"It is indeed," said the Distressed One. "No sooner had we said our farewells to the queen, than over her grave there appeared her cousin, the giant Malambruno, riding a wooden horse. Malambruno, who is a cruel enchanter, avenged the queen by turning the princess into a brass ape and Don Clavijo into a metal crocodile on the spot. Between them he put up a pillar on which is inscribed, in Syriac, the words: *These two shall not recover their former shape until the brave man from La Mancha comes to fight me.*

"He then summoned all the palace duennas and, denouncing duennas in general for their plotting and scheming, said he would not kill us but would punish us appropriately. At that instant, we felt our faces pricking as if being jabbed by needles. Feeling our chins, we found what you will now see."

All the duennas raised their veils to reveal faces bristling with beards of every description.

"See what Malambruno did to us," sighed the Countess Trifaldi. "Oh woe! What is to become of us?" And she looked as if she was about to faint.

"It's terrible," said Sancho. "I bet they can't even afford to pay anyone to shave them."

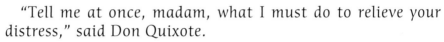

"Tell me at once, madam, what I must do to relieve your distress," said Don Quixote.

The Distressed One said, "It is five thousand leagues, give or take a couple, to Kandy by land, but only three thousand two hundred and twenty-seven in a straight line by air. Malambruno told me that he would provide a magical flying wooden horse to take you there by the fastest route. The horse, which is said to have been made by Merlin and whose name is Clavileño, can be steered with a wooden peg in its forehead."

"Well," said Sancho, "my master's welcome to go if he wants, but I'm certainly not flying through the air on a wooden horse just so that some duennas can get rid of their beards."

"You're very hard on duennas," said the duchess. "It seems you're in agreement with that Toledo chemist."

"Ah," sighed the Distressed One. "What a terrible time we duennas have, sneered at by squires, loathed by chemists, the butt of every pageboy's joke."

And she became so upset that Sancho relented, and declared he was prepared to accompany his master to the ends of the earth in order to relieve the duennas of their bristly burdens.

≈ Don Quixote and Sancho make a long and dangerous journey on the wooden horse Clavileño and, strangely, end up exactly where they started

Night came, and Don Quixote anxiously awaited the appearance of Clavileño. Suddenly four men covered in green ivy appeared, bearing a large wooden horse. One of them said, "Let any knight who is brave enough mount this machine; and let his squire, if he has one, mount behind him. But they must be blindfolded and remain sightless until the horse neighs, which is a sign that the journey is over."

Sancho said that he was too much of a coward to mount the horse, but was finally persuaded to do so by the duke. Don Quixote asked for a word or two with Sancho in private and drew him aside.

"Friend Sancho," he said, "we have a long journey ahead of us, and we don't know when it will be over. So I ask you now to retire at once to your bedroom, on the pretence of fetching something you've forgotten, and give yourself five hundred lashes or so out of the three thousand three hundred you owe. It won't take a second."

"Dear God, you must be mad if you think I'm going to tenderize my backside before sitting on a rock-hard horse without a saddle for goodness knows how long," responded Sancho. "Now let's be off to shave these duennas. I'll see about clearing my debt when we're back."

Don Quixote and Sancho had their eyes bandaged. They then mounted Clavileño and Don Quixote felt for the peg in the horse's forehead.

As soon as he touched it, all those watching shouted, "God be with you, most valiant knight and intrepid squire! You're off, flying faster than an arrow. Careful not to wobble, brave Sancho."

"It's strange," said Sancho, clinging tightly to his master. "How come their voices sound so close if we're high up in the air?"

"All sorts of odd things can happen on journeys like this," replied Don Quixote. "But I don't see what you've got to be frightened of – we're moving so smoothly that it feels as if we're completely still, although we're obviously flying into the wind."

"It's true," said Sancho. "It feels as if we are being blown at with a thousand pairs of bellows."

Which was indeed the case, as the duke and duchess's servants were busy pumping great bellows in their faces.

"We'll be approaching the realm of fire soon," said Don Quixote. And he and Sancho felt themselves growing warm, because of a lighted torch that was being waved in front of them.

"I believe we will shortly reach the kingdom of Kandy," continued Don Quixote. "Although it seems as if only half an hour has passed since we left the garden, I'm sure we've travelled a great distance."

The duke and duchess were very amused at Don Quixote and Sancho's conversation, but decided it was time to put an end to their game. A torch was applied to Clavileño's tail and the horse, which was stuffed full of firecrackers, immediately exploded with a great bang, throwing Don Quixote and Sancho to the ground, where they lay all singed. They got to their feet and, removing their blindfolds, saw with amazement that they were in the very garden they had set out from.

The bearded duennas and the Countess Trifaldi had disappeared, and everyone else was lying about as if in a faint. On one side of the garden was a lance stuck in the ground from which hung a parchment. On this was written in gold letters:

The brave knight Don Quixote de la Mancha, merely by setting out on the adventure of the Countess Trifaldi, has successfully completed his task. Malambruno is satisfied. The duennas are now all beardless and Don Clavijo and Princess Antonomasia are restored to their original form. Once the squire's whippings are completed, the white dove shall also be restored to her true form. So has the arch-enchanter Merlin decreed.

The others began to rouse themselves, as if waking from a deep sleep. The duke read the parchment and rushed over to Don Quixote, embracing him and declaring him to be the bravest knight ever. The duchess asked Sancho how he had fared on his long journey.

"Actually," he said, "I peeped out from my blindfold a couple of times. Once I saw the earth below me looking about the size of a grain of mustard seed, and once I found we were right next to the Pleiades, or the seven she-goats as we know them. Well, I'm very fond of goats, and so I quietly got off Clavileño and played with them for three-quarters of an hour, during which time Clavileño didn't budge."

"It is well known," said Don Quixote, "that the seven she-goats are in a part of heaven beyond the region of fire, and so we couldn't have got there without being burnt up. Either Sancho is lying or he was dreaming."

"Neither," replied Sancho. "Ask me about the goats and I'll prove I was there."

"Tell us about them," said the duchess.

"Well, two were green, two were blood red, two blue and one a mixture of all colours."

At this point, Don Quixote whispered in Sancho's ear, "Sancho, if you want us to believe what you saw in heaven, then you must believe what I saw in the Cave of Montesinos. I say no more."

≈ Don Quixote gives Sancho advice on how to be a governor

The next day, the duke told Sancho to prepare himself, as his island was finally ready. With the duke's permission, Don Quixote took Sancho aside to give him some advice.

"I am very pleased for you, Sancho," said Don Quixote when they were alone. "I had been waiting for success in my adventures to be able to reward you for your services, and now I find that, by a stroke of luck, you have achieved your heart's desire while I have yet to gain advancement. You must thank heaven for your good fortune.

"Now, it is important you take note of the following things when you are governor: first, never forget who you are – don't be like that frog who tried to puff himself up to be the size of an ox, but remember your humble origins and be proud of them. Always try to be virtuous, and if any of your relatives visit, be hospitable and treat them honourably. If you take your wife with you – which I would recommend you to do – then try to smooth out her rough edges, as a boorish wife can quickly undo the good of a wise governor.

"When you are handing out justice, treat everyone fairly, but be more indulgent to the poor than to the rich. Never forget that those who have done wrong are still human beings, and treat them as compassionately as you can. If you do all these things, you will live a long and contented life.

"And now, for some advice on how to look after yourself and your household. First, keep clean and tidily dressed, and make sure you cut your fingernails – long fingernails are an abomination. Don't eat garlic or onions. Walk slowly and speak carefully but don't sound pompous. Find out discreetly how much you might be paid, and if there is enough money to provide uniforms for your servants, make them neat and practical, rather than showy. If you can pay for six sets of uniform, provide three for your servants and clothe three poor men instead. Eat and drink in moderation. Don't chew on both sides of your mouth and don't eruct in public."

"What's *eruct*?" asked Sancho.

"It means *belch*," said Don Quixote, "but that's a vulgar word, so nice people use *eruct*, which is a Latin word, and so politer, although it describes the same thing."

"I'll remember that, as I'm always belching."

"Eructing."

"Eructing," said Sancho. "I promise I'll say that from now on."

"And be moderate in your use of proverbs," continued Don Quixote.

"I'll try," said Sancho, "but it won't be easy. And if I do use any, I'll make sure they fit. After all, in a house where there's plenty, supper is quickly cooked; and he who shuffles doesn't cut; and safe is he who raises the alarm."

"There you go, just as I'm telling you not to," said Don Quixote. "When you ride on horseback, don't loll about or stick your legs out sideways. Be moderate in your sleep. Never get into an argument between two families as to which has the best pedigree, as one family will always win and the other will then always hate you. And remember to wear long trousers. Finally, forgive me for saying this, but I do wish you could read and write, as it is not seemly for a governor to be illiterate."

"Well," said Sancho, "I can sign my name quite well as I learnt that once, and in any case I can pretend that I've hurt my right hand and make someone else sign things for me. For there's a cure for everything except death, as they say; and if anyone makes fun of me, they'll come for wool and be sent away shorn; and you're worth what you've got, as my grandmother used to say."

"A curse on you, Sancho, with all these damnable proverbs," said Don Quixote.

"But they're the only thing I've got," said Sancho. "And four really good ones have just popped into my head."

"And what might those be?"

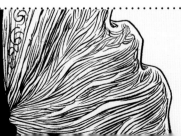

"'Never put your thumbs between two back teeth' and 'There's no answer to "Get out of my house" and "What do you want with my wife?"' and 'Whether the stone hits the pitcher or the pitcher hits the stone, it's bad news for the pitcher'."

"Well," said Don Quixote, "I wish you well in governing, though I confess I fear you might end up turning the whole island upside down. I could prevent it all by telling the duke that that fat little body of yours is nothing but a sack full of proverbs and cheek."

"If you think I'm not fit to be a governor, I'll give up the idea this instant," said Sancho.

"Just by saying that you've shown that you deserve to be made a governor," said Don Quixote. "Now, let us go and join the duke and duchess at lunch."

≈ Sancho Panza takes possession of his island and starts to dispense wisdom, and Don Quixote discovers a secret admirer

That very evening, the duke and duchess sent Sancho off with a large following to the village that was to be his island. The person in charge of the expedition was the duke's steward who had played the part of the Countess Trifaldi.

As soon as Sancho saw him, he turned to Don Quixote and said, "May the devil take me if this steward's face isn't identical to the Distressed One's. His voice is exactly the same too."

"You are quite right," said Don Quixote, "but the steward cannot be the Distressed One, so it is clear that something mysterious is afoot."

Don Quixote and Sancho had a tearful farewell and the party set off, with Sancho at its head dressed in a lawyer's outfit, and his donkey, kitted out in sumptuous fittings, following close behind.

After supper Don Quixote, low in spirits, retired to his room. He was undressing himself for bed when, to his horror, a great rip appeared in one of his stockings. And he could not afford a scrap of silk to repair it. Fortunately Sancho had left a pair of travelling boots behind, and Don Quixote could wear these the next day to cover his embarrassment.

Conscious of his poverty and sorely missing Sancho, he went glumly to bed. The night was warm, however, and he could not sleep. He got up and opened a window screen. As he did so he heard voices in the garden below.

"No, don't make me sing, Emerencia," one of them was saying. "I cannot sing, only weep, while that heroic man is in our midst asleep and ignoring me. And besides, our mistress is such a light sleeper. It would be terrible if she awoke and heard."

"Don't worry, Altisidora," replied another voice. "I'm sure the duchess is sound asleep. But the man you adore is certainly awake, for I have just seen him open his window."

After some more persuasion, Altisidora tuned her harp and proceeded to sing a long ballad proclaiming her love for the brave knight of La Mancha. Don Quixote listened agog at the window above.

When she had finished, Don Quixote cursed himself for having all these maidens fall in love with him and try to tempt him away from Dulcinea. "Whatever happens, and whatever tricks any enchanters try, I must remain true to her," he said to himself, and then slammed the window shut and went back to bed.

Meanwhile, Sancho and his attendants had arrived at a large, walled village of around one thousand inhabitants, one of the largest that the duke owned. Sancho was told that this was the island of Barataria, which would be his to govern. He was led first to the church and then, with great ceremony, presented with the keys to the town. Those who knew nothing of the joke were amazed at the sight of their squat, bearded new governor.

Once he had received the keys, Sancho was led to the courtroom, where he was installed on the judge's bench. Almost at once, two men appeared.

One, who was a tailor, said, "Señor Governor, please, I ask you to judge our case. Yesterday this man came into my shop with a length of cloth and asked me whether there was enough to make a cap. I told him there was. Obviously thinking that I would steal some of his cloth, he then asked me if there was enough for two caps. I again told him there was. This went on until he asked me if there was enough for five caps, and I said yes. And he's just come for them, but won't pay me."

"Is this true?" asked Sancho of the other man.

"Yes, it is," the man replied, "but I think your worship should ask to see the caps."

At this, the tailor took his hand out from under his cape and revealed five tiny caps, one on each finger. "Here they are," he said. "They're very well made and I promise there isn't a scrap of cloth left."

Everyone laughed. Sancho took it all in and said, "I don't think we need a complicated decision here. All I'll say is that the tailor should forfeit his labour and the customer should lose the cloth, and the caps can go to the prisoners in the jail."

Those in attendance were delighted at this judgement.

Two old men then came in, one using a cane as a walking stick. The other one said, "Señor Governor, some time ago this man asked to borrow ten gold crowns. I agreed, and waited a long time before asking for them back; but now he won't repay me, saying that I never lent them to him, or that if I did, he's paid me back and I've forgotten about it. I've no witnesses, and so I ask your worship to put him to the oath. If he swears that he returned them to me, I'll forgive him his debt."

"What do you say?" Sancho asked the other man.

"I admit that I borrowed them; but if you let me, I'll swear that I gave them back," the man replied.

Sancho lowered his staff of office for the man to swear on. The old man handed his walking cane to the other man and took hold of the staff. He swore that he had borrowed the ten coins, but had returned them. The man who had brought the case then agreed that he must have been mistaken. The debtor took back his walking cane and began to hurry out of the courtroom without saying a word.

Seeing this, Sancho thought for a while and called him back. "Sir," said Sancho, "give me that stick."

"Certainly," replied the man, and he handed it over.

Sancho gave the stick to the other man and said, "You can go now, for you have been repaid."

"What," replied the man, "is this stick worth ten gold coins?"

"Indeed it is," said Sancho, "or I'm not fit to be a governor."

He ordered the stick to be broken in two and there, hidden in the middle, were ten gold coins. All those watching were dumbfounded.

Sancho explained that he had seen the debtor give the stick to the other man when swearing his oath and had suddenly realized that the sum being argued about must be hidden in the stick — by handing it over he had made sure that he would not actually be lying when he swore. Yet again, everyone present was amazed at Sancho's good judgement.

≈ Sancho continues to dispense wisdom but has difficulty eating, Don Quixote is assaulted by cats and the duke writes to Sancho

Back at the duke and duchess's castle, we left Don Quixote brooding over Altisidora and her song. The next morning, he rose early and, walking down a corridor, passed Altisidora and Emerencia, who were lying in wait. Altisidora pretended to faint.

Don Quixote said to her friend, "Pray bring a lute to my room tonight, and I will attempt to comfort the poor maid and explain that I am promised to another."

That night, Don Quixote found a guitar waiting for him in his bedroom. Taking it up, he positioned himself by the window and started singing a song telling of his enduring love for Dulcinea del Toboso. All at once, a rope with more than a hundred bells on it was lowered from a balcony above his window and jangled up and down. It was quickly followed by an enormous sack full of screeching cats, each with a bell tied to its tail. The noise was terrible, and Don Quixote was paralysed with fear. Two or three of the cats managed to escape from the sack and get into Don Quixote's room, where they ran amok, knocking out the candles.

Don Quixote drew his sword and yelled, "Begone, you evil sorcerers!" while slashing wildly at the air.

All the cats escaped through the window except one, which launched itself at Don Quixote's face and clung there, scratching furiously with all four claws. Don Quixote began to bellow, and

the duke and duchess burst in. Don Quixote implored them to stand back, declaring that he himself would vanquish the demon that was attacking him, but the duke ignored him and seized the cat, flinging it out of the window.

Altisidora was summoned, and she bandaged Don Quixote's wounds. The duke and duchess left, feeling somewhat regretful at the outcome of their prank, which resulted in Don Quixote being confined to bed for five days.

To return to Sancho: having finished his judging for the morning, he was taken to a sumptuous palace and led into a room where a magnificent feast was laid out. He washed his hands and sat down. A man stood next to him holding a whalebone wand. With great ceremony Sancho was served with the first dish by a butler, but he had scarcely touched it when the man standing next to him tapped the dish with his wand. It was instantly whisked away. The next dish was presented, but the man tapped it and it was whisked away before Sancho had even tasted it.

"What is going on?" demanded Sancho.

"I am a doctor," replied the man, "and my job is to ensure that the governors of these islands eat healthily. That first dish was too moist and the second too hot and spicy."

He came up with a reason why Sancho could not eat any of the dishes laid out on the table, and Sancho became increasingly exasperated. He asked the man his name.

"I am Dr Pedro Recio de Aguero from Tirteafuera, and I have a degree from the University of Osuna," replied the man.

"Well, Dr Pedro Recio de Aguero from Tirteafuera," said Sancho, "I suggest you leave my presence at once or I'll take this chair I'm sitting on and break it over your head."

The doctor would have fled that instant, but a post horn sounded outside. A messenger ran in with a letter from the duke.

"Who here is my secretary?" asked Sancho.

"I am," said a man. "I can read and write, and I'm a Basque."

The secretary looked quickly at the letter and told Sancho it was a private matter. Sancho ordered everyone except the secretary, the duke's steward and the butler to leave the room. The secretary then read out the letter. It said:

Señor Don Sancho Panza,

I have learnt that enemies of mine plan to attack the island at night, so you must stay awake and on guard at all times. I have also learnt that four men have entered the town in disguise and plan to poison you, so do not accept any food offered as a gift.

Your friend,
The Duke

277

Sancho was astonished. "Well, the first thing to do is lock up Dr Recio, for if anyone wants to kill me, it's him," he said.

"And all this food must go," added the butler. "It was a gift from some nuns."

≈ Don Quixote receives a mysterious visitor, discovers something very strange about the duchess and is pinched black and blue

Back at the duke and duchess's castle, Don Quixote was feeling extremely downcast at his plight. He locked himself in his room for six days. One night as he lay awake brooding, he heard someone, whom he was sure would be Altisidora, unlocking his door. He stood up on his bed and waited.

Instead of Altisidora, the figure of a venerable duenna approached, swathed in a long veil and with the most enormous pair of spectacles perched on her nose. Don Quixote thought she must be some witch or sorceress. She slowly made her way across the room. She caught sight of Don Quixote standing on the bed, looking like a ghastly scarecrow, wrapped in a bedspread, with a cap on his head and his face and moustache all bandaged up. She let out a scream, dropped the candle she was carrying and promptly tripped over her skirts, sprawling full length on the ground.

Don Quixote said, "I order you, phantom, to tell me who or what you are."

The duenna replied, "I am no phantom, but Doña Rodríguez, and I come to you for assistance."

Don Quixote was very uneasy at having a duenna in his room, but he overcame his qualms and got back into bed. The duenna sat on a chair near the bed and began to tell Don Quixote the story of her life.

"I come from a good family in Asturias," she began, "but my parents were poor and I was left orphaned young. I ended up a servant in a house in Madrid and married a squire in the household who was considerably older than me. He died of shock after an unfortunate incident and left me a widow with a young daughter to bring up. Fortunately the duchess offered me a position here.

"Recently, the son of a rich farmer who lives near by fell in love with my daughter and promised to marry her, but he is now going back on his word. I beg you to take this in hand and force him to live up to his promise. My daughter is worth it – she is far finer than any of the other women around here. Take that Altisidora, for example; she's not bad compared with the others, but she's got more cheek than good looks, and her breath is terrible. And as for the duchess..."

"What, is something wrong with the duchess?" asked Don Quixote, aghast.

"Well," said Doña Rodríguez, "I have it on the highest authority that she's got two fountains in her legs that drain her of the nasty fluids the doctors say she's full of."

"Gracious heavens! I don't believe it," said Don Quixote.

At that moment, the door burst open with a bang. The duenna in her fright again dropped the candle, leaving the room in darkness. Two hands gripped the duenna's throat and she was briskly upended and given a good spanking with a slipper. Don Quixote's bedspread was hauled off him and he was pinched and scratched all over by unseen hands.

After half an hour the assailants fled. Doña Rodríguez picked herself up and left the room, sighing loudly but without saying a word. Don Quixote lay there in a daze, where we shall leave him and return to Sancho.

≈ Sancho finally manages to eat something, and dispenses even more wisdom

Against his better judgement, Dr Pedro Recio was persuaded to let Sancho have something to eat for his supper. The servants produced some cold chopped beef with onions and the feet of some not-so-young calves. Sancho fell on them with relish and told the doctor that that kind of food would suit him fine from now on, as his stomach was not accustomed to rich and expensive dishes.

After Sancho had eaten, he set off on a tour of his island, accompanied by his retinue. They had not gone far, when they heard the sound of clashing swords. Rushing to the spot, they found two men fighting, one crying, "Help! Someone stop this robber!"

The other one said to Sancho, "Señor Governor, I can explain. This man has just won more than a thousand reals in that gambling house. I was there and supported him more than once when people questioned his honesty, although in truth my conscience went against it. He left with his winnings, and I asked him for at least a gold crown in reward, as is only fair and proper. But he refused point-blank, so I was going to make him hand it over by force."

The other man agreed with this account but said that he had offered the man four reals, which he thought quite sufficient as he often gave him money, and the man should be thankful for anything he could get.

Sancho looked at them both and said, "I decree that you, the gambler, should hand over one hundred reals to this man, and thirty more to the poor prisoners in the town jail." Turning to the other man he said, "And as for you, you idle layabout, tomorrow you must leave this island with your money and stay away for at least ten years, on pain of death."

Sancho was just thinking that perhaps he ought to shut down all the gambling houses, as they seemed to cause nothing but trouble, when a constable came up holding a young man by the collar.

"Señor Governor, sir, this youth was coming towards us and as soon as he caught sight of us he turned and ran off, a sure sign that he's been up to no good."

"Why did you run away, young man?" asked Sancho.

"To avoid answering the questions that constables always ask," the boy replied.

"And what is your trade?"

"A weaver, sir."

"And what do you weave?"

"Iron lance heads, sir."

"I see we have a joker here," said Sancho. "And where were you off to just now?"

"To take the air, sir,"

"And where do people take the air on this island?"

"Wherever it's blowing, sir."

"Well, I think it's about to blow you into the town jail, where you'll be sleeping tonight," said Sancho.

"With all due respect, sir, you can as soon make me sleep in jail tonight as make me king," replied the boy.

"Don't be ridiculous! Of course I can make you sleep in the jail if I choose," said Sancho.

"Ah, you can lock me up in the jail, but you can't make me sleep if I decide not to," said the boy triumphantly.

"Ho ho," said Sancho. "Well then, I won't rob you of your sleep. Be off home, but don't fool around with the authorities in future, as not all of them will have such a good sense of humour."

Shortly afterwards, two constables arrived holding a finely dressed man in custody.

"Señor Governor," they announced, "this here person appears to be a man, but is in fact a woman."

She was indeed a beautiful girl of about sixteen. Sancho asked her who she was and why she was going about dressed as a man.

The girl blushed and looked down, saying, "Sir, I cannot tell you in front of so many people."

Sancho made all his retinue withdraw except for the duke's steward, the butler and the secretary.

"I am the daughter of Diego de la Llana," she began. "As you know, he is a rich and important man in the town. His wife, my mother, died ten years ago, and since then he has kept me shut up in our house. I have become desperate to see the outside world, or at the very least the streets of the town in which I was born. I have been trying to convince my younger brother to dress me up as a man in a suit of his clothes and take me out some night when our father was asleep.

"Tonight I finally succeeded, and we left the house about an hour ago. He dressed himself in clothes of mine – he has a very beautiful face and could easily pass as a young girl. We have been wandering the streets and were about to return home, when we saw a group of people approaching. My brother said it was the officers doing their rounds and that we must flee at once. I started to run, but tripped and fell, which is how the officers caught me."

One of the constables then returned with the girl's brother, dressed in a patterned petticoat and short silk cloak. Out of earshot of the girl, the brother told the same tale, proving beyond a doubt that the girl was telling the truth.

"You have both behaved very childishly," said Sancho when the boy had finished, "but no harm has been done. We will take you back home. Perhaps your father will not have missed you."

At the house they threw a pebble at a window. A maidservant who had been waiting up for them opened a door and they slipped in, leaving the rest of the party out in the street. The butler had been completely smitten by the girl and determined to ask her father for her hand in marriage. Sancho even thought that the boy might make a good match for his daughter, Sanchica.

≈ WE DISCOVER THE IDENTITY OF DON QUIXOTE'S ASSAILANTS, SANCHO'S WIFE TERESA RECEIVES A VISIT, DON QUIXOTE WRITES TO SANCHO, SANCHO WRITES TO DON QUIXOTE AND TERESA WRITES TO THE DUCHESS

To return to the castle, Cide Hamete explains the attack on Doña Rodríguez and Don Quixote as follows. When Doña Rodríguez left her own room to go to Don Quixote's, she was seen by another duenna, who in the way of all duennas immediately told the duchess. The duchess and Altisidora went to listen at Don Quixote's door. When they overheard Doña Rodríguez being rude about them, they could not contain themselves, and burst in, punishing Doña Rodríguez and tormenting Don Quixote.

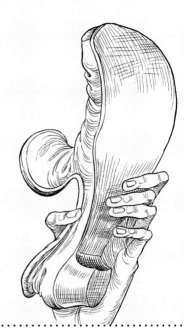

The duchess described all this to the duke, who thought it was hilarious. To continue in her entertainment, the duchess sent the page who had played the part of Dulcinea to Sancho's wife, Teresa. He carried with him the letter Sancho had written, as well as one from the duchess and a string of coral beads as a present.

At the outskirts of Sancho's village the page came across some women doing their washing in a stream. He asked for directions and a young girl stood up and said that she was Sanchica, Teresa Panza's daughter. She led him to their house, where Teresa came out to greet him.

The page leapt off his horse and knelt in front of Teresa, saying, "Let me kiss your hand, Señora Doña Teresa, wife of Señor Don Sancho Panza, governor of the island of Barataria."

"Do get up, sir," said Teresa. "I'm no court lady, just a poor countrywoman."

The page got to his feet and produced the two letters and the coral beads. "Here is a letter from your husband, and another, along with a coral necklace, from my lady the duchess, who has sent me here."

Teresa was astonished and asked the page to read out the letters. The one from the duchess said:

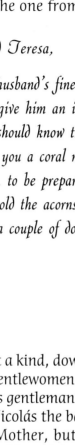

Friend Teresa,

Your husband's fine qualities encouraged me to ask my husband, the duke, to give him an island to govern. I am told he governs very well, and you should know that good governors are extremely hard to find.

I send you a coral necklace as a present. Tell your daughter, Sanchica, to be prepared, for I intend to find a good match for her.

I am told the acorns in your village are particularly big, so please send me a couple of dozen or so. Do write to tell me how you are.

Your loving friend,
The Duchess

"What a kind, down-to-earth woman that duchess must be, not like the gentlewomen around here," said Teresa. "Quick, Sanchica, see to this gentleman's breakfast while I run and tell the priest and Master Nicolás the barber the news of our good fortune."

"Yes, Mother, but you will give me half that string of beads, won't you?" said Sanchica.

"It's all yours," replied her mother, "but do let me wear it for a day or two first."

"And here's a fine suit of hunting clothes from your husband, worn only once," added the page.

Teresa marched off and quickly found the priest and Sansón Carrasco the graduate. She began dancing up and down with excitement. The two men read the letters and were overcome with amazement. They could not believe that Sancho was a governor, or that a duchess had actually written to Teresa Panza, let alone asked for acorns.

"Let's go and see what the messenger has to say for himself," said Carrasco.

The page confirmed that it was all true, and that Sancho was proving to be a very good governor, although he couldn't say for certain that what he was governing was an island.

Teresa and Sanchica began to get carried away with the idea of being a governor's wife and daughter.

"I'll keep a coach and horses, if I must," said Teresa.

"Of course you must," said Sanchica, "and even if people poke fun at us, who cares, as we'll be warm and dry."

The priest invited the page to his house for a meal and Teresa went off and found an altar boy who, for the fee of two eggs and a bun, wrote out two letters that she dictated: one to the duchess and one to her husband. Sansón had offered to write them out for her, but, knowing his waggish sense of humour, she preferred to ask someone else.

The morning after the night of the governor's rounds, Sancho took a meagre breakfast of a spoonful of jam and four sips of cold water, Dr Pedro Recio maintaining that a light and delicate diet was good for the brain. Still starving, the governor took his place on the judge's bench, where he listened to a particularly tedious case. The duke's steward, knowing that Sancho's governorship was coming to an end, then promised him a proper lunch, quite against all Dr Pedro Recio's rules and prescriptions.

They were just taking away the cloth at the end of the meal, when a messenger came in with a letter from Don Quixote for the governor. The secretary read it out:

Friend Sancho,

I was expecting to hear that you had made a terrible mess of governing, but all I receive is reports of your good sense. I also hear that you are being very humble. Do not be too humble, though, and remember to dress smartly, as befits your office. Most importantly, be polite to everybody (although I have already told you this) and make sure that there is always plenty of food cheaply available, as nothing angers the poor more than hunger and high prices.

Do not introduce too many regulations, but make sure that those you do introduce are obeyed. Do not be too strict or too lenient in your judgements, and make sure that you are often seen in public, especially in the marketplace. Write to the duke and duchess to show how grateful you are to them, for ingratitude is the worst of sins.

The duchess has sent a letter to your wife, with a present and your hunting suit. We are expecting a reply any minute. I have been a little indisposed from a certain cat-scratching. Let me know if the steward had anything to do with the Trifaldi performance as you suspected. I have been thinking up a plan, which might upset the duke and duchess, but it can't be helped.

Your friend,
Don Quixote de la Mancha

Sancho listened carefully to the letter, which was much praised by everyone present. He then shut himself away in his room with his secretary and dictated the following reply:

I am so busy that I have had no time even to scratch my head or cut my nails, which is why you have not heard from me before. I am hungrier now than I ever was when we were wandering through the countryside, all because of a certain Dr Pedro Recio. I think he is trying to starve me to death.

I have so far not collected any taxes or taken any bribes. I visited the marketplace, as you advised, and found a stallholder selling fresh hazelnuts, only she'd mixed a load of old, empty rotten shells in with them. I confiscated the lot and sent them to the orphanage, where they'll easily sort through them, and banished her from the market for two weeks. Everyone says I was very brave to cross a market woman.

I'm glad the duchess has written to my wife. Please, sir, think hard about doing anything that might upset her and the duke, as I may suffer the consequences. I don't understand about the cat-scratching.

May heaven preserve you from evil enchanters.

Your servant,
Sancho Panza the Governor

The letter was sealed up and immediately sent off. Sancho then spent the afternoon drawing up a series of regulations for governing the island. He ordered that no one could profiteer from selling food, and that wine could be imported from anywhere as long as its origin and vintage were declared, so that it could be fairly priced. Anyone who watered it down, or falsely declared its origin, would pay with their life. He lowered the prices of all footwear, especially shoes, which seemed to him exorbitant. He established very heavy penalties for anyone caught singing rude songs, by day or night, and forbade blind men from singing about miracles unless they could produce written evidence for the miracle.

All in all, he made so many good rules that they remain in force there to this very day and are known as *The Constitution of the Great Governor Sancho Panza*.

Cide Hamete tells us that once Don Quixote had recovered from his scratching, he soon decided that the idle life he was leading was completely unsuited to a knight errant. He determined to go at once to Zaragoza, as the tournament there was drawing near. He was at the dining table, about to tell the duke and duchess of his decision, when two women dressed in mourning came into the dining hall. They turned out to be Doña Rodríguez and her daughter. With the duke's permission, Doña Rodríguez turned to Don Quixote and repeated her tale of the rich farmer's son having betrayed her daughter.

"I ask you, sir, to see that justice is done," she ended.

Don Quixote immediately said that he would challenge the youth to a duel. The duke accepted the challenge on the boy's behalf, with the duel to take place in the castle courtyard in six days' time. If Don Quixote won, the boy would be made to marry Doña Rodríguez's daughter; but if he lost, the boy would be freed from his obligation.

At the end of the meal, the page who had taken the letters and presents to Teresa Panza returned. He gave Teresa's letters to the duchess, who read out the one addressed to her, "the duchess so-and-so of somewhere or another":

Thank you, your highness, for your kind letter and the presents. Nobody here believes that my husband Sancho really is a governor, but I don't care; although in truth, if you hadn't sent the presents I wouldn't have believed it either.

With your permission, madam, I've decided to go to court and travel about in a coach, although I'm a bit worried about how expensive it all gets.

I'm afraid there were no acorns collected in the village this year, but I'm sending you some I gathered in the woods myself. I wish they were bigger. I beg your highness to write again and I will be sure to reply.

Your servant,
Teresa Panza

Everyone was highly entertained, and the duchess then asked Don Quixote if they could hear the contents of the letter addressed to the governor. Don Quixote agreed and read out the following:

I got your letter, Sancho, and nearly went mad with happiness. Who would have thought that a goatherd could become a governor of islands? Her highness the duchess will tell you that I would like to go to court in a coach. Let me know what you think. Neither the priest nor Sansón Carrasco, nor the barber, can believe that you are a governor, and they think the whole thing is a fantasy, like everything that your master Don Quixote is mixed up in. I only laugh, and look at my string of beads and your fine hunting suit.

Here is some news from the village. La Berrueca married her daughter to a good-for-nothing painter who turned up and hasn't painted anything.

A company of soldiers came through and when they left, three girls ran away with them, though I won't tell you who they are as they might come back. There are no olives this year and not a drop of vinegar anywhere.

Sanchica is making lace. She puts all her earnings in a box to help with the housekeeping. Soon she can stop work as you'll be able to give her an allowance. The fountain in the square has run dry.

Let me know what you think about me going to court.

Your wife,
Teresa Panza

At this point, Cide Hamete tells us that all things must come to an end, including Sancho's governorship, and this is how it happened.

≈ How Sancho Panza left his island

On the night of the seventh day of his governorship, Sancho lay in bed, full not of bread and wine, but of listening to cases, passing judgements and making laws. He was just dropping off to sleep, when he was startled awake by a sudden, deafening clamour of bells, closely followed by the sound of trumpets, drums and people shouting.

He leapt out of bed and rushed to the door of his room, to see a band of more than twenty people waving swords and torches and all crying, "To arms! To arms! The enemy is among us! Without your brave leadership we will be lost."

"I know nothing of arms," retorted Sancho. "You'd be better off leaving this to my master, Don Quixote."

"That won't do at all, Señor Governor," said one of the men. "It is your duty as our governor to lead us in battle."

"Very well, arm me then."

The men produced two large shields and proceeded to sandwich Sancho between them, leaving his arms sticking out at the sides. They bound the shields tightly with rope and then handed Sancho a lance, telling him to march forward to the town square.

"How can I walk like this?" he asked. "I can't even bend my knees."

"Nonsense, Señor Governor," cried a man, "it is only fear that prevents you from moving."

Sancho tried to advance a step or two, but toppled over with a crash. He lay there helplessly, like an upended boat or a tortoise on its back. The party of jokers did nothing to help him, but instead began to shout louder than ever, swinging their swords about and slashing at Sancho. They knocked against him, and tripped over the shields. One even stood on top of him for a while like a sergeant on a watchtower, issuing orders to the others.

Sancho prayed for it all to end, and for the whole island to disappear. Eventually he heard voices calling, "Victory! The enemy is retreating!"

The men raised Sancho to his feet and freed him from his bonds.

"I'm not interested in the spoils of victory," said Sancho. "All I want is a glass of wine and someone to rub me down."

He sat down on his bed and promptly fainted away from fear and exhaustion. The jokers were rather alarmed at this, thinking they might have pushed their joke too far, but fortunately Sancho soon came to. He asked what time it was.

"Nearly dawn," they said.

Sancho got up and dressed himself very carefully, as he was badly bruised. He went to the stable and found his donkey. "Come, my friend," he said. "I was much better off when I only had you to worry about."

After fitting the packsaddle, he heaved himself onto the donkey with great pain and difficulty. He turned to those who were present, who included the duke's steward, the butler, the secretary and Dr Pedro Recio. "Make way, gentlemen," he said, "and let me return to my freedom. I was not born to be a governor – I'm more suited to ploughing and digging. God's blessings on you all, and tell my lord the duke that I arrived on this island without a cent and I'm leaving without a cent, unlike the way most governors leave their islands, I gather."

Much taken by Sancho's words and firm resolve to leave, the others agreed to let him go. They asked him if he wanted anything for himself or for the journey. Sancho said that as the distance back to the duke and duchess's was short, all he needed was a little bread and cheese and some barley for his donkey.

≈ Sancho meets an old friend

They set off, Sancho half sad and half happy, and had not gone far when Sancho saw six pilgrims walking towards them. They were foreigners, and as they drew near they arranged themselves in a line and began singing in a strange language, evidently asking for alms. Sancho took out the bread and cheese he had been given and handed it to the pilgrims, indicating with gestures that he had no money on him.

He was about to move on, when one of them suddenly rushed over and embraced him, saying in perfectly good Spanish, "Gracious heavens, can this be my old friend Sancho Panza?"

Sancho stared at the man in surprise.

"Goodness," said the man, "do you not know your neighbour Ricote, the Moorish shopkeeper from your village?"

Sancho looked even more closely at the man. "How the devil could I have recognized you got up like that?" he said. "Tell me, who turned you into a foreigner and how have you dared to return to Spain? It'll be pretty bad for you if you're found out."

"Unless you betray me, I should be safe," replied Ricote. "No one will recognize me in this outfit. But come, join my companions for a meal – they're all fine fellows. I'll tell you everything that has happened since the king's edict against my people caused me to leave Spain."

They made their way to a grove some distance from the road, and spread out a sumptuous picnic. Once they had eaten and drunk, Ricote explained to Sancho that before the deadline in the edict for all Moorish people to leave the country had passed, he had decided to go and find somewhere safe for him and his wife and daughter to live. He had first gone to North Africa, expecting to find refuge there, but had met with nothing but insults and ill-treatment. Next he had gone to France, then Italy and then Germany, which at last seemed somewhere it would be possible to live without persecution. He had returned to Spain in the company of some young German pilgrims and was intending to go back to retrieve some treasure he had buried outside his home town. He would then go to Algiers to look for his wife and daughter, who had gone there with his brother-in-law.

He asked Sancho to help retrieve the treasure. "I'll give you two hundred gold crowns," he said.

"I would help you, but I don't want any money," replied Sancho. "I'm not greedy – only this morning I resigned from a post that would have made me rich if I'd stayed for six more months. And besides, I'd be unhappy helping someone going against the king's law."

"What job was it you resigned from?" asked Ricote.

"Governor of a nearby island called Barataria," replied Sancho.

"Don't be ridiculous," said Ricote. "Islands are found in the sea. There aren't any on the mainland. And in any case, who on earth would give you an island to govern? You're talking nonsense."

Ricote could not persuade Sancho to help him retrieve his treasure, so after exchanging news of their village they embraced each other and went their separate ways.

≈ SANCHO AND HIS DONKEY FIND THEMSELVES IN A HOLE

The meeting with Ricote had delayed Sancho somewhat, and darkness fell before he had made it back to the duke and duchess's. He turned off the road to find somewhere for the night. Through a stroke of misfortune, his donkey pitched into a deep dark hole among some old buildings.

Sancho thought that his end had come, but, after falling about five metres, the donkey landed at the bottom of the hole and Sancho found himself still seated on the packsaddle, completely unscathed. He felt along the sides of the pit but could find no way out, so he and his donkey were forced to spend the night there, Sancho bewailing his fate and the donkey, which was very bruised and battered, listening in silence.

The next morning, Sancho saw that it would be impossible to get out of the pit without help. He shouted himself hoarse but no one came.

Eventually he found a small hole low down in the side of the pit, just big enough to squeeze through. On the other side was a large space with light coming through from above. Taking a stone, Sancho chipped away at the hole until it was large enough for the donkey to pass through. Leading the donkey by the halter, Sancho made his way through a series of tunnels, sometimes in light and sometimes in darkness, but always in fear.

"This would be a good adventure for my master," said Sancho to himself. "He would take these dungeons for flowery gardens or exotic palaces and would be sure to come out in some lovely meadow, whereas all I expect is that at any moment another pit will open up in front of me and swallow me up for good."

After journeying for what seemed like hours, Sancho thought he could detect some light coming in at one side of the tunnel.

Up above, Don Quixote had been out exercising on Rocinante, in preparation for the duel he was about to fight. Rocinante had been cantering along, and Don Quixote had had to pull him up sharply to stop him falling into a pit. Don Quixote was peering into the pit, when he heard cries from below. He thought he recognized the voice.

"Who is that complaining down there?" he called.

"No one but Sancho Panza, unlucky ex-governor of the island of Barataria and once squire of the famous knight Don Quixote de la Mancha."

Don Quixote was amazed, and decided that Sancho was dead, and that this was his tormented soul calling up from below. "I command you to tell me who or what you are," he said, "and if you are a soul in torment I will try to help you – it is my job as a knight errant to help those in distress, alive or dead."

"In that case you must be my master, Don Quixote," returned the voice, "and I am your squire, who has never died in his life but has given up being governor, for reasons I'll explain in a minute."

Don Quixote was not convinced until Sancho's donkey began to bray loudly.

"I recognize that bray as if it were my mother," he said. "And now I recognize your voice too, Sancho. Wait here while I go to the duke's castle for help."

Don Quixote hurried to the castle and returned with a large group of people carrying rope and tackle. With some effort they managed to haul Sancho and his donkey out of the hole.

"That's how all governors should end their governorships," observed a watching student, "starving, pale and evidently penniless."

They returned to the castle, where Sancho gave the duke an account of his time as ruler of the island of Barataria. He told him he had left the island as he had found it, had taken no money and had tried to pass some useful laws, but had found the responsibility of governing too much, and was happy to give it up.

Don Quixote listened in dread to Sancho's speech, fearing that at any moment he would make a fool of himself, and was hugely relieved when he did not.

≈ THE DUEL THAT NEVER HAPPENED

The day of the duel arrived. The farmer's son who had betrayed Doña Rodríguez's daughter had in fact fled to Flanders, to avoid having Doña Rodríguez as a mother-in-law. In his place the duke had substituted one of his servants, a Gascon called Tosilos. The duke had given Tosilos detailed instructions on what to do, telling him to make sure he overcame Don Quixote without doing him any harm.

All the spectators seated themselves, and with great ceremony Don Quixote and Tosilos rode out onto the tournament ground, Tosilos in a shiny suit of armour with his visor down. As he took his place, Tosilos looked up and caught sight of Doña Rodríguez's daughter. He fell instantly head over heels in love. He was so smitten that he completely ignored the trumpet signalling the start of the duel and just sat there, staring. Don Quixote, on the other hand, set off as fast as Rocinante could carry him, with Sancho cheering him on.

When Tosilos saw Don Quixote approaching, he called to the marshal, "Sir, this battle is to decide whether or not I should marry that lady, is it not? Well, I consider myself already defeated and agree to do so at once."

When Don Quixote saw that Tosilos was not going to fight, he pulled Rocinante up. The marshal went over to the duke and reported what Tosilos had said. The duke was furious.

Meanwhile Tosilos rode up to Doña Rodríguez and said, "Madam, I am willing to marry your daughter."

On hearing this, Don Quixote said, "In that case I am released from my duty and we need no longer fight."

Tosilos took off his helmet and revealed his true identity. Doña Rodríguez and her daughter were aghast.

"A trick! A trick!" cried Doña Rodríguez. "This is not the man who promised to marry my daughter, but some servant of the duke."

"Calm yourselves, ladies," said Don Quixote. "I am sure this is no deliberate trick on the part of the duke. Those evil enchanters who plague me must have given your fiancé the face of one of the duke's servants. Take my advice and marry him whatever he looks like, as he's definitely the one you want."

When the duke heard this his anger evaporated and he roared with laughter. "The things that happen to Don Quixote are so extraordinary that I half believe this really isn't one of my servants," he said. "Let's put the marriage off for a fortnight and see if he turns back into his original shape."

"I've seen all this before," said Sancho. "Those enchanters are good at this sort of thing. They turned the Knight of the Mirrors into the shape of the graduate Sansón Carrasco, and the lady Dulcinea del Toboso into a common peasant girl, so if they've turned that man into a servant, I bet he stays a servant for the rest of his days."

At this point, Doña Rodríguez's daughter put in, "I don't mind who he is; I'm prepared to marry him, for I'd rather be an honest servant's wife than be cheated on by a gentleman."

With this happy outcome, Don Quixote was declared the victor and everyone dispersed, although many in the crowd were disappointed not to have seen a real fight.

≈ Don Quixote and Sancho leave the Duke and Duchess

Don Quixote decided it was time to put an end to the idle life he was leading at the castle, and so one day he asked the duke and duchess's permission to leave. They agreed, although they were sad to see him go. The duchess gave Sancho his wife's letters and Sancho wept over them, thinking of how he would have to explain to Teresa that her ambition of becoming a court lady would now come to nothing.

Early one morning, Don Quixote and Sancho appeared in the castle courtyard, Don Quixote in full armour and Sancho on his donkey, extremely happy because the duke's steward had given him two hundred gold crowns for the expenses of the journey ahead.

They were saying goodbye to everyone, when Altisidora raised her voice and began to chant a poem in which she accused Don Quixote of abandoning her and of stealing three of her nightcaps and a pair of garters.

When she had finished, Don Quixote turned to Sancho and said, "Sancho, my friend, do you know anything of these nightcaps and garters?"

"I've got the nightcaps," replied Sancho, "but I know nothing of any garters."

The duke, thinking to keep the joke going, said, "Sir Knight, I do not think this is a good way to repay my hospitality. I ask you to return my maid's things, or I shall challenge you to a duel to the death."

"I would not dream of taking up arms against one who has been so kind to me," replied Don Quixote. "I will certainly return the nightcaps, as Sancho says that he has them, but I cannot return the garters, which I am sure the maid has mislaid. I have not taken them – I am not and never have been a thief. Now I beg you to let me continue my journey."

"Well said," put in the duchess. "Go safely on your way as quickly as possible, for you can see the effect you are having on my maid."

Altisidora broke in. "Oops, silly me," she said. "I seem to have had the garters on all the time. I'm frightfully sorry."

With that Don Quixote saluted the duke and duchess, and he and Sancho rode out of the castle.

≈ DON QUIXOTE AND SANCHO MEET SOME BRIGHT YOUNG THINGS AND HAVE AN UNFORTUNATE ENCOUNTER WITH SOME BULLS, AND DON QUIXOTE RAISES THE VEXED QUESTION OF DULCINEA'S DISENCHANTING

They were both delighted to be on the open road again. They met a party of labourers carrying some statues to be put up in the local church and Don Quixote amazed Sancho with his knowledge of the saints portrayed.

Shortly afterwards they were travelling through some woods, discussing Altisidora's saucy behaviour, when Don Quixote suddenly found himself entangled in a green net stretched across the path. He could not understand what was going on but suspected some kind of enchantment.

Just then two beautiful young girls appeared, dressed in shepherdesses' costumes of very fine material.

"Please don't break those nets, sir," one of them said. "They're just there for our amusement – we're trying to catch birds in them. We're from a village near here and are out with some of our friends playing at being shepherds and shepherdesses."

Don Quixote introduced himself and the other girl exclaimed, "How lucky we are to have the famous knight errant in our midst! And I bet this is his squire, Sancho Panza."

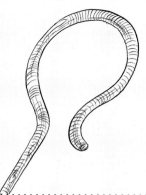

The brother of one of the two girls appeared, dressed as a shepherd, and begged Don Quixote to allow himself to be entertained in a marquee they had put up near by. Don Quixote consented and they all made their way to a clearing, where they found a party of about thirty men and women, all dressed as shepherds and shepherdesses. Don Quixote and Sancho were treated to a splendid feast, with Don Quixote as guest of honour.

At the end of the meal, Don Quixote rose and said, "Although some say that pride is the greatest sin, I say that it is ingratitude. To show my thanks for your hospitality, I propose to take up position in the middle of the road to Zaragoza and for two days and nights declare to all who pass that these two ladies disguised as shepherdesses are the most beautiful and politest maidens in the world, except for the fair Dulcinea del Toboso."

The others protested that this was quite unnecessary, but Don Quixote could not be dissuaded. They all followed him to the road to see what would happen. Don Quixote stopped in the middle of the road and repeated his declaration in a loud voice. He did this twice more, but there was no one on the road to hear him.

Soon, though, a party of men carrying lances came into view, riding in a tight group. Sancho immediately took refuge behind Rocinante's hindquarters.

One of the men, seeing Don Quixote, shouted, "Get out of the way, you devil, or these bulls will knock you to pieces!"

"What do I care for bulls?" said Don Quixote. "Confess at once that what I say is true, or you shall deal with the consequences."

The man had no time to reply, for in an instant a great herd of bulls came charging through, knocking Don Quixote, Sancho, Rocinante and the donkey to the ground and trampling all over them. The four picked themselves up and Don Quixote began to run after the disappearing herd, crying, "Stop, you rabble, and answer for yourselves," but to no avail.

Bruised, battered and miserable, Don Quixote and Sancho continued on their way, without saying goodbye to the fake shepherds and shepherdesses.

They found a clear spring in a grove of trees and stopped to refresh themselves. Sancho brought out some food. He began to tuck in with gusto, while Don Quixote ate scarcely anything.

"Eat, Sancho, my friend," he said morosely. "Your life is more important to you than mine is to me. Look at me! My deeds are famous, and just as I was looking forward to great victories, I find myself trampled underfoot by filthy beasts. I have no appetite, and am of a mind to starve myself to death."

"Things aren't that bad, sir," said Sancho. "Eat something and then have a sleep on this comfortable grass. You'll feel much better for it."

Don Quixote decided to follow Sancho's advice, but before he did he said, "Sancho, one thing would ease my mind greatly, and that is if you would take yourself off while I am sleeping and, exposing your flesh to the air, give yourself four or five hundred lashes with Rocinante's reins, to help with the disenchanting of Dulcinea."

"There's a lot to be said about that," said Sancho. "Let's both sleep now, and we'll see what happens afterwards."

≈ Don Quixote discovers to his horror that a false version of his adventures is in circulation

It was quite late when they woke up, and they hurried on to an inn which they could see in the distance. To Sancho's great relief, Don Quixote did indeed consider it an inn, and not a castle as he normally did.

Don Quixote was sitting in his room, about to start on his supper of cows' heels and calves' feet, when he heard a voice in the room next door saying, "Señor Don Jerónimo, while we're waiting for supper, let's read another chapter of the second part of *Don Quixote de la Mancha*."

At the sound of his name, Don Quixote leapt to his feet and listened all agog.

"I don't see what you want with that, Don Juan," replied the man who was evidently Don Jerónimo. "It's rubbish compared with the first volume."

"I agree, but it's better than nothing," said Don Juan, "though I do hate the part where it says that Don Quixote is cured of his love for Dulcinea."

Don Quixote immediately cried out in a loud voice, "Anyone who declares that Don Quixote de la Mancha has forgotten or will ever forget Dulcinea del Toboso can answer to me!"

"Who's that?" asked the men through the wall.

"It is Don Quixote de la Mancha himself," replied Sancho.

The two men burst in and warmly embraced Don Quixote. "From your appearance it must be you," they said. "And this must be Sancho Panza, your squire."

"None other, and proud of it," said Sancho.

The men then showed Don Quixote the book they had been reading. He ran his eyes over it and handed it back, saying, "This so-called history is full of errors. It even says that Sancho Panza's wife is called Mari Gutiêrrez, when her name is Teresa Panza. Any book that makes such an important mistake clearly cannot be trusted at all."

The two men then invited Don Quixote next door to share their supper, while Sancho and the landlord sat down to help themselves to the meal that Don Quixote had left behind. The men asked Don Quixote for news of Dulcinea, and he told them of her enchantment and all that had happened in the Cave of Montesinos, as well as of Merlin's declaration regarding her disenchantment.

They went on talking about the false book for much of the night. The two men tried to persuade Don Quixote to read more of it, but he refused. They then asked him where he was going next. He replied that he was going to Zaragoza to take part in the jousting tournament. Don Juan said that this was described in the new book, although in a dull and stupid way.

"In that case I shall not set foot in Zaragoza," declared Don Quixote. "That will show what a liar the author of the book is."

"Good plan," said Don Jerónimo. "Why don't you go to Barcelona instead? There are jousting tournaments there."

Don Quixote replied that he would follow Don Jerónimo's advice.

≈ Don Quixote and Sancho have a serious disagreement about Dulcinea's disenchanting, get a nasty shock under some trees and meet the famous outlaw Roque Guinart

Don Quixote and Sancho set off early the next morning, taking the road for Barcelona and carefully avoiding all routes that went anywhere near Zaragoza.

Nothing of any interest happened for six days, at the end of which they found themselves in a grove of live oak or cork oak trees – Cide Hamete doesn't specify which. They dismounted and settled down for the night. Sancho quickly went off to sleep but Don Quixote lay awake, brooding over the disenchantment of Dulcinea. It seemed to him that his good-for-nothing squire was not making enough progress in this, and after some deliberation he decided to take the matter into his own hands. He fashioned Rocinante's reins into a kind of whip and then crawled over to where Sancho was sleeping.

He began tugging at Sancho's breeches, but Sancho immediately woke up, shouting, "Who's that?"

"It is I," said Don Quixote, "come to give you your lashings as you seem to show no interest in giving them to yourself."

"Don't you touch me," said Sancho. "Those lashings have to be performed by me and of my own free will."

But Don Quixote would not give in. The two began struggling. Eventually Sancho forced Don Quixote to the ground and pinned him there, his knee planted firmly in his chest.

"What, traitor, do you rise up against your master?" gasped Don Quixote.

"I rise up against nobody, but only stand up for myself," replied Sancho. "If you promise to be quiet and not whip me, I'll let you go. If not, you'll perish on the spot."

Don Quixote reluctantly agreed to leave Sancho alone and let him decide where and when he should whip himself.

Sancho got up and moved away a short distance to find another tree to lean against. Something touched his head and, reaching up, he felt two human feet with shoes on. Trembling with fear, he made for another tree, where he felt another pair of feet. He shouted out to Don Quixote to come and rescue him. Don Quixote came over and asked what had happened. Sancho explained and Don Quixote guessed immediately.

"I'm sure those are the feet of brigands and outlaws who've been hanged from the trees," he said.

When first light came they found out that this was indeed the case. As they were recovering from the shock of seeing the dead outlaws, they were suddenly surrounded by about forty live ones, who told them in Catalan to stand and wait for their leader. Don Quixote was nowhere near Rocinante and his lance was propped up against a tree some way off, so there was little he could do.

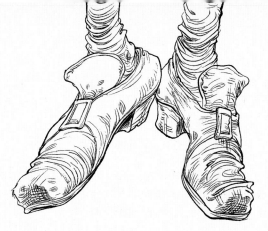

The outlaws rifled through the packsaddle on Sancho's donkey and took everything they could find. Fortunately Sancho had hidden the gold crowns the duke's steward had given him in a money belt, otherwise those would certainly have been taken too.

The outlaws' leader arrived and showed himself to be a powerfully built man with a stern expression, about thirty-four years old. He stared in wonder at Don Quixote, who was in full armour and looked utterly dejected.

"Don't look so sad, my good man," he said. "You have not fallen into the hands of some cruel tyrant, but into those of Roque Guinart, who is more merciful than brutal."

"I am not downcast because I have been captured by you, brave Roque, whose fame knows no bounds. I am in despair because I have been negligent in my duty as a knight errant and allowed myself to be taken unprepared. I should have been waiting for your soldiers on Rocinante with my lance and shield. I would then not have been easily overcome, as I am Don Quixote de la Mancha, whose deeds are known throughout the world."

Roque had heard of Don Quixote and was very pleased to meet him, as it gave him a chance to find out if all that he had heard was true.

"Do not despair, valiant knight," he said. "Fortune works in mysterious ways, and perhaps this misfortune will do you good in the end."

≈ The strange and tragic story of the impetuous Claudia Jerónima

Don Quixote was about to thank him for his words, when a horse came galloping into view, ridden by what appeared to be a young man, but turned out to be a woman in men's clothing.

The woman came up to Roque and said, "I have come to seek your aid, brave Roque. I am Claudia Jerónima, the daughter of your good friend Simón Forte, who is the sworn enemy of your enemy Clauquel Torrellas. This Torrellas has a son, Don Vicente Torrellas. Unknown to my father, he courted me and I fell in love with him. We became secretly engaged.

"Then yesterday I heard that he was planning to marry someone else this very morning. I was livid. I got up and dressed in these clothes, armed myself and set off in pursuit. I caught up with him a short distance from here and without waiting for him to say a word, fired my musket and two pistols into him. Now I need help to flee to France, where I have relatives and can escape from Torrellas's family."

Roque was filled with admiration for the young woman's spirit and said, "First, madam, let us go and see if your enemy is dead." He ordered his men to return to Sancho everything they had taken from Sancho's donkey, and set off with Claudia to find Don Vicente. They soon caught up with him; he was sorely wounded and being carried by his servants.

Claudia dismounted and, taking Don Vicente's hands, said, "This would never have happened if you had kept your promise to me."

"So it is you who did this," said Don Vicente. "Why?"

"Were you not about to marry Leonora, the daughter of the rich Balvastro?" asked Claudia.

"No, that was some false rumour," replied Don Vicente.

When she heard this, Claudia fainted away, and at the same instant Don Vicente breathed his last. Roque and Don Vicente's servants sprinkled water on Claudia's face. She came to and, seeing Don Vicente's dead body, burst out crying. She berated herself for her cruelty and impetuousness and then fainted again. Eventually she recovered enough to declare that she would go into a nunnery where an aunt of hers was abbess. Roque ordered Don Vicente's servants to take the body back to Don Vicente's father's village to be buried.

≈ DON QUIXOTE AND SANCHO WITNESS ROQUE GUINART IN ACTION

Roque Guinart returned to where he had left Don Quixote and Sancho. He called his men together and distributed the goods and money that had recently been obtained, carefully ensuring that each man got his fair share. He had just finished when two lookouts came running up to report that they had spotted a party of people on the road to Barcelona. Roque ordered his men to go and fetch them.

While this was being done, he turned to Don Quixote and said, "Ours must seem a strange way of life to you, sir. It is certainly an unsettled and difficult one. In truth it goes against my nature and troubles my conscience. I was drawn into it by a thirst for revenge for a great wrong that had been done to me. I have not abandoned hope of escaping from it some day."

Don Quixote was amazed to hear a highwayman saying such things. "To recognize the disease is the first step in the cure," he said. "I can help you turn away from wrongdoing by showing you how to become a knight errant if you so desire."

Roque laughed when he heard this and, changing the subject, gave an account of Claudia Jerónima's tragic affair. His men then returned, bringing with them two men on horseback, a couple of servants on mules, two pilgrims on foot, and a coach full of women with six servants in attendance. Roque's men surrounded the group and everyone stood in silence waiting for Roque to speak. He asked the party who they were and how much money they had on them.

The two men on horseback said they were infantry captains heading for Naples, where their companies were stationed; they had around two or three hundred crowns on them. The pilgrims said they were going to Barcelona to take a ship to Rome, and had about sixty reals on them. One of the servants accompanying the coach said that the women in the coach were the lady Doña Guiomar de Quiñones, wife of a senior judge in Naples; her daughter; a handmaid; and a duenna. They were carrying about six hundred crowns in all.

Roque said, "That makes some nine hundred crowns and sixty reals in total, and I have sixty men. That's a difficult sum." He kept the group in suspense for a while and then, turning to the captains, said, "Gentlemen, I would be very pleased if you would lend me sixty crowns." He then asked Doña Guiomar's servants if her ladyship would be willing to lend him eighty crowns.

The money was handed over and Roque called his men together and said, "Here are two crowns for each of you with twenty left over. Give ten to the pilgrims and the other ten to Don Quixote's worthy squire so that he is sure to speak well

of this adventure in future." He then wrote out safe passages for all the people in the party in case they should run into any of his other gangs. He handed these out and told the people to continue on their journey.

One of his men, rather disgruntled by this, said, "Our leader would be a better friar than a highwayman, being so generous with what's really ours."

Roque overheard and furiously smashed his sword down on the man's head, virtually splitting it in two. "That's how I deal with impudence," he said, cowing the rest of his men into silence. He then went to one side and wrote a letter to a friend of his in Barcelona, telling him that he intended to send Don Quixote and Sancho there in four days' time.

Don Quixote and Sancho spent the next three days with Roque and his men. They were amazed at their way of life, constantly on the move and always on watch. Finally, by way of little-used back roads they made their way to Barcelona, arriving the night before the Feast of St John. Roque presented Sancho with the ten crowns he had promised him and then said goodbye to him and Don Quixote, embracing them both.

≈ Don Quixote and Sancho arrive at Barcelona, see the sea and meet Don Antonio Moreno

The sun rose, and Don Quixote and Sancho found themselves on the beachfront just outside the city. They saw before them, for the first time in their lives, the sea. They could not get over how big it was. They were overwhelmed too by the great ships arrayed along the beach, all alive with activity preparing for the celebration of the feast day. The ships started to perform manoeuvres in the bay at the same time as a horde of knights rode out of the city. A mock battle took place, with those on board ship firing volleys at the walls of the city.

In the middle of all the noise and confusion, a group of horsemen came galloping up to Don Quixote and Sancho. Wheeling around the pair, the horsemen shouted, "Welcome to our city, brave and valiant Don Quixote de la Mancha!"

"These men obviously recognize us," said Don Quixote. "I'm sure they've read our history."

One of the men said, "Come with us, Señor Quixote; we are all friends of Roque Guinart."

They started to ride into the city. As they did so, some street urchins crept up and stuck prickly bunches of gorse under the tails of Rocinante and Sancho's donkey. The two animals started bucking wildly and soon pitched both their riders onto the ground. Don Quixote and Sancho picked themselves up, removed the gorse and remounted. The men with them tried to find the boys to punish them, but lost them in the crowd.

Don Quixote's host was a certain Don Antonio Moreno, a rich and intelligent man who set about finding ways of encouraging Don Quixote's eccentricities without doing him any harm.

First he made Don Quixote take off his armour and led him, dressed in his tight chamois leather undersuit, onto a balcony overlooking one of the main streets of the city. Everyone passing gawped up at the strange figure. Then he entertained him to a fine meal at which several of his friends were present. They treated Don Quixote with great respect, as if he were a true knight errant, leading to him becoming rather puffed up with pride.

After the meal, Don Antonio took Don Quixote into a room that had no furniture in it except a table on a pedestal, both apparently made of some dark stone. There was a head that seemed to be made of bronze on top of the table.

"I paid a great magician from Poland a thousand crowns for this head," said Don Antonio. "It has the ability to answer any question put to it, but not on Fridays. As today is Friday, you must wait until tomorrow to put it to the test."

They returned to the dining room, where Sancho had been regaling the others with tales of their recent adventures.

That afternoon, Don Antonio and his friends took Don Quixote out into the town, dressed in ordinary street clothes. They put him on a fine mule and gave him a great woollen overcoat to wear. On the back of the overcoat, unknown to Don Quixote, they fixed a sign which read: *This is Don Quixote de la Mancha.*

As he paraded through the streets, passers-by read out the words on the sign to one another, making Don Quixote think that everybody recognized him.

Finally one man rounded on him, saying, "The devil take you for Don Quixote de la Mancha! How come you're not dead after all the beatings you've received? Go home now, you madman, and take care of your own affairs."

After this, and with the crowd of people pressing in on all sides, they surreptitiously took the sign down and led Don Quixote back to Don Antonio's house.

That evening, Don Antonio held a dancing party. Two of the ladies in attendance appeared to take a great shine to Don Quixote and kept him dancing late into the night, wearing him out in body and in spirit. Eventually he could take no more, and sat down on the floor in the middle of the room. Don Antonio's men carried him upstairs and Sancho helped put him to bed.

≈ The talking head

The next day, the mysterious talking head was put to the test. There were eight people in attendance: Don Antonio, his wife, two of Don Antonio's gentleman friends, the two ladies who had exhausted Don Quixote the night before, Don Quixote himself and Sancho.

Don Antonio approached the head and said in a low voice, "What am I thinking?"

The head replied in a clear voice, without moving its lips, "I cannot read thoughts."

Don Antonio then asked who was present, and the head named them all.

One of the women then asked the head, "What should I do to be very beautiful?"

"Be very virtuous," replied the head.

The others asked similar questions, to all of which the head replied.

Then Don Quixote came forward. "Tell me, head," he said, "whether what happened to me in the Cave of Montesinos was real or a dream. Also tell me whether my squire, Sancho, will carry out his whippings, and whether Dulcinea will soon be disenchanted."

"There is much to be said about the cave," replied the head. "There is something of both in it. Sancho's whipping will proceed slowly, and Dulcinea's disenchantment will eventually happen."

It was now Sancho's turn. "Head, shall I ever be governor again?" he asked. "Shall I ever escape the hard life of a squire? Shall I return home to see my wife and children?"

The head replied, "You shall govern in your own home. If you return home you will see your wife and children; and as soon as you stop serving, you will cease to be a squire."

"Good grief," said Sancho, "I could have provided those answers myself."

"What answers would you have the head give?" asked Don Quixote. "Are you not satisfied?"

"I could have done with a bit more detail," said Sancho.

All were left in wonderment at the head, except for Don Antonio and his two gentleman friends, who were in on the secret. The head had been made by Don Antonio and was hollow and had been painted to look like bronze. The table and pedestal were also hollow and made out of wood painted to look like stone. Hidden in them was a metal tube running from inside the head down into the room below. Downstairs a nephew of Don Antonio's, who was a sharp-witted student, sat listening to the questions and responding through the tube. He had been briefed by Don Antonio to provide answers to most of the questions that were likely to be asked.

≈A JOUSTING TOURNAMENT IS ARRANGED, DON QUIXOTE MAKES SOME OBSERVATIONS ON TRANSLATION, AND HE AND SANCHO ARE TAKEN ON BOARD SHIP

At Don Antonio's request, the gentlemen of the city agreed to hold a jousting tournament to give Don Quixote a chance to show his prowess. One morning, while waiting for the day of the tournament, Don Quixote decided to go on a quiet walk around the city. He came across a printer's and went in to talk to the man in charge. The printer showed him some books he was printing, including one that was translated from the Italian.

Don Quixote did not really approve of translation. "It seems to me that translating a book from one language to another is like looking at a tapestry from the wrong side," he said. "You can make out the general picture, but it is all blurred and indistinct. Still, I admit that there are worse ways to use your time."

That same day, Don Antonio made arrangements for Don Quixote and Sancho to be shown around the ships lying at anchor off the beach. Sancho in particular was delighted as he had never seen one at close quarters. Don Antonio sent a message to the commander of the ships, an admiral from Valencia, telling him that he was bringing the famous Don Quixote de la Mancha as a guest.

As soon as Don Quixote and Sancho appeared, trumpets were sounded and a small boat was launched from one of the ships to collect them. They were piped on board the ship with great ceremony. At a signal from the captain, the crew stripped to the waist and took up positions. Sancho was standing on the captain's right, when suddenly the nearest crew member picked him up and, holding him high in the air, passed him to the crew member behind him, who passed him on in turn. He was whirled all round the deck in this fashion, at such a rate that he was convinced that devils were flying away with him.

When Don Quixote saw what was happening to Sancho, he leapt to his feet and grasped his sword, declaiming, "This may be the traditional way of greeting someone who has never been on a ship before, but no one is going to treat me like that."

At that instant, the sailors lowered the yardarm with a great crash. Sancho thought the sky was falling in and crouched down in terror, his head between his knees. Even Don Quixote turned pale and could feel his knees knocking together. The anchor was raised and the crew seized their oars and started rowing the ship out to sea, the first mate lashing them on the shoulders with his whip.

When Sancho saw all these red feet moving across the surface of the water – for that is what he took the oars to be – he thought, This is a truly enchanted thing, not like the ones my master talks about. And what can those wretches have done to deserve being whipped like that?

Don Quixote said to Sancho, "If you joined those gentlemen, you'd soon finish disenchanting Dulcinea, as I'm sure one lash from that man's whip would be the same as ten that you'd give yourself."

The admiral was about to ask about Dulcinea and her disenchanting, when a lookout cried out, "A foreign vessel has been spotted in the west."

The ship set off in hot pursuit, accompanied by three others from the fleet. After a long chase they ran down the foreign ship and called on it to surrender. Two Turks on board let loose with their muskets and killed two of the sailors on the ship that Don Quixote and Sancho were on. The ship then tried to make off again, but was overtaken once more.

This time it surrendered and was taken to the beach, where the viceroy of Barcelona was waiting. The admiral ordered the yardarm to be lowered so that they could hang the crew of the captured ship from it, as punishment for their having killed two Spanish sailors. First he asked who the captain of the foreign ship was. One of the prisoners pointed out a handsome young man who scarcely looked twenty.

The viceroy came on board and asked what was happening. The admiral explained that he was about to take revenge for his murdered sailors, but the viceroy was much taken by the appearance of the young captain, and resolved to save his life at least if he could.

"Are you a Moor or a Turk?" he asked.

"Neither, but a Spanish woman and a Christian," replied the captain. "I ask you to delay my execution briefly while I tell you the story of my life."

≈ The strange story of Ana Félix

The captured ship's captain began her story. "I was born of Moorish parents here in Spain. As I was growing up, a young gentleman from a nearby village, Don Gaspar Gregorio, fell in love with me. When those of our race were banished from Spain, Don Gregorio chose to join me in exile. My father had left the country beforehand to try to find a safe refuge for us. Before he had gone, he had buried a great quantity of treasure outside our village for safe keeping. He told me where it was, but commanded me to keep its location a secret.

"Don Gregorio and I, in company with two of my uncles and other neighbours and relatives, made our way to Algiers. News of my beauty and my family's wealth reached the king, who summoned me. He persuaded me to return to Spain disguised as a man to retrieve the treasure. To protect Don Gregorio while I was away, I convinced him to disguise himself as a woman.

"The king of Algiers provided me with a ship and ordered two Turks – the ones who killed your soldiers – to accompany me. The rest of the crew are just oarsmen. They are Turks and Moors, except for one Spaniard who is secretly a Christian. Our orders from the king were to land in secret as soon as we could, find the treasure and then return, but these two Turks had other ideas and decided to see if we could capture a ship or two on our voyage. That is how we came to be out here, and that is the end of my sad story."

All the while she had been telling her tale, an elderly pilgrim who had come on board the ship at the same time as the viceroy had been watching her intently. As soon as she had finished he threw himself at her feet and said, sobbing, "Oh, my unhappy daughter, Ana Félix, this is your father, Ricote, come back to look for you!"

At these words, Sancho looked round and recognized the man he had met the day he had resigned his governorship. Ricote recounted his adventures to the company, and explained that he had now retrieved the treasure, but had virtually given up hope of finding his daughter. Sancho confirmed that he knew Ricote well, and that Ana Félix was indeed his daughter.

The admiral freed Ana Félix and the rest of the crew, but was still determined to hang the two Turks. The viceroy begged him to spare their lives, and the admiral finally relented. They all then tried to think of a plan for rescuing Don Gaspar Gregorio. It was finally decided that the Spaniard who had come back with Ana Félix would captain a small boat that would cross to North Africa and try to find him. Ricote said he would willingly pay Don Gregorio's ransom if that proved necessary.

All this was agreed and the party returned to shore. Don Antonio offered to put up Ana Félix and her father while they waited for Don Gregorio's return. Don Quixote privately told Don Antonio that the rescue plan was not a good one, as it was too risky. It would be much better if he, Don Quixote, were to land with his arms and horse in North Africa. He would easily rescue Don Gregorio, no matter how many Moors tried to stop him. Don Antonio agreed that they would try this if the first expedition failed.

≈ DON QUIXOTE'S DEFEAT

One morning, as Don Quixote was out riding along the beach, dressed as usual in full armour, he saw coming towards him a knight, also in full armour, with a shining moon painted on his shield.

The knight approached and said in a loud voice, "Illustrious Don Quixote de la Mancha, I am the famous Knight of the White Moon and have come to do battle with you. I intend to make you admit that my beloved, whoever she is, is more beautiful by far than your Dulcinea del Toboso. If you acknowledge this now, we shall not have to fight. If you do not, and I defeat you in battle, all I ask is that you lay down your arms and return to your village to live in peace and quiet for a year."

Don Quixote replied, "I have not heard of you, and I am sure you have never set eyes on the fair Dulcinea, but I accept your challenge."

The Knight of the White Moon had been seen from the city, and the viceroy, Don Antonio and several others came hurrying out to the beach, just in time to see the two knights prepare to engage in combat. The viceroy could not make out whether this was all one of Don Antonio's jokes or not, but gave the two knights permission to fight.

They withdrew and then both wheeled round and began to charge at each other. The Knight of the White Moon's horse was much faster than Rocinante, and the two knights met almost before Rocinante had begun to move. The Knight of the White Moon did not touch Don Quixote with his lance, which he seemed deliberately to be keeping pointed up in the air, but still clashed so heavily with him that both Don Quixote and Rocinante were thrown to the ground.

The Knight of the White Moon leapt off his horse and, placing the tip of his lance on Don Quixote's visor, said, "Admit that you are defeated, sir, or you shall die."

Don Quixote replied in a week and feeble voice, "Dulcinea del Toboso is the fairest maiden in the world and I am the most unfortunate knight on earth. It would be better for you to end my life now, sir."

"I will not," said the Knight of the White Moon. "And I am happy to let the fame of the lady Dulcinea live on for ever. All I ask is that the great Don Quixote retire to his home for a year."

Don Quixote agreed to this. He was lifted up and carried into the city in a sedan chair provided by the viceroy, as Rocinante was lying on the beach quite unable to move. Sancho sat in silence, utterly dejected and not knowing what to say or do.

Don Antonio was burning with curiosity to find out who the Knight of the White Moon was, and followed him back to the inn where he was staying. The stranger explained that he was a graduate, Sansón Carrasco, from Don Quixote's own village. He then told of the plan that he, the priest and the barber had come up with to cure Don Quixote of his madness, and recounted the story of his first failed challenge.

"Oh, sir," said Don Antonio when Sansón had finished, "may you be forgiven the wrong you have done the whole world in trying to bring this entertaining madman to his senses. There will be no fun any more if he becomes sane, although personally I think he is too far gone ever to do so."

Don Quixote kept to his bed for six days, feeling extremely miserable. Sancho did his best to cheer him up, at the same time trying to persuade him to return home.

One day, as they were talking, Don Antonio came in. "Good news! Don Gregorio has been rescued and is this very minute coming here."

This did cheer Don Quixote a little. "I was almost wishing that he was still there," he said, "for then I would have been forced to take up arms and rescue him. But what am I saying?

Am I not the one who has been defeated? Have I not promised not to take up arms for a whole year?"

"That's enough of that, sir," said Sancho. "After all, tomorrow is another day. Now let's go and greet Don Gregorio."

Don Gregorio was reunited with Ana Félix. It was immediately obvious that the two were very much in love with each other. Don Antonio said that he would go to Madrid to see if there was any way that the king could be persuaded to allow Ana Félix and her father to remain in Spain.

≈ DON QUIXOTE AND SANCHO BEGIN THEIR JOURNEY HOME, SANCHO DISPENSES ONE LAST BIT OF WISDOM, DON QUIXOTE AND SANCHO MEET AN OLD ACQUAINTANCE, DON QUIXOTE RETURNS TO THE QUESTION OF DULCINEA'S DISENCHANTING, AND HE AND SANCHO HAVE AN UNFORTUNATE ENCOUNTER WITH A HERD OF PIGS

Two days after Don Gregorio's arrival, Don Quixote and Sancho took their leave and began the journey back to their home village, Don Quixote in ordinary travelling clothes and Sancho on foot, as his donkey was laden down with Don Quixote's armour. For five days they travelled, discussing Don Quixote's defeat and the twists and turns of fate.

On the sixth day, they came to a village where there were a number of people gathered around the inn enjoying themselves, as it was a holiday. One of them said, "Here's some people who can help us decide what to do about this bet, as they don't know either of the two involved."

The man then explained that a man in the village who weighed one hundred and twenty-five kilos had challenged a man who weighed sixty kilos to a race, with the only condition being that they should both carry equal weight. The fat man was insisting that the thin man should run the race with sixty-five kilos of iron strapped to his back. The villagers were not sure if this was right or not, and the thin man had objected.

Before Don Quixote had a chance to speak, Sancho butted in. "I've just been governor of an island where I had to pass judgement on this kind of thing the whole time," he said. "It's obvious that what should happen is that the fat man should lop flesh off himself until he weighs the same as the thin man. Then they can run the race on equal terms."

"That's brilliant," said one of the other men gathered around, "but I bet the fat man won't part with a single gram of his flesh, let alone sixty-five kilos."

"It'd be better if they didn't run the race at all," said another, "then the thin man won't be crippled and the fat man won't lose his flesh. We'll spend the money from the bet on wine instead."

They invited Don Quixote and Sancho to drink with them, but Don Quixote politely declined.

Don Quixote and Sancho spent that night out in the open air. The next morning, they saw someone running towards them with a knapsack on his shoulder. On reaching them he embraced Don Quixote's leg, saying, "Don Quixote de la Mancha, sir, how pleased the duke will be when he hears you are returning to his castle."

"Who are you?" asked Don Quixote. "I don't recognize you."

"I am Tosilos, the duke's servant who refused to fight you over marrying Doña Rodríguez's daughter."

"You aren't the man whom my enemies the enchanters turned into a servant, are you?"

"There was no enchantment involved at all," replied Tosilos. "A servant I was and a servant I shall be. Unfortunately, though, the whole thing didn't really turn out as I'd hoped. As soon as you'd left the castle, the duke gave me a hundred lashes for disobeying his orders over the fight. Doña Rodríguez's daughter has become a nun, and Doña Rodríguez has gone back to Madrid. Now I'm on my way to Barcelona with a package of letters from my master to the viceroy. I have some wine and cheese here I'd gladly share with you."

Don Quixote declined the offer, but Sancho eagerly accepted it. Don Quixote retired to the shade of a nearby tree while Sancho and Tosilos ate and drank. He sat brooding over all that had happened to him, the behaviour of Altisidora at the duke's castle and the disenchantment of Dulcinea.

Sancho joined him and they continued their journey. Soon they came to the very spot where they had been trampled by the bulls. Don Quixote recalled the rich young men and women who had been playing at being shepherds and shepherdesses.

"We shall do the same," he declared, "at least for the year that I am supposed to spend in retirement. I'll buy some sheep and call myself the shepherd Quixotiz, and you can be the shepherd Panzino, and we'll wander around the woods singing songs all day."

"A fine idea," said Sancho, "and perhaps Sansón Carrasco, the priest and Master Nicolás the barber will join us."

"Yes," said Don Quixote, "Sansón can call himself Sansonino; the priest, Curiambro; and Nicolás, Niculoso."

They turned off the road and settled down for the night. Sancho was soon fast asleep, but Don Quixote lay awake. Eventually he woke Sancho and said, "I do not see, Sancho, how you can sleep there so unconcerned while I, your master, lie here sad and suffering. Rouse yourself and give yourself three or four hundred lashes towards Dulcinea's disenchantment."

"I'm no monk to inflict needless suffering on myself in the middle of the night," said Sancho. "Now please let me sleep."

At this point both master and squire became aware of a harsh, indistinct noise echoing around the valley. It grew louder and closer. Sancho, terrified, took shelter under his donkey, piling Don Quixote's armour on one side and the packsaddle on the other.

It soon became apparent what was causing the noise, for a herd of about six hundred pigs on their way to market surged past, knocking Don Quixote, Sancho and their animals to the ground. Sancho picked himself up and, enraged, asked Don Quixote for his sword, saying he wanted to kill half a dozen of the pigs to teach the rest of them some manners.

"Leave them be," said Don Quixote. "It is only right and proper that a defeated knight should receive this kind of treatment." He told Sancho to go back to sleep while he kept watch for the rest of the night.

≈ The duke and duchess organize one last jest at Don Quixote and Sancho's expense

The following morning, Don Quixote and Sancho gathered together their scattered possessions and resumed their journey. Towards evening they encountered a party of ten well-armed men on horseback and four or five on foot. They surrounded Don Quixote and with menacing gestures but in complete silence indicated that Don Quixote and Sancho should go with them.

The men led the way, never letting Don Quixote or Sancho open their mouths. About an hour after midnight they reached a castle, which Don Quixote immediately recognized as the duke's.

"What can this mean?" he said. "We have been treated so well here in the past."

The men led Don Quixote and Sancho into the courtyard, which was lit up with hundreds of candles. In the middle, there was a great bier on which was laid out the body of a beautiful woman. On one side of the courtyard was a sort of stage. Sitting on chairs on the stage were two figures who, from the fact that they were wearing crowns, appeared to be kings of some sort. Don Quixote and Sancho were made to sit in chairs at one side of the stage.

At this point Don Quixote saw that the body was none other than Altisidora. A pair of figures whom Don Quixote recognized as the duke and duchess appeared and took their place in chairs on the stage next to the kings. Don Quixote and Sancho rose and bowed deeply to them. An official then threw a black robe painted with flames over Sancho, and put a conical cardboard hat on his head, covered in pictures of devils. Sancho was not particularly concerned, as the flames did not burn, nor did the devils try to carry him off.

The sound of flutes was now heard and a young man dressed in Roman costume sang a song about Altisidora and how she had died through the cruelty of Don Quixote. He was interrupted by one of the kings saying, "Enough of Altisidora's praises. Let us talk of the penance that Sancho Panza must undergo if she is to be restored to life. What is your opinion, Rhadamanthus, my fellow judge?"

The other king said, "I call on all the servants in this house to come forward and give Sancho two dozen smacks on the face, a dozen pinches and six jabs with a pin on the back and arms. Only then will Altisidora be restored."

At this Sancho cried out, "No one's touching me! I don't see what smacking my face has got to do with restoring this young lady."

"Obey in silence, or you shall die!" roared Rhadamanthus. "What's asked of you is not too much."

A procession of duennas started to make their way across the courtyard. As soon as Sancho saw them he yelled, "I'll put up with a lot, but I'm not going to be touched by any duennas! I'd rather be stabbed by daggers or pinched with red-hot pinchers."

Here Don Quixote broke silence and said, "Have patience, friend Sancho, and give in to these demands. It is not everyone who can restore the dead to life."

Sancho relented and allowed himself to be smacked and pinched by the duennas, but when they began jabbing him with pins his patience snapped. He jumped to his feet and, grabbing a burning torch, began chasing after his tormentors.

At this instant Altisidora rolled over onto her side and the bystanders shouted out, "Altisidora lives!"

When Don Quixote saw this, he went down on his knees in front of Sancho and said, "Now is the time to give yourself some lashes for Dulcinea's sake."

Sancho retorted that he would do no such thing.

Altisidora rose from her bier and bowed to the duke and duchess. "Cruel knight, to have caused me such suffering!" she said to Don Quixote out of the side of her mouth as she passed him. "As for you, the kindest squire in the world, you can have six of my smocks to make shirts out of. They're not completely intact, but they are clean."

Sancho made his bed that night in Don Quixote's room. After discussing what had happened, both men fell asleep.

Cide Hamete, the author of this great history, explains it all as follows.

Sansón Carrasco, determined to be revenged for his defeat as the Knight of the Mirrors, had acquired new armour and a new horse and had set off to track down Don Quixote. He had reached the duke and duchess's castle, where the duke had told him of all the tricks that had been played on Don Quixote and Sancho while the two were staying. The duke had also told Sansón that Don Quixote was heading to Zaragoza, and had asked the graduate, if he caught up with him, to return and recount what happened.

Sansón had gone to Zaragoza but, not finding Don Quixote there, had gone on to Barcelona. Having found and defeated Don Quixote, he had gone back to the duke's castle and told him everything. When the duke heard that Don Quixote was returning to his own village he decided to play one last trick. He set up the stage in the castle courtyard and had his men scour the countryside to track down the knight and his squire, with orders to bring them to the castle as soon as they were found.

Cide Hamete says at this point that he thinks that in going to all this trouble, the duke and duchess showed themselves to be as foolish as the two men they had been so determined to make fools of.

Dawn came and Don Quixote was about to rise, when Altisidora came into the room and sat herself down on a chair next to Don Quixote's bed. She began lamenting her fate, explaining how Don Quixote's coldness to her had made her die of grief.

She went on in this vein for some while until Don Quixote said to her, "I have already told you I am sorry that you have fallen in love with me, as I am sworn to Dulcinea del Toboso and can love no other."

Altisidora appeared to fly into a rage. "Don Codfish, Don Kicked-in-the-Face, did you really think that I died for your sake? Let me tell you that everything you saw tonight was make-believe. I'm not the sort of woman who'd let her little fingernail suffer for the sake of a camel like you, let alone die."

"That I can believe," said Sancho. "All that stuff about lovers pining to death is nonsense."

The duke and duchess now came in. They all had a delightful conversation and the duchess asked whether Altisidora was now in Don Quixote's good favour.

"Madam," replied Don Quixote, "it is my belief that this young lady's troubles arise entirely from her being too idle. She should be put to work to take her mind off it. I recommend lace-making."

"There's no need for that," said Altisidora. "Just thinking of what this ugly brute has put me through is enough to make me forget about him." She then left the room, pretending to wipe the tears from her eyes as she went.

≈ DON QUIXOTE AND SANCHO REACH AN AGREEMENT CONCERNING THE DISENCHANTING OF DULCINEA AND CLEAR UP SOME CONFUSION REGARDING THEIR TRUE IDENTITY

Don Quixote and Sancho set out that same evening. Don Quixote was both downcast and happy. He was downcast at the thought of his defeat, but happy because the raising of Altisidora from the dead had shown him that Sancho possessed magical powers. This meant that he could easily accomplish the disenchanting of Dulcinea.

Sancho was most unhappy, because Altisidora had not kept good her promise to give him six of her smocks. Don Quixote commiserated with him and then said that he would gladly pay Sancho a fee for the lashings needed to disenchant Dulcinea. Sancho jumped at this. They agreed a price of one quarter a real per lash. With three thousand three hundred lashes outstanding, that made eight hundred and twenty-five reals in total. Sancho said he would get on with the lashings that very night.

Don Quixote was overjoyed. "Sancho, my friend, Dulcinea and I will be in your debt for the rest of our lives," he said.

Night arrived and they found a pleasant spot just off the road. They ate a meal and then Sancho, having turned his donkey's halter into a whip, walked off and took up position among some nearby beech trees. Don Quixote called on him to administer the lashings carefully and not cut himself to pieces – not just for Sancho's sake, but because if he killed himself in the attempt, Dulcinea would never be disenchanted.

Sancho then stripped off his shirt and began to lash himself, with Don Quixote keeping count. After six or eight Sancho began to think that this wasn't funny, so he stopped and said, "I think we settled on too low a price. Each of these is worth half a real at least."

"Agreed," said Don Quixote. "I'll double the fee."

With that Sancho continued, but this time, instead of lashing himself, he began to hit the nearby tree trunks, letting out a groan every now and again as if he were really suffering.

Don Quixote began to grow worried. "By my reckoning you've given yourself over one thousand lashes," he said. "I'm sure that's enough for now."

"No, no," replied Sancho, "never let it be said that I was paid for something I didn't do." And he laid into the trees so forcefully that he stripped several of them completely of their bark. At one point he let out a particularly dramatic cry as if he were about to expire.

Don Quixote could not bear it, and, rushing up to Sancho, seized the whip saying, "That's quite enough. You can't possibly kill yourself for my sake. Dulcinea can wait another day."

"If you insist, sir. But would you be so kind as to lend me your cloak – I'm sweating terribly and don't want to risk catching a chill."

Don Quixote obliged and spent the rest of the night in his shirtsleeves, while Sancho wrapped himself warmly in the cloak and slept soundly until sunrise. They resumed their journey and the next day came to a village where they stopped at an inn, which Don Quixote recognized as an inn and did not think was a castle. They spent the whole day there, Don Quixote desperate for night to come so that Sancho could finish his disenchanting.

While they were waiting, a gentleman arrived at the inn accompanied by four servants.

"Señor Don Álvaro Tarfe, here is a suitable place for you to stay," one of the servants said.

Don Quixote overheard this, and as soon as the man was settled in went up to him and said, "Good sir, are you perchance that Don Álvaro Tarfe who appears in the recently published second part of the *History of Don Quixote de la Mancha*?"

"I am indeed, and Don Quixote is a very good friend of mine," replied Don Álvaro.

"Tell me, sir, am I at all like the Don Quixote you speak of?"

"Not at all," said Don Álvaro.

"And did he have a squire called Sancho Panza?"

"He had," said Don Álvaro, "but he was a greedy, boorish fellow and not at all amusing as he is supposed to be."

At which point Sancho said, "Well, sir, you should know that I am the real Sancho Panza and this is the real Don Quixote de la Mancha, the famous, the brave, the protector of widows, the stealer of damsels' hearts, the worshipper of the fabulous Dulcinea del Toboso."

Don Álvaro was amazed by all this, but quickly became convinced that these were indeed the real Don Quixote and Sancho Panza. He still couldn't understand how he'd managed to get mixed up with the false ones, but put it down to the work of the enchanters who constantly plagued the true Don Quixote.

Don Álvaro and Don Quixote dined together, and by chance the village notary came in. Don Quixote asked him to draw up a certificate which Don Álvaro would sign declaring that he agreed that these were indeed the true Don Quixote and Sancho Panza. This was done, to the immense satisfaction of Don Quixote and Sancho.

That evening, they continued their journey and again spent the night in a wooded glade, where Sancho continued his lashings at the expense of the nearby trees. Don Quixote kept careful count, and calculated that in total three thousand and twenty-nine lashes had now been administered.

They travelled on through the next day and night, when nothing of interest happened except that Sancho completed his total of lashings, to the inexpressible delight of Don Quixote.

The next day, Don Quixote eagerly examined every woman who came near, in the hope that she might be the restored Dulcinea, but without luck.

≈ DON QUIXOTE AND SANCHO ARRIVE HOME

And so, finally, they descended a slope and came to their own village. They stopped at the outskirts to see two boys quarrelling.

One said to the other, "Do shut up; you'll never see it as long as you live."

Don Quixote turned to Sancho. "Did you hear that? It means I'm never going to see my beloved Dulcinea."

Sancho was about to answer, when he was distracted by the sight of a hare flying towards them with some greyhounds and hunters in pursuit. The terrified hare took shelter under his donkey. Sancho caught it alive and handed it to Don Quixote, who regarded this as another omen, saying, "A hare flies, but Dulcinea appears not."

It turned out that the boys were arguing about a cage full of crickets that one had taken from the other. Sancho paid a few coins for the cage and handed it to Don Quixote. "See, that omen is undone. You should not be so superstitious."

The hunters then appeared and asked for the hare, which Don Quixote gave them.

Don Quixote and Sancho went into the village and ran into the priest and Sansón Carrasco the graduate. They embraced warmly and made their way to Don Quixote's house, where the housekeeper and his niece were already waiting for them. Sancho's wife had also heard of their arrival and came running up, dragging Sanchica by the hand. Seeing Sancho bedraggled and on foot, she said, "This doesn't look like the way a governor should be arriving home."

"Hold your tongue, Teresa," said Sancho. "Let's go home and I'll tell you all about it. I bring money, earned by my own labour, and that's the most important thing."

Don Quixote went indoors with the priest and the graduate and told them about his recent adventures, of his defeat and his promise to remain in the village for a whole year. He then described his plan for them all to play at being shepherds and shepherdesses, and how he intended to call himself Quixotiz and Sancho Panza, Panzino. The two were amazed at Don Quixote's new craze, but decided to humour him for the time being.

The conversation was overheard by the housekeeper and the niece, and as soon as the priest and Sansón had gone they came in and told Don Quixote not to be so foolish.

"It's a very tough life being a shepherd," said the house-keeper, "what with the cold of winter and the heat of summer, and the wolves. You're too old for that sort of thing."

"Yes, yes," said Don Quixote wearily, "now help me to bed as I don't feel very well."

≈ The end of Don Quixote de la Mancha

Whether it was his continuing sadness at his defeat, or just the normal order of things, Don Quixote fell into a fever which lasted for six days. He was often visited during this period by his friends the priest, the barber and the graduate, and Sancho stayed by his bedside the whole time. He came out of his fever but still remained very melancholy. The others tried to cheer him up but Don Quixote could not shake off his sadness. His friends called the doctor, who examined him and stated that things did not look good.

Don Quixote remained quite calm at this news, but not so his housekeeper, niece and squire, all of whom began to cry piteously. He fell asleep for around six hours, and when he awoke he seemed quite different.

"I am cured of the madness that afflicted me," he declared. "I see now the terrible effect that those detestable books on chivalry had on me. Niece, I feel I am on the point of death, and I ask you to call my good friends the priest, Sansón Carrasco the graduate and Master Nicolás the barber."

The three men soon arrived.

"Good news, gentlemen," said Don Quixote. "I am no longer Don Quixote de la Mancha but Alonso Quixano, who was thought a good man."

The men could not quite believe that Don Quixote was cured, but Don Quixote was adamant and asked for a lawyer so that he could dictate his will. He then sent out the graduate and the barber, and took confession from the priest. The lawyer arrived and Don Quixote set out the terms of his will.

"Sancho Panza, whom in my madness I made my squire, has in his hands some money of mine, which I bequeath to him," he began. And turning to Sancho he said, "You deserve no less for your loyalty and simple good nature, my friend. Forgive me for leading you astray and making you seem as mad as I was."

Sancho began to weep. "Don't die, master, but take the advice of a simpleton and live for many more years, for the daftest thing a man can do is die for no good reason. We might find Dulcinea disenchanted yet, and you can always blame me for your defeat at the hands of the Knight of the White Moon."

"It is no good," said Don Quixote. "All that might have meant something to me when I was mad, but now I am sane. I was Don Quixote de la Mancha, but now I am Alonso Quixano the Good. Let us continue with the will. I leave twenty ducats for a dress to my housekeeper, as well as the wages I owe her. All the rest I leave to my niece, on the condition that, if she marries anyone who has ever heard of a book on chivalry, she forfeits it all."

With that he ended his will and, feeling very faint, lay down full length on his bed. He lived for another three days and then died peacefully and quietly. That was the end of the Ingenious Gentleman of La Mancha, whose village Cide Hamete would not name precisely, so that all the towns and villages of La Mancha could argue for ever more over the right to claim him as their own.

for Amelia, Caz & Phil ~ MJ

for my brother Rick ~ CR

First published 2009 by Walker Books Ltd,
87 Vauxhall Walk, London SE11 5HJ

This edition published 2010

2 4 6 8 10 9 7 5 3 1

Text © 2009 Martin Jenkins
Illustrations © 2009 Chris Riddell

This book has been typeset in Cerigo and Cancione
Printed in China

ISBN: 978-1-4063-2430-3

www.walker.co.uk